ASYLUM IN THE MIND

DOCTOR WISE BOOK 6

ARJAY LEWIS

MIND
BENDER
PRESS

Asylum In The Mind: Doctor Wise Book 6

Cover Design: Marianne Nowicki: www.premadeebookcovershop.com
Editing: Brandi Salazar: www.brandisalazarediting.com

ISBN-13: 978-1732659315
ISBN-10: 1-732659311

Published by:
Mindbender Press
474 South Main Street
Phillipsburg NJ 08865
www.mindbenderpress.com

DEDICATION

To Brandi Salazar, my wonderful editor
and a great part of my team.
Her eye catches the many mistakes
that this wordsmith creates.

"A casual stroll through the lunatic asylum shows that faith does not prove anything." —*Friedrich Nietzsche*

"The world sometimes feels like an insane asylum. You can decide whether you want to be an inmate or pick up your visitor's badge. You can be in the world but not engage in the melodrama of it; you can become a spiritual being having a human experience thoroughly and fully." —*Deepak Chopra*

PROLOGUE

She surfaced slowly from the fog of unconsciousness, her eyelids fluttering as if reluctant to reveal the world again.

How long had she been out? Minutes, hours, days? The disorientation clung to her mind like a choking veil, thick and suffocating.

She fought to gather her scattered thoughts, clutching to the fragile fragments of her identity.

I'm Mary Gillian. I'm a nurse.

The words felt distant and unreal, like echoes from a life that belonged to someone else.

A hazy memory flickered: her cramped, cluttered apartment bathed in the cold morning light, the worn bathroom mirror. It reflected an image of an attractive dark-haired woman with fair skin, a roundness of cheek and chin, perhaps carrying a bit too much weight.

Then came the painful sting of recollection: the bitter argument with Todd, the boyfriend she had broken up with days — or was it weeks? — ago. It was a stupid fight, another stupid fight on top of all the other ones, but they decided it would be best to end it. She wished he was here with her in this horrible place, where she would beg his forgiveness.

How perfect her life had been before all this darkness swallowed her whole.

She glanced around the room, struggling to determine whether it was night or day. But the chamber was perpetually shrouded in darkness, broken only by a faint sliver of cold light sneaking beneath the door.

A frigid shiver ran down her spine — not from the chill, but from dread. If night had come, then the torment would begin again.

He would return. He always did. What fresh horrors awaited her this time? She flexed her bound hands and legs, feeling the raw bite of the strips of torn bed sheets wrapped tightly around her. The knots were cruelly precise; the more she struggled, the tighter they constricted, threatening to steal the feeling from her fingers as they had before.

He had made that painfully clear — his twisted parting gift on the first night, leaving her bound so long that numbness had blotted out sensation for two agonizing days.

Better not to resist, she told herself.

He seemed to savor her defiance, inventing new ways to break her spirit, pushing her to the edge where resistance felt like a desperate gamble. He feigned escape routes — mocking traps designed only to crush hope and twist her agony anew.

This wasn't how her life was supposed to be. A week ago... maybe less... her days had been filled with mundane joys: the doctor's office where she worked, the comforting chatter of coworkers, the occasional laughter of friends. Now, nothing remained but the horror of his face and the perpetual nightmare of his hands on her body.

She shifted her injured ankle slightly. Pain shot sharply up her leg — broken, surely — but over time the torment had dulled to a merciless throb.

Her face — her beautiful face — was a ruin. He had carved into her with a scalpel, cruelly fast, making deep slices that burned and stung, branding her with violence. Was the damage permanent? She dared not hope.

Suffering had become her sole companion, a shadow that clung to her with merciless persistence.

A faint glow spilled beneath the door, casting eerie shadows on grimy walls slick with dirt and neglect. She spotted the chair she was tied to, centered in a disturbing pattern scrawled on the floor — no mere circle, but a pentagram, dark and ominous beneath her.

She had awoken here after the attack. That terrible, senseless moment in the parking lot outside the office — a man had approached out of nowhere, striking her down with a heavy blow.

She remembered nothing beyond the pain and darkness swallowing her.

He fed her scraps, brought water, but mostly left her tied to that chair. Once a day, if he was merciful, he'd escort her to the filthy bathroom — if not, she was forced to soil herself.

The humiliation was endless.

"Oh God... Fluffy? Who's feeding Fluffy?" she whispered hoarsely.

An image — her black and white long-haired cat — flashed into her mind. He had always curled around her feet at night, a silent guardian. The thought of him suffering alone, hungry and scared, broke something inside her.

Tears welled unbidden, salty and hot, and she cloaked her sobs in a fragile whisper, afraid he might hear.

Or perhaps he wasn't here at all. But she couldn't stop crying. The tears came in helpless waves just as they had that first night — until his harsh slap silenced her, searing pain exploding across her face.

Now, a faint sound stirred from the other room. She swallowed hard, her breath catching in her throat. Panic clenched her heart.

It was going to start again.

The door creaked open, and he appeared: tall, menacing, his white lab coat stained dark with blood — her blood. Her gaze locked on the gloved hand that held a gleaming instrument, sharp and cruel.

"Please... no," she whimpered, her voice raw and trembling.

"Shh. It'll be all right," he said, an unsettling smile curving his lips — a smile she knew too well. The smile that promised pain.

"No, no, let me go. I swear, I won't tell anyone—"

"No, you won't," he replied coldly. "You've been an excellent plaything, perhaps the best yet. But it's time I moved on. Fairness demands I share myself with others."

Her eyes darted to the glinting scalpel. Panic roared in her throat, choking the words out.

"No, please!" she said, just a whisper.

He stepped closer, his gloved fingers trailing lightly over her cheek like a venomous touch.

"One last night together, sweetheart," he said, his voice low and terrifying. "And know this: of all the women I've ever had, you are — the most recent."

In one fluid, horrifying motion, the scalpel flashed.

The screaming began.

1. IVORY TOWER

A heavy sense of foreboding settled over me as I steered my van into the nearly empty parking lot of the Mountainview Police Station.

I'd been summoned here countless times before, but something in Bill McGee's voice today hinted at deeper trouble. He hadn't outright said it, but I could read between the lines when a case was spinning out of control — and Bill was probably grasping at straws.

Fortunately, grasping at straws was my specialty.

The handicapped parking spots were free, so I pulled in, opened the van door, and swung my specially modified bucket seat around to help me ease my stiff leg out. Gripping my cane that rested behind the passenger seat, I planted myself firmly on the asphalt.

At six foot four, I probably looked like a genie emerging from a bottle — no matter how large the vehicle. I ran a hand through my short brown hair as I closed the door behind me.

Outside, it was a perfect late May day: the temperate air neither stifling like July nor biting like March, but alive with fresh greenery and the intoxicating scents of spring in full bloom. I took a long, deep breath, letting the crisp air fill my lungs and calm my nerves.

The moment I stepped inside through the back entrance using my special ID card, the springtime tranquility evaporated. Sergeant Tice emerged from the locker room — a sour-faced, balding man whose gruff exterior seemed impenetrable, though I sometimes wondered if he ever remembered what courtesy was.

"So, the witch doctor's been summoned again," he sneered, flashing a smile tight enough to look like a clenched fist. "Must be desperate on a case. Guess they really don't have squat, do they?"

I kept my voice measured, knowing that pushing back against Tice rarely ended well. "And good afternoon to you, Sergeant Tice. Lieutenant McGee asked me to stop by."

"Tarot cards today, or just some tea leaves? Which is it?"

"Tea would be nice," I said with forced politeness, while a string of less courteous retorts rattled through my mind. I chastised myself silently. Years of discipline had taught me to maintain a quiet mind — yet lately, the edge of anger gnawed at me like an unwelcome companion. It wasn't like me.

Still, I reminded myself, I was at a high point in my career. Dr. Leonard Wise: top of my medical school class, psychiatry fellowship following the tragic loss of my fiancée. Eventually, I accepted that the strange visions and fleeting insights I experienced were more than coincidence. That realization led me to study under Dr. Fritz Kohl — in the country's only parapsychology program — where I refined my unusual gifts and learned to harness them.

Looking back, it was a pretty impressive résumé.

That background landed me a position as associate professor and head of the new Parapsychology Department at Garden State University. In that capacity, I researched and taught psychic phenomena, and through such studies helped this work gain acceptance.

On top of that, I was fortunate to assist Lieutenant McGee regularly on challenging cases.

I limped down the corridor toward the administration area, where McGee's office sat alongside Captain Harris' and the department's communications center.

At one of the wall desks sat CeeCee Carter, our vivacious head dispatcher. She had pushed her headset down around her neck and was munching on a sandwich. Her dyed-blonde hair spilled over strong shoulders, and though her sharp features and even sharper personality could be off-putting, I found her presence comforting.

"Hey, Len!" she greeted warmly between bites.

"Hey yourself, CeeCee," I replied, my mood still dragging.

She cocked an eyebrow. "Why the gloomy Gus routine today?"

I forced a smile. "My first year at GSU is wrapping up, and I'm not sure if the program will be renewed."

"Oh, no worries," she said enthusiastically. "You could always work here! You're here a lot anyway."

I chuckled. "And what would my job be?"

"If it were up to me, I'd want you to be my personal secretary — with benefits, if you know what I mean."

I couldn't help but smile.

CeeCee grinned. "See, you *can* smile!"

"You know I'm dating Assistant District Attorney Emery."

"Oh, so formal," she chided. "You guys still together? I'm willing to wait — but not forever."

That was CeeCee, always a flirt, but I knew it was all just bravado.

I said, "We've had a few ups and downs, but we're working it out."

She snorted. "Probably going up to Maine over New Year's. Chicks hate when you leave them on New Year's."

I couldn't imagine my six-foot-tall, beautiful African-American girlfriend being a 'chick,' but I just nodded.

"Right. I'll keep that in mind," I said. "Is McGee in?"

"His majesty awaits," she said with a gesture to McGee's office.

"Thanks, CeeCee." I stepped forward and knocked.

"Come in," came Bill's gruff voice.

Inside, his desk was buried beneath a chaotic mountain of papers and cardboard boxes, resembling one of those stories you hear about eccentric collectors who hoard every scrap of paper they ever touch. I wondered how he managed to wade through the mess to his chair at all.

Bill was tall, like me, but broader — built like a football player in peak shape. His suit was large enough to cover his broad shoulders but rumpled and dirt-stained from frequent work at crime scenes, where he often knelt in the dirt searching for clues.

If he ever looked too shabby, his wife would sneak his clothing out under cover of darkness and replace it with crisp new outfits — whether he wanted her to do so or not.

He was astonishingly perceptive when it came to tiny details at a murder scene but completely oblivious to how he presented himself to the world.

"Bill," I nodded, stepping inside.

"Len, good to see you," Bill McGee's deep, commanding voice echoed through the hallway as he grasped my hand with a grip that was firm and resolute.

"It's been a few weeks since I heard from you," I replied, noting the absence.

"Yeah," he admitted with a chuckle, "we've been tackling cases the old-fashioned way lately — with police work."

I raised an eyebrow. "A novel concept these days."

He chuckled and then a shadow of seriousness crossed his face. His steel-blue eyes flashed with determination as he continued, "But I'm afraid we've hit a tough one."

"Murder?" I guessed.

"It's a missing person case. She's been gone for about a week, and so far, not a single clue has emerged."

"A week? Why didn't you call me sooner?" I asked, concern in my voice.

McGee ignored the question and instead said, "Come with me, Len," as he strode purposefully toward the door.

I followed quickly, stepping into the main hall and moving with him toward the detective's bullpen. I got a strong feeling of *déjà vu*, rather like I did the very first time I walked into this police station and sat down with McGee. I had been lecturing at the college — I wasn't yet a professor, just a guest speaker. When my address was over, he came to me and asked me if I really believed that psychic abilities could be used to solve crime.

I was taken aback. It wasn't the kind of question one gets from someone who claims to be a policeman. But something genuine in his tone compelled me to offer my help.

That case was a success, and gradually, I found myself called in more and more. Meanwhile, McGee climbed the ranks, from detective to lieutenant, through his relentless dedication.

Pulling myself out of the memory, I followed him into the bullpen and then into Interrogation Room B. The large one-way mirror on the far wall tried to make the small, cramped room feel less confining. In the center stood a rectangular table, scarred and worn from years of use. Draped on its surface lay a woman's blue blazer, crumpled and lifeless, next to a sizable black purse.

Chuck Norman, the MPD sketch artist, occupied one of the chairs. His glasses caught the harsh glare of fluorescent lights overhead, and he wore his customary all-black attire, clothes slightly rumpled and his hair freshly trimmed close to the scalp. With a nod, he acknowledged my arrival.

"Hey, Chuck," I greeted warmly. "Glad to see your leg's finally healed."

Chuck gave a weary smile. "Still aches when it rains," he said, bending to extend his knee.

"Wish I could do that with mine." I tapped my leg, cane in hand. The gesture earned a small, half-hearted smile.

McGee stepped forward. "Len, the reason we didn't call you earlier is simple — I've only had the case since yesterday. The missing woman's a nurse. She left work early one night because she wasn't feeling well. She lives alone, and at first, everyone thought she'd just skipped her shift the next day due to illness."

"Eventually, someone must have checked on her — and realized something was wrong," I said.

"Exactly. That was this week. Her car's still in the parking lot of the doctor's office where she works. We checked her apartment; her landlady didn't know a thing. The cat was pretty hungry — now in a no-kill shelter. She was a bit of a loner, as it turns out. She did have a boyfriend, but they broke up about a month ago."

"You think he had something to do with it?"

"Partners or ex-partners are always our first suspects, but he was out of town during the time in question. We checked his alibi, and it was good. Besides, we don't even know if she's been harmed."

"So that's where I come in — your trained pet psychic?"

McGee chuckled. "Len, I wouldn't call you trained. Hell, I wouldn't say you're housebroken. But you've had successes on missing persons cases before."

He pointed to the purse on the table. "Found this near the trash cans in the parking lot, not in them — otherwise it'd be gone for sure."

"Is it hers?"

"Had her ID and credit cards, but no money. The parking lot's pretty secluded, so robbery probably wasn't the motive."

"So you think she was grabbed there?"

"Most likely." He looked at me earnestly.

"And where did the jacket come from?"

"It was hanging on a door at the doctor's office. The staff all said it was hers. You always ask for something owned by whoever you're trying to reach—"

He almost said 'victim,' paused, and moved on. The word hung unspoken but heavy in the air. He went on. "Think you can sense anything?"

I sat down, took a breath, and tried to center myself.

"You know the drill," McGee said. "If you see any faces, tell Chuck here, and he'll sketch them out."

"I know," I said, quiet but firm. "What I need is a few minutes of silence."

"Sorry," McGee said as he activated a recorder. A faint beep announced it starting up. "May sixteenth, five p.m. Session with Doctor Leonard Wise, police civilian consultant."

He settled into the chair nearby. I was already focused on my breathing, to bring my mind down into an alpha state.

In…out, in…out…

I relaxed the mental barriers and opened myself to any impressions that might come. I reached out my hands and touched the soft wool of the jacket, its faint scent of perfume drawing me deeper.

"A face," I whispered. "A woman's face."

The image formed clearly in my mind's eye: Caucasian, a pleasant nose, a softly rounded chin, straight brown hair cut with bangs. And the eyes — gray and unmistakably sharp.

I heard Chuck's pencil moving on his pad as I described the subtle details in shorthand meant for him.

Then I shifted focus to the purse. I ran my fingers carefully over its contents — lipstick in her favorite shade, a worn nail file long overdue for replacement, and a hairbrush she'd had since college.

Gently, I threaded my fingers through the bristles and extracted several loose hairs — perfect. Something from her body, a tangible link I could use to reach her.

Holding the hair between my fingers felt like grasping a tiny living thing, a wriggling thread of connection. I opened myself further, inviting the images hovering just beyond my conscious mind.

Suddenly, a sharp, searing pain stabbed my ankle.

"Ahhhhh!" I cried out, startled by my own voice.

"Len, you okay?" McGee barked.

"It's my ankle — it hurts," I whispered, somewhere dark and suffocating. The pain was intense. I reached up to my face — and felt wetness. Warm, sticky.

"Blood," I moaned, struggling to sit upright. Though my eyes remained closed, I was overwhelmed with images of a room: unlit and old, it smelled bad and I knew it was a bad place where terrible things were done.

"Oh God, he cut me. He cut my face," I said, seeing only that dark, terrifying room.

"Who? Describe him!" the voice roared.

"He's coming. Oh God, he's—"

A terrified shriek tore from my lips, and suddenly I was back in the interrogation room. The visions slammed shut behind an invisible door in my mind.

Breathing hard, I sat motionless for several moments. Then, blinking, I opened my eyes.

"What did you see, Len?" McGee asked gently as he leaned in.

"Water," I whispered.

McGee stepped out and returned moments later, placing a small bottle of water in front of me, cap already removed.

I took it gratefully and tilted my head back, the cool liquid soothing the shock and pulling me fully back to the present.

"Len?" McGee's voice cut through the tense silence. "Did you get anything we can use?"

I shook my head, though it hardly required the movement — my whole body was still trembling. "No. I disconnected."

"Did you get a location?"

I exhaled slowly, trying to steady my racing heart and wipe away the sweat dripping down my brow. "I couldn't focus on a place. It was too dark."

"Well, at least we have something." Chuck's grin was faint but genuine as he turned his tablet toward me, revealing the sketch he'd drawn. The face was exactly as I'd described it.

McGee reached into the worn leather purse and pulled out a similarly beaten wallet. He flipped it open and produced a New Jersey driver's license with a photo that matched the sketch — though the chin was a bit different, and she wore glasses in the photo. Still, my description and Chuck's drawing had captured the likeness well.

"Pretty good, Chuck," McGee nodded approvingly. "Len, can you tell me anything else? Is she still alive?"

I hesitated. "I don't know. It felt like I was about to get close, really close, but then — just like that — I was shut off. Tell me more about her."

McGee gave me a curious look. "Len, when we do this, you always tell me not to reveal what I already know."

I nodded, recalling our usual approach. "Yeah, I prefer not to have preconceived information influence the reading. But maybe this time it would help."

"Alright," McGee said, "her name is Mary Gillian—"

"You mentioned she's a nurse," I interjected.

Chuck cut in abruptly as he stood. "If I'm not needed anymore, I've got other work."

"Of course, Chuck. We'll call you if we need anything else," McGee said, watching him leave.

As he disappeared, I couldn't help but think Chuck was the kind of guy who'd excel at poker. His expression never gave away a thing.

"So, Len," McGee started, returning his full attention to me. "What else can I do? I'm really stuck on this one."

I looked deep into his steady blue eyes, picking up a subtle hesitation.

Something he's not telling me…

I felt a 'buzz' — the small psychic impression that sometimes slips unexpectedly into my mind like a silent alarm. It can be a warning or a subtle insight, depending on its intensity.

"There's something you're holding back," I said gently.

McGee sighed heavily, closing the door behind him as he walked over and sat down across from me. His usual calm demeanor was gone; he looked troubled.

"Are you reading my mind now?" he asked half-jokingly.

"Never tried, Bill."

He ran a hand over his face. "It's just… what I have is mostly conjecture."

"Bill, you don't have to apologize. Something's bothering you. Tell me."

He pressed his lips together for a moment, then reached into his jacket pocket and pulled a large folded paper and laid it carefully on the table between us. He unfolded it to reveal a map, but it appeared strange. There were brightly colored roads in reds and blues, cities in orange, and places marked with small red dots.

I leaned closer. It was a detailed blowup of the Morris, Essex, and Union County area.

"Don't tell me you spilled spaghetti sauce all over this," I joked.

"Very funny, Len. It arrived in the mail — addressed specifically to me." His finger traced a black spot near the edge of Mountainview, close to Bloomdale, New Jersey.

"That's where Mary Gillian was taken."

I scanned the map, noting the numbers scrawled next to each mark — dates. Nearby, next to the black dot, was a date next to it that included May of this year.

"Did the sender include the date?" I asked.

"No, I added those." He gestured to other dots, each marked with similar dates.

"What are the other dots?"

"At first I didn't know. That black spot made me dig deeper. I contacted some state police connections and got disturbing info. Those other marks are disappearances that match ours in nearby towns."

"Seriously? You went through their database?"

McGee nodded. "You have no idea. These were young women — mostly loners, recently divorced or separated from long-term partners. Snatched in open areas they frequented, on routes they used regularly. Someone was watching."

"Sounds like a predator."

"Yes, and many were taken right before planned vacations. Nobody noticed they'd gone missing for weeks. Trails went cold. Never found, presumed dead." He tapped the map again. "I'm trying to spot a pattern."

"This came in the mail? Was there anything on the envelope? Fingerprints?"

"No, wiped clean. Address printed in block letters — impossible to trace. It was mailed at the Mountainview Post Office."

McGee stood, moving behind me to point out three yellow marks alongside the red ones.

"Notice the color difference?" He pointed to a few green marks too, each marked 'found' with dates next to them.

"The state police found bodies at those locations. Horrifically mutilated. Like here, just outside Chester — the woman's legs were crushed with a sledgehammer. And there's more."

"How could it get worse?" I shuddered.

"Bill watched me carefully. "The bodies they found were decapitated."

I gasped, staring at the dots spread across the map. "There must be over a dozen."

"Seventeen in total, including Mary Gillian," McGee grimaced and began pacing, his mind wrestling with the weight of these horrors.

"Seventeen," I repeated slowly. "That's... awful."

"Over six years. About three a year." He pulled another paper from his pocket — a list of names, dates, and locations.

"All women?" I asked, scanning the list.

"Yes. Each listing when and where they disappeared."

I furrowed my brow. "Seems random."

"Maybe, but whoever sent me that map knew every abduction site like the back of their hand. Mary's case is the first to happen under my watch." He took a seat beside me, voice low. "Len, if this is the work of a serial killer and he mailed this to me, he's daring me to catch him."

The thought was chilling. A serial murderer in sleepy Mountainview.

"I forget you're FBI sometimes," I offered a weak smile.

"Not something I try to remember," he said ruefully. "I prefer small-time crimes — go home to my wife and kids without nightmares. I didn't want to drag you into this, but from the few bodies that were found, this guy is a monster."

"If it's the same person," I added, a cold shiver running down my spine.

"Same MO, Len." McGee's face darkened. "From the found bodies, this guy severed fingers, cut off toes... the medical examiner believes the mutilations happened while they were still alive."

I trembled at the mental image. "That's unimaginable."

"If Mary Gillian was taken by him, the same horrors likely await her. She's probably dead by now, given what you perceived during the reading."

I nodded slowly, my voice barely above a whisper. "I sensed pain in her ankle, maybe broken. And blood... on her face." The memory faded like a dim echo.

"That's not much to go on, but it's something. Len, can I ask a favor?"

"Of course, Bill."

"I contacted the FBI New Jersey Task Force."

"Stan Frazier's team?"

"Yes. Stan ran it until that near-fatal incident in the case you worked on in March. I want to bring in the woman we worked with on that abduction case."

"Kate Yearling," I said. "I didn't think she cared much for me."

"You won her over, at least a little. She's an expert profiler and hypnotherapist — helped with deprogramming after the Vanya case. I think she could use hypnotherapy to guide what you're seeing."

I nodded resolutely. "I'll do whatever you need."

Bill smiled warmly. "That's great to hear. You do realize time is of the essence, right?"

"Of course," I replied.

"She's driving up from Baltimore today," he said.

"Baltimore?" I echoed, raising an eyebrow.

"She was assisting on a case down there. I'm expecting her to arrive around eight o'clock this evening."

"And you want me here when she gets in?"

"To be honest, I was hoping our session this afternoon would have given me some leads for her," Bill admitted.

"Sorry, nothing came through," I said quietly.

"No, it's fine. Could you possibly come by tonight?" he asked hopefully.

"I'll have to call Jyanette. We were supposed to meet up," I answered, pushing myself up from the chair with the help of my cane. "By the way, would you be able to make me a copy of that map?"

"I was actually planning to make full-color copies for tonight's meeting. Can you wait until then?" Bill offered.

"That's perfect. I'll see you in a few hours," I said, shaking his hand and heading toward the door.

Despite the arrangement, I couldn't shake the frustration creeping in. Usually, it was effortless for me to pick up impressions about a person's whereabouts. But today, something had blocked me completely.

I shuffled down the hallway, passing the locker room, and as I approached the exit to the parking lot, Tice caught my attention.

"Hey, Doc, next time you're here, go easy on the screaming," he said as I passed.

A sudden flush of embarrassment warmed my cheeks — I hadn't realized I'd been that loud. I gave him a small wave in acknowledgment.

Let it go, let it go, I told myself.

But beneath the surface a simmering anger lingered.

2. SOLO SANCTUARY

I drove back to Garden State University and parked in the handicapped-reserved space near my office in College Hall. The building was quite empty by six o'clock, as the semester had ended and professors were no longer coming in. Most students were preparing to leave for home or getting a beer at a nearby bar.

I recalled a memory from when I was a student at this college, a long time ago in the spring. I had finally reached the age where I could go out and have a beer. I didn't get drunk; I just had one and felt...powerful. That was before I became a full-blown alcoholic.

I often wished I felt that invincible now, at thirty, but I was also grateful that I didn't. It's why so many young men die in car accidents. They just felt too damn invincible.

I reached my office, flicked on the overhead light, and pulled out my cell phone.

"Hello," came a pleasant female voice with a hint of an Irish accent.

"Mrs. Higgins, it's Leonard."

"Halloo, Doctor! You must be calling to tell me you're not coming home at your usual time."

I smiled. By this time, I was sure that this sweet Irish lady, my landlady for months, was a far better psychic than I would ever be.

"How do you know that, Mrs. Higgins?"

"It's just my women's intooition."

"As usual, your intuition is correct. I have to go to police headquarters at eight."

"Ah, that nice Lieutenant McGee needs you, then?"

"Yes, so I might be home late."

"What're ye do for supper? You get worn out so easily."

I chuckled. This tiny little fireball of a woman was worried about *me* getting worn out. "I'll grab something. I'll be fine, Mrs. Higgins."

"Just make sure you do, Doctor. Being sick now wouldn't be good. You need your strength."

"I'll eat," I implored. "I promise."

"Very well. Good night, Doctor."

"Good night, Mrs. Higgins, and thank you."

"Just watching over me charge."

I shook my head and ended the call. So I was her *charge*? You would think she worked for me, instead of the fact that I was renting a part of her house for a very reasonable rent.

The house was truly her domain. We were roommates in the sprawling Victorian. It was a wise investment when she bought it, and with the repairs and upgrades I'd helped with, it was now more valuable than when she purchased it.

Mrs. Higgins and I each had our designated areas and knew who would handle which tasks. We divided the chores: she took care of cleaning and cooking, while we shared the laundry. I managed the major renovations and minor repairs, although I wasn't particularly good at working on ladders.

The only thing we disagreed on was that she strictly prohibited me from leaving papers in the 'common area.' She had once thrown out important documents because they made the house 'unpresentable.'

It was a trade-off. I had learned to be cautious to avoid losing valuable work, and I thoroughly enjoyed the benefits of Mrs. Higgins' culinary skills.

My next call was the most important one.

"Hello?" came the female voice on the other end. I could hear the smile in her voice.

"Hello, lover," I said.

"Big talk from a man who hasn't been available for weeks."

"I was under the impression that it was your early court appearances that got in the way."

"Yes, because of your late nights grading final exams. But I'm looking forward to tonight," she said with a throaty chuckle, conjuring images of physical bliss.

"That's why I'm calling. McGee has a hot case of a missing person, possible foul play."

"Damn, I was hoping to get lucky."

I smiled. "Oh, my dear, I am always the lucky one…because I have you."

"Mm, that was a good save." She sighed dramatically. "Oh well, I do have court early tomorrow again—"

"Big case?"

"Len, you are my favorite man, but you know I can't talk about it."

"Favorite? You have more?"

"Not that I'm sleeping with."

"I have no doubt they want to."

"And I might let them, if you don't take care of business soon. A girl's got needs, you know."

"I promise — Friday night. And maybe Saturday night, just to be sure."

"I expect to be ravished in the mornings as well."

"How could I possibly refuse?"

"You won't if you're smart. Have a good night, darling. I'll just be eating a sandwich and going over case files."

"I love you."

"You too. Good night."

She ended the call. I looked at her photo on my phone for a moment. Her beautiful ebony features, so much darker than my pale flesh, her full African nose, and amazing curly-kinky hair that fell to her shoulders.

I'd had a lot of bad luck with women since the night my fiancée died in the car crash where I'd experienced my first vision.

That was eight years ago. But this time, I'd been lucky to be dating Jyanette for over six months.

We'd had a few fights, a big one on her birthday when I showed up with a black eye.

She didn't speak to me for a week after that, then texted me when I was at the point of despair. We met over coffee and talked half the night away, finally going to her place and sharing fantastic make-up sex. Despite the bumps in the road, we both really wanted to be together.

Feeling lighter, I booted up my laptop. Then I heard a rather raucous 'beep' down the hall.

I walked out the door of my tiny office and two doors down to the shared computer room all the professors used. The lights were out, but a dimly lit computer screen threw flickering shadows on the ceiling as a figure tick-tacked away at the keys.

Silently, I walked closer. My cane was more for balance than need, so I held it off the ground as I snaked closer to the person at the computer. He had long hair, shoulder-length from the back, and clothes that were remarkably reminiscent of the 1990s.

"Hi, Teddy," I said quietly.

The figure jumped — no, *propelled* himself out of the chair with so much force, I expected him to hurt himself. He made some noises, not really words, as I turned on the overhead lights.

Teddy Santos, my teaching assistant, stood before me, trying to compose himself.

"Doc!" he said, shielding his eyes from the sudden onslaught of light. "What the hell did you do that for? You practically gave me a heart attack."

From the look on his face, I wanted to laugh, but I controlled myself. Santos was panting from the shock.

"How did you get in here so quietly?" he asked.

"I can move without a lot of noise when the need arises," I explained. "Sorry, Teddy, I really didn't mean to frighten you. You know it's past six?"

"It is? Oh, I was just surfing the net, trying to get some information for my last paper."

"The joy of being a Teacher's Assistant. You work here for me, then you have to still do all your college work." I sympathized. "Plus, you're taking summer classes this year, aren't you?"

He shrugged. "It's that or help my father rebuild the house."

Teddy's parents had bought a rambling Victorian in Dover, and every visit usually entailed that he helped with the room-by-room renovation his father had planned out.

"I dunno, I guess I like it." Santos sat back in the chair and leisurely moved the mouse on the table to print a document. "I also like the stipend the college pays me."

"When I studied with Doctor Kohl in California, that TA stipend was a lifesaver. So, what's the paper about?"

"The Incas, for my computer science class. Did you know they used knots on string in a binary code to keep records?"

This surprised me. "Uh, no."

"Yeah. They were the most powerful culture in South America, and then one day they were just gone. It's fascinating."

"Find anything good on the Internet?"

"There's a lot out there. I'm assembling what I can as source material, and then I'll make my own conclusions."

I shook my head. "The way you can find specific information, it's quite impressive."

"It's easy, Doc."

I straightened up and took a step back. "Don't say that. I might realize that you aren't irreplaceable."

"Then forget I ever said anything."

I chuckled. "Teddy, I have to go back to the police station in a couple of hours. If I give you some money, will you get us both dinner? Unless, of course, you have a date?"

"Yeah, right," Santos scoffed. He turned away from the computer as the printer hummed and spat out paper. "I haven't had a date since New Year's." He looked up at me, his thick glasses distorting his bright brown eyes as if under a magnifying glass.

I grinned. "That's okay. I was alone on New Year's too."

"Oh yeah, that's when you were out of town. But you've got ADA Emery."

"You can just call her Jyanette, Teddy," I said as I gave him a twenty, which made his eyes light up. "I want a salad, even if you get pizza."

"You won't eat pizza? Isn't that a crime or something?"

"I'll have one slice. After all, I don't want to be accused of being a criminal. But I promised Mrs. Higgins I would eat right."

"Oh yeah. Don't make her mad." Teddy grabbed his jacket off another chair in the computer lab and strolled to the door. "See you in a few," he said without looking back.

I pivoted on my cane and went back to my office. Poor Teddy, he had little chance to meet people. He was studying for his

Master's in computer science, being my teaching assistant, and running my office so I could go wherever I was needed, often at a moment's notice.

When I got this job from my old college friend, Jonathan Baines, I made one thing very clear. I was a working researcher in the field of parapsychology, and as such, I needed to go off and *do* research. Over the last year, I'd been called in to find missing people, investigate haunted houses, odd cults, and criminal cases including murders. The only way to learn was to go out and study phenomena.

It's like being a paleontologist: you spend a lot of time digging in dirt to find an occasional bone. Sometimes, you find an entire skeleton, and it changes your concept about dinosaurs.

In a way, parapsychology was like that. I go to dirty old buildings where phenomena exist and I do research. Sometimes, what I learn is a tiny fragment. Then again, I could stumble across a big discovery that would change people's concepts of the supernatural.

I considered the dating situation. Santos last had a date on New Year's when he was visiting his parents and large family. Probably an old girlfriend with whom he got reacquainted. The years after Cathy died, I was involved in several troubled relationships because I was such an emotional mess.

Another woman with whom I was involved ended up dead. Wendy Wallace burned to death before my eyes. In my professional life, I had seen Carole Winslow shot, and then Stan Frazier stabbed...

I stopped myself.

I had been over each incident repeatedly, and every time I wondered what the outcome would have been if I could've moved faster, done something more—

"Stop!" I said out loud, surprised by the volume of my own voice. Maybe that was why I'd been on edge and little things made me angry. I was repressing my guilt that people I'd worked with had died or gotten seriously injured.

I'd recently faced a crazed chemist who made a drug that opened up his mind and led him to communicate with an ancient goddess who could've been a demon. He had made frescoes of her as a beautiful woman and as a horned demon. Scrawled on the wall of one shrine he'd made were the words, "Sacrifices must be made."

Those were the exact words I had heard in a vision — Jyanette hanging upside down in a car crash, exactly as my fiancée had when she bled to death. In my vision, Jyanette had said those very words.

There was no way the chemist could've known those words. Unless his goddess told him. Or he read my mind.

I meditated daily, but even that wasn't helping. Not enough to keep my temper in check. I was working very hard not to let it slip out when around either Mrs. Higgins or Jyanette, but I was having more and more trouble controlling it.

I put my laptop into sleep mode and leaned back in my chair. Maybe a bit of meditation now would help. I closed my eyes and tried to relax.

I still couldn't understand why I froze up with McGee earlier. It was like having a door slammed in my face. The only other time this happened was with the hypnotized minions of Doctor

Vanya. They had blocks in their minds, preventing deprogramming.

A memory slipped by my conscious mind. I gingerly reached into my pocket and found several long hairs.

I looked at the fine strands in my fingers. These were Ms. Gillian's hairs from her brush. I had slipped them into my pocket, under the idea that without the pressure of McGee watching and waiting, I might have better luck.

I leaned back in my chair a bit more and once again felt the hair between my fingers. I focused on my breathing, trying to descend into that alpha state again.

Thoughts passed through my head — 'cloud thoughts' we called them in meditation. I let them pass through my mind and did not attach to them, just let them slip past harmlessly. I was sinking deeper into an altered state.

I felt the pain stabbing through my ankle again. My face grimaced from the pain, but I quickly detached myself from it. I had to observe, not take on the experience. But I couldn't see very much. I exhaled, trying to go deeper... deeper...

I was in an old, neglected room; paint peeled off the walls. Boards covered the windows, and no light streamed through them.

It was night and I was frightened.

Night is bad. Night is dangerous. Night is when it all starts again.

Cords dug into my wrists, binding my hands together behind me. No, not my hands, her hands. I needed to detach more, to move away, to see the room, but not as a participant.

I went deeper.

Observe the room; don't become a part of the events. My view grew a little darker as everything shifted and slowed down. I heard a noise like a great wind. No, it was breathing. I heard someone breathing.

I looked around the room. I saw a woman tied to a chair. It was her breath I'd heard. She glowed, surrounded by luminescence. I moved a little closer to see her face. The glow was her aura, but it was a sickly green color. Around her ankle was a red haze so dense I could barely see her leg through it. Other spots on her body were leaking the same blood-red energy that poured from wounds on her face, her stomach, her breasts.

No, no, I was still involved. I needed to detach… detach…

It's not happening to me. It's something she felt.

I focused on regaining my composure. I looked at her face and almost lost it again. Strips of skin were hanging loose, cut with a surgical instrument, exposing the red muscle underneath. I turned away.

Oh God, the pain must be unbearable.

But, like all pain, it faded with time. She cried quietly; the tears running down her face. Her shoulders heaved. But it was all so slow, her crying impossibly loud.

I wanted to walk to her, help her, hold her until the tears stopped, and then take her to a hospital to save what remained of her face.

But if I wanted to help, I was wasting my chance. I needed to look around to find out where she was. I moved to the boarded window. There was a knothole in one sheet of plywood that covered the broken glass. I gazed out the hole in the window into the night, but I couldn't see much. The windowsill was brick. This was a brick building. But where?

All at once, she stopped crying as a thunderous noise came from the next room. I guessed it wasn't thunderous; it was just amplified in my level of existence. The girl stifled her sobs and looked at the door with horror as it opened.

"*Pleeeeease, nooooo!*" she said as if amplified through a bullhorn. The door pushed open and a figure wearing a white lab coat stepped through. He had gloves and something metal in his hands; I could see it clearly.

A scalpel.

I lifted my perception to look at his face, to memorize it so that Chuck could do a sketch and McGee could catch the sick bastard. I stared at his face.

I jolted awake out of my chair, my eyes open. I sucked in the air, trying desperately to fill my lungs. I was clammy, covered in sweat.

"Dammit!" I yelled as soon as I possessed the air to do so. It was the same as last time. I had gone further, but I still ran into a wall, completely shut off from the vision, shunted back into reality.

"Hey, Doc!" I heard in the next room. "Pizza's here. Salad, too. You eat cheese, right? Doc?"

My mouth felt like a foreign object as I tried to form words.

"That's fine, Teddy—"

"Extra vinegar on the salad, the way you like it, Doc. I'll set us up at the table in the computer room."

"That's great." I was indeed hungry. But after what I saw, I definitely didn't want to eat alone.

I thought for a second about the man at the door in my vision. I could see his body clearly, but as I moved to the face, I lost it. There was something about the face. I tried to focus on that last moment. Something on his head... a hat, perhaps?

I suddenly felt an overwhelming need to relieve myself and walked down the hall to use the men's room. A part of me also wanted to vomit, if there were anything in my stomach to throw up. As I relieved myself at the urinal, the memory clicked in.

There was something *on* the head.

Was it... horns?

3. SECURE HAVEN

W hen I returned, Santos was halfway through the largest pizza I'd ever seen. Fortunately, he had brought a bottle of my favorite water along with my salad.

For reasons I'd never understood, using my abilities always drained me literally, as well as figuratively. Having visions made me thirsty, like a drunk the day after, which was something I was familiar with.

"Slice?" Santos offered.

"No, thanks."

"Criminal!"

I didn't feel like eating, but I went through the motions, lightly picking at my salad while we discussed the lesson plan for my intermediate class in the following year, assuming I remained employed.

"C'mon, Doc," Teddy started. "Your classes have done very well, and the assistant dean is your best friend."

He was referring to Jon Baines, who took the risk to offer college-level courses in the study of parapsychology with myself as the man in charge. But things had not always gone swimmingly this first year, and I was unsure I would still have a job.

"We should probably eat," I suggested.

Santos went back to the pizza, and he was in heaven, his fingers covered with grease and cheese. I rarely saw him eat a substantial meal, so it was satisfying to see him filling himself with something besides gum and pork rinds. His appetite was contagious. Soon I'd finished my salad. I even got the last slice away from him. How could someone so thin eat so much at one sitting?

Eating with Santos was very grounding. It gave me the illusion that I had a normal life. There was something to be said for the immediacy of a meal.

At about seven-thirty, I left Santos to do his research. Within minutes, I had driven back to the police station.

Bright lights lit the department's parking lot. There wasn't another soul anywhere nearby. As I got out of my vehicle, I couldn't shake the feeling I wasn't alone. I felt extremely vulnerable, something I wasn't used to.

My original teacher, Doctor Kohl, used to say that feelings like this came from second-level senses: a stage of awareness that collected information we weren't consciously noticing, but that we tapped into when needed.

Still, there it was, that oppressive feeling that made me glance over my shoulder to see if there was anyone behind me. But this didn't feel like my usual warning — the buzz that had saved me more than once. My visions had seriously spooked me, and perhaps they affected me more than I wanted to admit.

Either way, I felt better as I walked into the well-lit station. It was quieter now. And thankfully, Tice was off duty, so I didn't have to deal with him. I could see Bill standing nearby, and he ushered me into the interrogation room we had used earlier.

A familiar woman sat at the table, and as always, her hair was her most striking feature — red, curly, cascading to her shoulders like a waterfall of fire. She was attractive. Not a fashion model, but in the 'real world' sense of the word. She had green eyes, as bright as emeralds, and as I got closer, I could see the faint freckles on her face. She rose to shake my hand.

"Len," McGee said, "you've met Doctor Kate Yearling."

"On the missing person's case months ago," I said, as a smile crept to my face. "A pleasure."

"Doctor," she responded, her jaw set, giving me the impression that the feeling was not mutual. "You helped on that other case, but I have my doubts if you can be of much use here."

"I'll do what I can, and please call me Leonard."

"If you like. Let's get to it, shall we?"

Was it getting colder in the room? People already dead had given me warmer receptions.

McGee and I sat, as Kate picked up some blue binders and handed them to us. I flipped mine open. The copy of the mysterious colored map I'd asked for earlier lay loosely on top.

Kate spoke up. "Doctor Wise, before we begin, I want you to understand that the FBI doesn't officially sanction the use of 'psychics' or people who call themselves such. I should tell you, I've read your paper about the Mishan case."

"I'm flattered."

"Don't be. Not to be rude, but I'm no believer. You write well, but the paper was far too sensational for a scholarly work. I want you to know, up front, that unlike *that* experience, this matter is strictly confidential. The FBI will not publicly comment on the matter outside this room."

"I understand," I said defensively.

"Let's go over the basic facts," Kate went on as she looked from Bill to me. "I'm going to give a synopsis of the common traits established about this criminal type. I'm sorry if this is old ground for you, Bill."

"No problem, Kate, I could use the review."

"Very well. Serial killers tend to be white males, ninety percent of the time. They are usually intelligent, highly interested in sadomasochism and voyeurism—"

"They like to watch," McGee said with deadly seriousness in his voice.

"Yes, but in a detached way. Just like their killings, they watch their victims' reactions but don't become involved in their suffering."

I shifted uncomfortably in my chair. "How can they not be involved with someone they're torturing?"

"They're engrossed in a fantasy, Doctor. They're watching each reaction to their specific action. But they are *emotionally* indifferent," she explained. "In fact, in all aspects of their lives, they have a lack of attachment toward other people on every level."

I noticed McGee was 'Bill,' while I remained 'doctor.'

She looked at her notes. "Although very smart, they often have trouble staying employed. They work at menial jobs that are far beneath their abilities, in places where they think they won't get caught. In fact, people like this are methodical about avoiding entrapment."

"That sounds like this guy," McGee suggested. "Except… why did he send me the damn map?"

Yearling shook her head. Her tresses shimmered in the fluorescent light. "I could write an entire book about that, Bill. On one hand, he's bragging, daring you to catch him."

"Like the Unabomber?" I asked. "I read about him. He often would brag about what he did."

"Yes, but I would suggest his psychosis is of a different strain. On another level, perhaps your perp wants to get caught. Other than that, he fits the profiles. He even has the 'cooling off' period after each murder."

"Cooling off?" I asked.

"Yes," McGee took up the conversation. "There's time between each abduction. That's what made me suspect it was a serial killer we were dealing with."

Kate nodded. "The killer often acts out a psycho-sexual fantasy. This one seems to create a story that requires him to seek his prey, research them, find out their comings and goings, and then pick a perfect time to strike. The target's death fulfills the adventure, providing him with an emotional and often sexual release.

"In some cases, Len, rape can be involved," McGee said.

Kate responded. "From what you've told me of this case, he has heavy sexual ramifications: fixation on the nipples, removal of skin. But penetration isn't part of his particular fantasy."

"What causes someone to do this?" I grimaced, sickened.

"I could give you the song and dance about domineering mothers or childhood sexual abuse," she clarified with a polite shrug.

"But no one knows for sure, Len," McGee finished for her.

"That's right." She gave McGee a smile, which faded completely as she looked back at me. "All we can do is try to catch him with the information we have."

"If I recall my psychiatric training," I said, "we would technically classify this type of action as a mental disorder."

"He's been disordering a lot of innocent people," McGee added grimly.

"Actually, three victims a year is pretty slim for some of these guys," Yearling surmised, looking at her notes again. "Anatoly Onoprienko killed fifty-two people in Russia between 1989 and 1995. Pedro Alonso Lopez, the 'Monster of the Andes', went on a spree in South America killing three women a week. Authorities believe he murdered over three hundred women before they stopped him."

"Oh good, our guy isn't in the big leagues," I muttered.

"No, but he scopes out victims and covers his tracks. There's not a lot we're going to find with traditional police techniques, especially without a body."

I nodded. "I get the problem. Forensics uncovers things we're not aware of."

McGee gave me a reassuring smile. "As it is, I've requested the forensic files on the cases where they discovered the bodies."

"Good," Kate acknowledged. "You see, Doctor, forensic psychiatry builds a profile, which helps focus the search."

I stared right at her. "And that must be where I come in."

"I've seen you demonstrate abilities that suggest you're a psychic." She stared at me as if I were a new kind of bug. "After our last case, I had to reconsider the 'advantages' you brought. You may have just been lucky."

It was my opportunity to push a point. "With all due respect, Doctor Yearling, we could use some luck right now."

"I hope you don't mind." She pulled a thin file out of her shoulder bag, which lay on a chair out of sight. "Since our last encounter, I did a little research on you."

"I assume more than my author's bio from the paper I wrote?" I smiled.

"You were also a medical student?" Kate said, sticking to business.

"Correct, first in my class."

"And you studied to be a clinical psychiatrist."

"Why, Len, I always knew you possessed a shady past," McGee joked. "What's next, a lawyer?"

"No, I just date one," I assured.

"I have to tell you," Kate continued. "It is very rare to find a psychic with a medical background."

"Even harder to find a parapsychologist with a science background. I'm working to change that."

She watched me, and her look softened. "I have to say, compared to most people who call themselves psychics, you have a unique history."

"'Unique' meaning 'scientifically based' in my case? Like Bill, I prefer facts over intuition, but I also have to rely on my abilities, and I'll tell you, something in this case is affecting them."

"I don't understand." Kate frowned and glanced at Bill.

"Neither do I," I said.

"Len, you only tried once," McGee reassured.

"No, I tried again before I came here. I got closer, actually felt as if I was with Mary—"

"Is she still alive?" McGee sat up in his chair.

"I don't know. She is in an old room, peeling paint, boarded-up windows, and in a lot of pain. But I lost it again."

Doctor Yearling gazed at me. It was fascinating having those emerald circles inspect me as if she could peer into my soul. If I made eye contact, I could actually peer into hers.

"Leonard, as you know, I have only limited personal experiences with psychics."

"Limited?" I repeated.

"Very well… it's non-existent, except for the case I did with you. As I told you, the Bureau doesn't put much credence in the idea of Extrasensory Perception—"

"Except for some very impressive clinical trials," I observed.

"You know about—" she stopped, catching herself. "That was years ago, and they went nowhere. But, tell me, what do you mean you 'lost' it? How did you get there in the first place?"

"I did a reading. I held a few strands of hair from the woman's purse."

"Hair, why?"

"It helps if I hold something from the crime scene, or a personal object of the victim—"

"Or missing person," McGee added.

"Victim, Bill. If this woman isn't dead, she will be soon."

Yearling looked back at me. "Let's stay focused. How do you get impressions?"

"I put myself into an alpha state through controlled breathing and meditation. It helps to focus on an object. My mind tunes into the vibration of that specific mental energy and my mind interprets that energy as a vision."

She nodded her head. "Alpha is a self-hypnotic state. I could recreate that. Is that your only technique?"

"There are others. Often I get hunches — sometimes precognition. I call them buzzes. Those show up where and when they choose."

"Doctor Yearling, when we tried earlier, Len seemed to be with the girl and experiencing the same things she did."

"I did better at my office," I said. "There, I brought myself down to a very low level, and I could see the room around her. I could detach from her feelings — her pain."

"Any sense of where she was?" Yearling asked.

"No, it was an old building, some abandoned structure."

"Great!" McGee muttered. "There's only about ten thousand empty buildings in northern New Jersey."

"I got a quick glimpse of someone in a white lab coat, and that's when I disconnected."

"Leonard, I have to ask you, did you feel you were really there? Is the memory strong?"

"It's faded a bit," I conceded, leaning back. "That's the problem with the visions: the images depart quickly."

"If you're willing to try, I can probably pull that memory up to the surface."

"But I told you, I ran into—"

"Whatever stopped you when you were seeing the vision shouldn't affect you if it's only a memory. I could attempt to regress your mind and help you see in more detail."

"Are you game for it, Len?" McGee said.

I felt a shudder run through me as the wispy memory of that room passed through my head, the horror and pain I tapped into when I was with Ms. Gillian. Plus, that shadowy figure, whose presence caused my mind to rush back to my reality. I swallowed hard and shrugged my shoulders.

"I'll do anything you want," I offered, looking directly at Kate. "But I have to warn you: a psychopath was in control when she hypnotized me."

"Ah, you were one of Vanya's?"

"Yes," I said, recalling Doctor Anika Vanya, the hypnotherapist, who used a combination of drugs and deep hypnotic techniques to turn ordinary people into killers.

"That actually might speed things up," Kate considered. "Have you ever done guided meditation?"

"Often."

"What I will do is very similar." She pointed to a small gooseneck fixture on the table next to McGee. "Bill, can we kill the fluorescent lights? Maybe turn on that lamp?"

Kate glanced back at me and watched my reaction. "Do you remember your key, or the lock she programmed you with?"

I nodded. Vanya had used a two-step technique to manipulate her victims. First, she had a code word, a 'key' which put you in a mesmerized state instantly. Then she would use a 'lock', usually a poem, to gain access and control of your mind. "No. I mean, not exactly. My key was a character from *The Manchurian Candidate*."

"Who?" Kate questioned. "Raymond Shaw?"

"I'm here." The words sprang from my mouth unbidden.

A moment later, Kate snapped her fingers in front of my face.

"Ah, welcome back, Doctor."

"What happened?" I wondered. "Any luck?"

"Well, we found your key," Kate disclosed. "Now if I only knew your lock."

I shook my head. "The others were children's poems, but I have no idea—"

A memory struck me.

"Queen of Hearts!" I blurted.

"What?" McGee challenged.

"The last time Vanya tried to activate my lock, she talked about the Queen of Hearts," I concluded.

Kate smiled. "That could be the famous poem. It also makes sense. In the film, Ray — I mean the lead character — would obey any order he heard after he saw a playing card, the Queen of Hearts."

"It's worth a try," I offered.

Yearling went on. "Okay. If we succeed, I'll make sure you remember everything that happens."

"That would be nice," I remarked.

"Oh yeah," McGee said. "And remember, only give commands. Part of the programming causes people only to respond to commands."

"I de-programmed Tom Harrigan and Tylissa Booker, Bill. I know the rules," Kate offered, a bit condescendingly.

McGee walked over and closed the door, shutting us off from the rest of the station.

"Are you ready, Leonard?" she told me in a calm and reassuring tone.

I smiled at this. "At least you're calling me Leonard now."

"And you can call me Kate. Raymond Shaw."

4. RUGGED REFUSE

"I'm here," I said immediately.

"The queen of hearts, she made some tarts—" Kate began.

"All on a summer's day," I responded.

"The knave of hearts, he took those tarts—"

"And stole them clean away," I finished.

"Where are you?" Kate asked.

"In my retreat," I stated.

The term 'mental retreat' was another technique Vanya had programmed into her people. It was a part of their subconscious that allowed them to be commanded to do almost anything, given the right motivation. But your conscious mind did not know about this 'retreat', unless the hypnotist ordered you to remember.

"Good. You will remember everything we say while we are here, and you will listen only to my voice. Tell me if you understand."

"I understand."

"Now, close your eyes and relax… Breathe… There is only the sound of my voice… Breathe…"

I was weightless, floating. I knew Kate had hypnotized me, but it certainly was not what I expected. It differed from the image I had of the hypnotist, as well as differing from the destructive methods of Doctor Vanya.

I could hear her speak to me, her voice guiding me.

"Think back to the images you saw. You were in contact with Mary Gillian. You were in a room…"

I sank back into the memory of the vision. Or was I going back to that room? I couldn't tell, but I was there again and able to watch Mary's form. It must be the memory of what I had seen earlier, as she was in exactly the same position.

"Concentrate on the room around you," Kate's voice told me. "Try to bring it into focus."

I could see the room in much sharper detail. During my previous vision, I must have been so centered on Mary that the room was secondary. I felt a quick twinge of the remembered pain Mary felt.

"Stay the observer," I heard Kate say. I must have winced at the flash of Mary's pain, and Kate tried to keep me to the task at hand.

"You can speak," she ordered. "Tell us what you scc."

"I'm in a dark place, a room," I testified. I described the peeling paint and boarded window, which I could see in much greater detail than I had earlier.

"Focus on your surroundings. Is there anything you missed the last time?"

"Is there?" I responded dreamily.

"Watch that," McGee warned.

"Oops," Kate apologized. "Focus. Tell me if you see anything you missed the last time."

I looked at Mary, noticing how she didn't seem to move. As I observed the vision from memory, time seemed to stop. It was so odd being there in this way. Every time I experienced a vision on my own, it was more like a dream. I observed what I could, and it was quickly gone from my mind and memory.

But with Kate's guidance, the room was much clearer than before. I could see places where the ceiling had fallen, leaving piles of plaster and dirt on the floor. I could see every board of lathe in the wall where there was a hole, and the linoleum of the floor, an old pattern worn and faded.

I noticed something behind Mary.

"I see something in the room's corner. A collection of metal tubes—"

Kate instructed me. "In your mind, move towards the tubes. Try to get a good look at them, to see what they are."

I saw myself move around Mary as I drew close to the metal. It formed a shape, a familiar one.

"It's a bed," I realized. "There's a support, like a cot. No, no, it's too high to be a bed. And there are wheels…"

"Put the pieces together, Leonard. Tell me what it is."

"It's a gurney," I said, perhaps a little too enthusiastically. "A bed they wheel patients in a hospital. But it's in terrible shape — one wheel broken, there's no mattress. And there are straps hanging." I shook my head. "I've never seen a gurney like it."

"Tell me if those straps could be restraints."

"Yes, yes… that's it."

"Tell me what else you see."

"I looked out the window when I was last here."

"Excellent." Her voice stayed calm and even. "Go to the window and look out."

"Yes," I responded, and moved toward the window to peer through the same opening as before. "I see grass and a tree — nothing else."

"Is the grass long or short?"

"No, it's cut. But there are spots where it's overgrown, close to the building."

"Allow the picture to become clear. Don't force it. Just see as much as you can."

I glanced around the limited view from the window, and it became a little sharper.

"I can see a wall… no, the corner of a building. It's dark, but it looks like brick — two colors of brick. The corner of the building is lighter. I see a door—"

"A door?"

"Yes, a rusted metal door. They painted it white, but the rust leaked through. It's got letters on it."

"Tell me what letters you see."

"It looks like a W... then an A... and an R, and under the letters are numbers '39' and another '48'. I can't see any more."

"That's fine. Come back into the room."

I backed away from the window.

"What else do you see?"

"There's broken glass on the floor. It's so dirty. And there is a shape in white paint under the chair Mary is on. She's in the center of a circle, in the middle of... a pentagram."

"A five-pointed star?"

"Yes, it's inverted." I could feel the terror rising within me.

"Calm, Leonard, stay the observer. Listen only to my voice."

"Yes."

"Turn and look around."

"I'm turning and looking at the door. It's so — Ah!"

"What do you see?"

A chuckle rose from my throat, more a relief response than anything funny.

"Tell me what you see," she urged in her calm, even voice.

"I'm sorry, there is a drawing on the wall. I guess it kind of surprised me."

"Tell me what you see. Keep it small, just the details."

"It's a man with horns," I said, knowing now that this must have been what I saw in the vision when the man came into the room. I realized how images mixed when you were in an altered state. With Kate to guide me, I avoided the pitfall of sensory overload. She kept me focused on the specifics.

Mary must see that drawing every day, and the image may have become mixed in her mind as well. I confused this image with her pain and perceptions. When I was in touch with her both times, I was too easily swept into her interpretation of events.

Suddenly, I felt the hairs on the back of my neck stand up. Fear gripped me and filled me with terrible dread.

"He's coming," I whispered. "I've got to get out of here."

"You're safe," Kate told me.

"No, I'm not. Get me out of here!" I demanded.

"Stay the observer. Try to see him."

"But he'll see me. I need to get out of here!" I heard myself shout.

I looked at the door, which I could see in greater detail than before. In fact, it appeared huge. I could see it slowly open, and I could detect the gloved hand holding the scalpel appearing.

"No!" I yelled, and my eyes pushed open as I jumped to full consciousness in the interrogation room. I was standing upright, as if I had bolted from my chair. I breathed heavily with my armpits moist.

"Jesus, Len, are you okay?" McGee said, his firm hand clamped onto my arm, as if to hold me from flying up to the ceiling.

"Yes, yes," I said, as I blinked and tried to calm down. I could hear my heartbeat racing in my ears.

"Kate, you have to be more careful!" McGee stormed.

Kate rose from her chair as well. "That wasn't me. It was him." She faced me. "You have to know — coming out of an altered state in that way—"

"I know, I know," I muttered.

"That's no reason to—" Bill started to say.

"It's okay, Bill." I lifted my hands with my fingers spread to calm everyone down. "Kate's right. I lose the images when the man comes into the room. If I could push past it, I might see him."

"Perhaps you're still too involved," Kate conceded. "But to come up like that from a trance state… it could be dangerous."

"I don't know what it is." I straightened and tried to loosen up my stiff shoulders. "But every time I get close, I panic. The odd part is that in a trance state, I shouldn't panic at all."

"You have to shut it off," Kate said, and watched me for a reaction, probably to help me work through whatever it was.

At that moment, however, it just annoyed the hell out of me that she was staring. I snapped, "You don't have to stare at me like that!"

"Hey, easy, Len," McGee said.

I realized I had spoken with a lot of vitriol.

I was immediately contrite. "I'm sorry, Doctor."

"No, it's me that should be sorry. I didn't mean to keep pushing at you. It was a very successful session."

"Successful? I didn't seem to get much."

"That's where you're wrong, Len." She turned to McGee. "Bill, in Leonard's vision, he saw a gurney. What does that suggest to you?"

"A hospital."

"Good. Now, the building looked empty, unused."

I looked at McGee, his face lost in his own inner vision; the detective was re-examining clues in his mind.

"An abandoned hospital," he said. "There aren't a lot of those in New Jersey—" He got up and paced.

"But Leonard saw restraints on a gurney—"

"A mental hospital!" Bill realized. "A sanitarium!"

"Very good," Kate praised him.

I could tell from the excitement on their faces that they had done this before. For a moment, I felt like I was intruding.

"Abandoned mental institutions exist all over the state," he said. "The state cut funding, which caused a bunch of them to close. "There must be three or four in North Jersey alone."

"Also, Leonard saw a word on the corner of another building that started 'W-A-R,' which could be 'Wards.'"

"Yes, it all makes sense," McGee enthused. "The guy wears a white coat, like he's a doctor. He kidnaps these women, takes them to an old hospital. Then he does his own brand of 'surgery' on them."

Kate nodded. "Filled with sexual overtones and torture. He's one sick puppy."

"Or mad dog," McGee said, his merriment calmed.

"So what's the next step?" I asked.

They both looked over, as if surprised I was still there. They immediately went back to business, the intimacy gone.

"It's after ten," Kate sighed, "and I had a long drive up from Baltimore today."

"Of course, Kate, you're tired," McGee apologized. "Besides, it's in my ballpark now."

"How far do you want to take this?" she asked. "Nothing against Leonard, but all we have are these impressions. That's not evidence."

"True, but the map he sent me is solid evidence. It will help me get the FBI New Jersey Task Force involved and permission to go to some of those abandoned sites."

"Bill, it's really not much," Kate interjected, as doubt crept into her voice.

"She's right, Bill," I pointed out. The last thing I wanted was McGee to get busted back to desk sergeant.

"If we get to work right away, we can start searching these places tonight," McGee suggested, a reassuring look in his eye.

"We should wait. I'll be working with the Task Force while I'm here. Allow me to make some connections tomorrow," Kate said.

"I'm worried that Mary Gillian may not last the night." McGee frowned. "Len says she's in bad shape."

I sighed. "If my vision was true, he's removed the skin from places on her face, possibly done some surgery. I'm convinced that Mary will die tonight."

"I will help in any way I can, Bill," Kate said. "If you need me to stay—"

"No, look, both of you should go, get some rest. You've done a lot. You've given me a place to start."

"More thanks to Leonard than me," Kate conceded.

"I only hope what I saw pans out," I noted. "Though I have to say, I've never seen a place so clearly as when Kate was guiding me."

"I think we've got a good team here," McGee boasted. "Kate, it's nice to see you again. I'll give you both a call tomorrow."

"If you can save Mary…" I said.

"Leonard, you'd best not get your hopes up," Kate warned. "This man has done this for years. He's good at covering his tracks."

"Which makes me wonder why he sent me that map. The police found three bodies, Kate," McGee said. "But then he just hands us the mother lode."

Kate nodded. "I'll start on a full psychiatric profile, but I would assume that he gets off on taunting the police. He thinks he's invincible. I hope you stop him, Bill."

"I hope *we* stop him, Kate."

"Can I walk you to your car?" I asked Kate.

"Please." She smiled.

We walked out of the interrogation room and out of the station, her in a pair of sensible shoes, and me tapping along with my cane.

"Sorry for getting so angry back there," I apologized, sheepish.

"You were in an agitated state."

"I usually have more control."

"As do I. I should apologize to you for being so unfriendly. I guess it's the idea of working with a psychic—"

"Worried about your reputation?"

"Since we last worked together, there have been people trying to convince me you're a fraud."

"I'm surprised. After our last success, I thought you appreciated what I brought to the table."

"Well, agents told me stories and gave pretty good explanations for how you did it last time."

"Do you think differently now?"

She stopped walking and turned to look at me. "Yes."

I smiled. "Ah, good qualities — intelligent and forgiving. Where do you usually work?"

We walked as she continued. "I have an office in Baltimore, but I spend a lot of time on the road, going wherever I'm needed each day. Profiling is a profession with a lot of traveling."

"I would think with your psychiatric background—"

"Don't start. I've told the story so many times that I can give you the overview. Yes, I was planning to be a regular psychiatrist, with some extra added hypnotherapy training to help patients—"

"—Quit smoking?"

A smile crept onto her face, only the second one I'd seen tonight. "I'm not above that. But it all changed when my sister — she got picked up by one of those monsters—"

"Oh, no."

"Yes," she said, her smile fading as memories overwhelmed her. "He kept her alive for three days. Raped her, stabbed her, and let her bleed to death. I helped the police catch him."

We were silent for a moment. I valued her honesty with me in the face of such a traumatic loss.

Finally, I spoke as we reached her car. It was a pale gray Mercedes, with a federal government license plate and tinted glass that seemed completely opaque in the dim light of the parking lot. "How did you do it?"

"I got into his head. I decided if I learned all the things about how a killer thinks, then I could catch him. I had help — the FBI got involved. We found a girl that survived an attack, and I used hypnosis to regress her and remember what the man looked like."

"That must have impressed them."

"We caught him, which did impress them. So, they offered me a job. I decided that if I could help another family not lose someone to one of these — that would be a good way to spend my life."

"I'm sure McGee appreciates your help. You two seem very… familiar with each other."

"We worked together, which is what I hope you mean. Bill was a member of our team. We got to be close."

"Should I ask 'how close' or will I lose any ground I've gained tonight?"

"Not as close as you think, Doctor Dirty Mind." Kate frowned, but she wasn't angry. "Bill was married back then. We were only friends, but he is great to work with: quick, fast, decisive. He was an excellent agent. So, when he called about this, I showed up."

"I meant what I said in there: you helped me."

"Your gifts, or whatever they are, interest me. And with that programming from Vanya, it made things easy."

I nodded and looked at my feet as I walked. "Bill and I have saved lives, and that's enough."

She reached into her purse and pulled out a card. "If you get any more insights, my cell number is here. I'm staying at the Holiday Inn on Route Three. Thank you for the escort. Good night, Leonard." She stuck out her hand, and I shook it.

"Good night, Kate." I watched her drive off before I walked back to my van. It was a dark night, but the stars glimmered brightly. I made a silent prayer that McGee would find Mary Gillian tonight.

If, indeed, she was still alive.

5. NIGHTMARE SHELTER

The darkness didn't just sit there; it pressed against my eyes, thick and suffocating. I tried to blink the world into focus, but the gloom was oily. Then the smell hit me—stale copper and rot. I knew this place.

The peeling paint hung from the walls like strips of dead skin. The windows weren't just boarded over; they had been sealed shut to keep the screams in.

I was in *that* room.

No. This is a dream. I can't be here.

A sound scraped through the silence—a wet, dragging noise from deep in the hallway. My pulse spiked, my heart beating like a frantic bird. I tried to get up, to hide in the shadows, but my wrists snapped back.

Leather straps bit into my flesh, anchoring me to a heavy wooden chair. I lunged forward, but the chair didn't budge.

"He bolted it," I rasped, my voice sounding thin and hollow as it bounced off the empty walls. "That's why he chose this room."

The logic was cold, but speaking it aloud was the only thing keeping my mind from shattering. The dragging sound grew louder. Scrape. Step. Scrape.

"Got to get out," I hissed, thrashing against the restraints. The leather tightened with every frantic jerk.

"I'm coming for you, boy."

The voice was a low, gravelly vibration that seemed to come from the floorboards themselves. I knew that voice—it lived in the darkest corners of my memory. He knew me. He knew exactly how much I could bleed before I broke.

"No!"

I lunged one last time; the world tearing apart as I sat bolt upright.

The ropes were gone. Sweat-soaked bedsheets merely tangled my wrists. Pale, jagged moonlight sliced through the room at unnatural angles. I gulped down the air, my lungs burning as if they were full of ash.

I heard a gentle knock on the outer door of my sitting room.

"Wh-who is it?" I breathed, the words barely escaping my throat.

"Doctor?"

The familiar, matronly voice of Mrs. Higgins cut through the dread. I let out a jagged breath, my muscles turning to water.

"Mrs. Higgins? What are you doing up?" I swung my legs over the side of the bed, my limp heavy as I staggered toward the door in the gloom.

"I heard voices. Are ye alright?"

"Just a nightmare. I'm sorry," I said, reaching for the handle and pulling the door open.

Mary Gillian stood in the hallway. The skin on her face hung in grey, tattered ribbons down to her collarbone. Her hair was a white shroud, and her eyes—void of pupils—burned with a rhythmic, bloody light.

"Some help you were," she hissed, the sound of wet gristle grinding together.

I shrieked, my body convulsing as I hammered at the bedside lamp. The light flickered on, harsh and blinding. I was back in bed, drenched in a cold, oily sweat.

"It was a dream," I whispered, my voice trembling. "Just a dream."

But as I sat there, I realized the room was still dead silent—and the smell of stale copper seemed stronger than ever.

I didn't go back to sleep. I spent a few minutes looking at the ceiling of my bedroom and pinching myself. Comforted that I was truly awake, I put on my robe and walked into my sitting room, and headed for the kitchen. I made a cup of Red Zinger tea to stop myself from shaking.

I desperately wanted to call Jyanette, and I wanted a drink to steady my nerves. Of course, as a recovering alcoholic, I wouldn't stop at one drink.

I'd gone on a bender on New Year's Eve, from a combination of self-loathing and the availability of my favorite tipple. It had been a personal failing, but I'd stayed away from alcohol since then.

I wandered, my tea in hand, through the living room, which had a huge green tile fireplace with a stunning stained wood mantel. When Mrs. Higgins bought this house, all the woodwork was here and not painted over, like in some older houses. With an eye for antiques that would give Martha Stewart a run for her money, and some brilliant purchases at garage and estate sales, she'd decorated the place nicely.

I walked back to my end of the house and went through the door into my sitting room that served as my home office. Going to my desk, I pulled out a notebook and transcribed notes for the book I was working on.

My first case with Bill had involved a pyrokinetic, and I wrote a paper about it for a renowned parapsychological society. A literary agent saw the paper and suggested it would make a good book. I was currently writing it up as a novel, changing all the names to avoid any problems or lawsuits.

I imagined I was quite a sight as I sat in my bathrobe and pajamas, my hair sticking up wildly. It didn't matter; I just kept typing, going back and forth to my handwritten notes.

The writing was very grounding, and I slowly felt normal. The book was about half-done and I would finish it over the summer break, which began in a few short days when all of my classes ended.

My first year as a teacher had been a great success, and I would've liked to believe it was because I didn't just expect my students to regurgitate what I told them. I always liked to get a good look at their papers, their writing, the *thought process* going on in their heads. I didn't need them to know all the ins and outs of parapsychological theory because new research and new concepts constantly changed it.

No, I was much more interested in students learning to *think*, to grasp concepts logically, and to put arguments in a coherent, orderly fashion, even if I didn't agree with it.

At about seven-thirty, I heard Mrs. Higgins in the kitchen, so I pushed myself up from the desk and went out to procure coffee.

"Good mornin', Doctor. Ye're oop early."

"Good morning, Mrs. Higgins. I had a nightmare. Did you hear anything?"

"I'm on the second floor of the house, dear. I wouldn't hear a thing."

"You made a guest appearance in my dream."

"Oh? I hope I looked presentable."

I shivered at the recollection. "You weren't quite yourself."

"Ye've been having a spot of trouble with this case that McGee called ye on?"

I eyed her suspiciously. "How do you know that?"

She shrugged innocently. "Ye said ye had a nightmare. Ye only have those when something's botherin' ye, in here." She tapped her head.

I poured the dark brown liquid into my awaiting mug. "So, if I am, what do *you* think I should do?"

"Ah, Doctor, now ye're playin' with me," she teased, as she got the cream from the refrigerator and handed it to me. "But there is a story that moight help."

I smiled despite myself. "One of your famous stories, Mrs. Higgins?"

"It's an ol' Irish tale about a young man who must go and foight a dragon in order to save his lady love. Did I tell you this?"

"Doesn't sound familiar."

"Now, this dragon is goin' to destroy the entoire village if he doesn't give the monster the one woman that he loves. Instead, he decides to face the monster and combat it. But he's a young man and must borrow a shield, a sword, and a helmet that don't quite fit."

Already pulled into the tale, I said. "He must've been a sight."

"Yes. Off he goes to face the beastie. Now, outwardly he's putting on a brave front, but inside he's nearly scared to death. In his mind, he imagines the dragon as this enormous lizard that can kill with his fiery breath and crush him with his huge talons. He gets more and more scared as he approaches the cave where it dwells."

"And it rips him to shreds?" I suggested ruefully.

She gave me a wry look. "It's my story, I'll tell it, thank ye. So he gets off his horse and walks into the cave and forces himself upright, when all he wants to do is run away. He's glad he only has the armor he does, so that the dragon can't hear his knees shake. He walks in and yells out, 'Come out, dragon. I'm here to face ye, man to beast.'"

"Not the most subtle way of handling it."

"Well, there's a long silence, and he yells again. 'Come, beastie,' he hollers, 'or I'll be in there after ye.' Finally, he hears a rustling, a scraping of talons on dirt. He can see something move in the dark. He raises his shield, lifts his sword, and out from the cave comes a lizard not much bigger than a dog.

"So what does he do?"

"He ends up taming the beastie and marrying his girl—"

"And they live happily ever after," I added. "A lovely story, Mrs. Higgins, but I don't see how it applies."

"Oh, ye will, Doctor, ye will," she said, and tottered over to the stove. "Can I cook ye some breakfast?"

"That would be lovely. Thank you, Mrs. Higgins."

"I'll bring it when it's ready."

I went back to my office, shaking my head. I honestly knew better than to dismiss her stories — they usually had a way of being relevant at some point.

Forty-five minutes later, I pulled into my parking space at Garden State University. The sky was ominous, as heavy gray clouds rolled overhead and threatened rain. Was it the day that made me nervous, or the remnants of my nightmare, which I could still remember far too clearly?

I walked into Williams Hall and carefully up the stairs, always a frustrating thing with only one good leg. I lifted my left leg up a step, pulled my right leg up to the same step, then repeated the process again and again. At least going downstairs was faster.

As I reached the top of the stairs, Jim Stevens was walking down the hall toward me. Jim had been the "custodial engineer" at the university for years. He never seemed to age. Tall and lanky, African-American, he was one of those people who seemed content with his life and was always in a good mood.

"Hey there, Jim."

"Doc Wise, how you doin'?"

"I'm getting by. How's the family?"

He considered this for a moment. "It's just Ronnie and me, these days. But she's out of town helping her sister right now."

"How is Ronnie?" I smiled as I recalled meeting her a year earlier when I first arrived at GSU.

"Fine, fine."

"You looking forward to the summer break?"

"I dunno. I still gotta work. Just at a different place. T'ain't as nice as the college."

I frowned. "What do you mean? Aren't you here during the summer?"

"No, just part-time, so the State of New Jersey assigns me to another facility, over in Morris Plains."

I frowned. "That's a ways from here."

"Don't I know it. It's one of those mental places."

I hated to admit I had been only half-listening, but suddenly my ears perked up. "A mental institution?"

"Yeah, y'know, the state facility."

Energy crackled up my spine, which made it difficult to form my next words.

"What's the name of this place?"

"Don't you know, Doc? It's been there a hundred years. It's called Blackshale."

As he spoke the name, the very palpable buzz screamed in my head.

Blackshale…

"You okay, Doc? You got a funny look on your face."

"Huh? No, I'm fine, Jim. I just was… thinking. Are any of the inmates dangerous?"

"Don't matter. I was a boxer in my younger days." He brought his hands up in the traditional defensive pose and feigned a few shadowboxing moves with a smile. "Besides, I just clean. They don't usually bother me."

"Good," I said, as I tried to put my manners back in place. "I've got to teach a class. I'll see you later, and my best to Ronnie."

"Sure thing, Doc." He wandered off with the big broom in his hand.

The word *Blackshale* repeated in my mind.

I focused on letting the psychic part of my brain know I got the message. I had a class to teach, and I couldn't do anything about the buzz until afterward.

I walked into my classroom, a small lecture hall with my desk in the room's front, like a stage, with the students sitting in elevated rows all the way to the back. It was only about half full but filling rapidly. My classes were always well-attended, even by students who majored in other subjects. They came in and sat down, a freshman class, youthful faces still so terribly unsure of themselves, even though they had been here since last fall.

"Good morning, everyone. Today we are finishing the history of psychic phenomenon in the Spiritualism Movement of the Nineteenth century by beginning with—"

And I began my lecture, a part of my mind still distracted.

An hour and a half later, back in my office in College Hall, I retrieved the blue folder about the case from my laptop bag. I stared at the map McGee had copied for me. Using a highlighter, I went over his marks a second time to focus on each location better.

I heard McGee from the previous night saying, "Time is of the essence." I pulled out my cell phone and hit the speed dial.

"McGee," his gruff voice said, as he picked up on the second ring.

"It's Len, Bill. Any luck?"

"We raided four abandoned places last night, and I was personally at two of them. There are a whole bunch of closed mental hospitals in this state. There was one in Caldwell, on Sanatorium Road, of all places. It was a real mess, and the smell… but we didn't find a thing, and we went through two buildings, top to bottom. Then I went to a place in Edison. Man, the entire neighborhood was a mess. I didn't get home until after four."

"And there you are, back at ten-thirty."

"I've got a madman to catch."

"I may have a lead. I'm going to check it out today."

"Want some help?"

"I think — no, I want to see if I'm actually onto something before I involve you."

"So, it's just a buzz, huh?" McGee chuckled, familiar with my terminology.

"Yes, and I feel I have to check it out on my own first."

"Don't get all bold and daring, Len. Take it slow and call if you need backup. You know how Jyanette feels about you taking risks."

"I do," I sighed. "When I showed up with a black eye on her birthday, she didn't talk to me for a week. You should probably keep working your leads."

"Doctor Yearling is coming in to give us a hand today. She got set up in an office in Morris Plains. So, where are you going?"

"Blackshale."

"The state mental facility?" Bill replied, confused. "But that's still open, isn't it?"

"Yes. I've found it on my map app."

"You'll see signs from Route Ten as well."

"Thanks, I'll call you if I have any luck."

"I thought we were looking for an *abandoned* place."

"So did I. I'll let you know, Bill."

"Good hunting, Len."

I looked down at the map in my hands. During the conversation, I drew lines connecting the different murder sites. It formed a large, oddly shaped circle. Near the center of the circle was Morris Plains, New Jersey.

Blackshale.

6. UNDISCLOSED HIDEAWAY

I had not planned to take Santos along; it just happened. He came into the office to talk about a speaking engagement I had booked. We had just received the contract. Santos worried about running my classes during my absence because it was a September engagement.

He saw me put my laptop away and asked where I was going.

"On a wild-goose chase," I said.

"Fieldwork?" Santos queried, all but drooling.

"Possibly. I'm following up on a hunch."

I knew better. I should have just made a lame statement and been out the door. Santos went into his complete song and dance that I never took him out on fieldwork, which would be an addition to his education.

"Teddy," I objected, "you're just trying to find an excuse to avoid finishing that paper you're writing."

"Yeah, that too."

I smiled. At least he was honest about it. So, I agreed. An extra pair of hands might be useful if I had to go exploring.

We drove through the murky day with the headlights on. We rode in silence as Santos wrote in a spiral-bound notebook.

"What are you doing?" I finally asked.

"I'm taking notes of our field research."

"We aren't doing any yet. All we're doing is driving. I'm not even sure where we're going to end up."

"When we get there, I'll be ready."

I nodded. I shouldn't spoil his fun. After all, he still had the enthusiasm of youth. And I knew what it was like, seeing every project as an adventure. Maybe I'd just wandered through a few too many musty old buildings, or I still wasn't over being featured in the National Inquisitor.

I was experiencing a persistent negative attitude. I felt annoyed with Santos, though I had to admit he was the best TA I could imagine. He knew how to help without getting underfoot. The guy actually wanted to do some research. Usually, when I have to investigate a phenomenon, it's at a location hundreds of miles away. When I was in Maine at a haunted house, I also needed him to cover classes.

Maybe what I was feeling was the result from the dark day and my dark dream.

I made the turn onto Route Ten, heading west. This route would take us through Livingston.

"Hey, Teddy. Let me buy you a Starbucks."

"Sure!"

His reaction brought a smile to my face. Even though he was in his mid-twenties, he still had the delight in things of an eleven-year-old. I hoped he wouldn't lose it.

As we parked and entered the Starbucks, I quietly brought Santos up to speed, telling him the details of the last few days as well as I could. I continued talking as we got our coffee from some perky young thing who was seriously giving Teddy the eye. Santos, of course, was oblivious. His attention focused on my story, as his quick mind analyzed all the possibilities.

Santos questioned me as we continued our drive, trying to get a different perspective. This annoyed me as well, even though challenging me helped me to be more thorough.

Finally, as if satisfied with my responses, Santos moved into review mode. He looked over the notes he'd made, going over what we did and didn't know.

"So, there's this missing woman."

"Check," I offered, to hurry the process along.

"You saw her in a vision, and now you're trying to track the place down."

"Check."

"So far, you have found little or no empirical evidence to support your readings, and you observed that something blocked them."

"Uh… yes," I confessed.

"Doc, if I went out on a case with no solid facts to back up my intuition, you'd be the first person to tell me that was bad science."

Apparently, Santos listened to my lectures. I was a big supporter of intuition; I thought some of our best thinking came not from our head but from our gut. I also stressed in class that parapsychology must meet the demands of any other science, and therefore, any research must have hard data to back it up.

Here I was, breaking that rule.

"Good point. But we have little else to go on. Sometimes, you can find the evidence later. With a haunting or some other metaphysical activity, you would encounter a situation with established facts. There would be witnesses, a location, people you could question, perhaps even documentation. Here, we don't have a place, and we may not even have a person. If we can find one of those, we will have more information for the investigation."

Santos nodded. "That makes sense, Doc."

I breathed a quiet sigh of relief.

We passed the Livingston Circle and shopping center after shopping center. Route Ten was a popular place to shop, being one of the first four-lane highways in the state. Now, compared to highways like 80 and 280, Ten was slow, with traffic lights every few blocks.

We passed under 287, another major artery, where cars flew over us on bridges high above our heads. Santos seemed to be content to review his notes, and I was happy for the break in the conversation. I didn't want my mood to get worse and snap at him.

As we came over a steep hill, I saw a small green sign with white letters:

BLACKSHALE STATE MENTAL FACILITY
THIS TURN

I got off at the jug handle and crossed the highway. We drove up a small hill, and the landscape changed drastically. From stores and mini-malls, it now was houses with large plots of property. They were all farms a generation or two ago. We turned onto a road named "Old Dover" and the pavement became the quality of a third-world country. I needed to slow down because of the terrible potholes and rough surface.

"Jeez!" I said. "What happened here?"

"It's construction, Doc. Look out my side of the van."

I glanced over, an easy trick now that we were only doing fifteen miles per hour. I could see large houses with two-car garages. They were huge but packed so close to each other that if you lived there, you would have to be careful undressing near a window.

"'The Commons,'" I said, as I read a large sign. "'Luxury one-family dwellings'. Driving a tank must be a pre-requisite."

"Oh, I don't know. A Jeep or a Humvee should work."

The road smoothed out and became half as wide, putting us safely back on the original Old Dover Road.

We came to a crossroads. Directly in front of us were several modern red brick buildings and a sign that read the same as the one on Route Ten.

Apparently this was Blackshale.

I turned right and slowly passed a series of small buildings.

"Is this it?" Santos asked, disappointed.

"I don't know," I said as we passed a building with an admissions sign. "It is certainly not anything like what I saw in my vision."

Santos pointed at a road ahead on our left. "Wait, Doc. Turn onto that street. It might take us into the facility."

I made the turn. It brought us past several small parking lots to a gracious building marked AUDITORIUM.

Teddy mused, "This place looks a lot more modern than I expected."

"Me too, Teddy. Look, there's one of the older buildings." I nodded to a structure on our left that was made from cut stone — all of it well maintained, with air conditioning units suggesting a central air and heating system.

"I guess I was wrong," I muttered, dejected but grateful I hadn't dragged McGee out here with us.

"Or maybe not. Look straight ahead."

I turned from the building on my left to see a white house straight ahead. It looked more like one or two of the haunted houses I'd researched. It was old, dilapidated, and surrounded by a high, rusty chain-link fence to keep anyone out.

"That certainly doesn't look like it belongs here," Santos suggested.

"I don't know." I turned to take the road off to our left. We approached a very tall building, at least five or six stories high. But we must have been approaching it from the back, as it didn't look like a front entrance. I quickly turned onto a minor road with a green sign marked 'Kitchen Street'.

"Where are we going?" Santos asked.

"I want to see the other side of this building — oh, my God!"

"What — oh shit!"

Santos and I were both looking out my window as I brought the van to a stop. There was an enormous building, or a section of the same one. Plywood boarded up the windows. We could see, even in the overcast sky, that the roof had a huge, gaping hole in it. A stucco section under one set of windows had fallen off the building, exposing brick underneath, in contrast to the cut gray stone.

"This section can't be in use," Santos considered.

"They're lucky it's still standing."

Santos pointed. "Doc, look at that!"

I followed the line of his finger and saw a white door. It was like the one in my vision, but the surrounding stone was wrong. It had words and numbers stenciled on it:

WARDS

22

24

28

I stopped the van, throwing it into park. Santos and I got out and approached the door. Under the numbers there was another sign that warned:

DANGER-AUTHORIZED PERSONNEL ONLY.

"Is that the door you saw, Doc?"

"No, it's similar. But the numbers are wrong." I looked around and tried to imagine the view from my vision. "There isn't anywhere you could see this door from."

Santos headed for the van. "Let's keep going."

I followed him back into the vehicle, and we continued around a curve in the road, which brought us up to another abandoned and boarded building, this one having a decidedly 'Tudor' look to it. Its base was red brick, but it had large flat sections of stucco with exposed wooden beams, which divided the squares diagonally. I made another left turn.

"I think we're coming to another main entrance," Santos said.

"How could that be…?" I said. My words ended as I saw the structure ahead of us, and the view was stunning.

The edifice loomed menacingly over the landscape, its façade crafted entirely from uneven, jagged blocks of local stone that seemed to absorb the very light around them.

The entrance was imposing great soaring upwards to a height of five stories, its sheer scale both awe-inspiring and unsettling. Towering smooth granite pillars thrust skyward, firmly anchoring the weighty space between the second and third floors, casting elongated shadows that danced like restless spirits in the dim light.

Intricate figures were painstakingly carved into the stone, grotesque and otherworldly, their forms twisting into dark shapes that resembled humans or possibly gargoyles.

Above, large windows of yellow glass dominated the fourth floor, their opaque panes shimmering ominously even in the absence of sunlight.

Above that was what appeared to be a bell tower or a clock tower, though neither bell or clock appeared to be within it,

Outside, billowing dark clouds swirled violently, their ominous presence intensifying the building's sinister allure and making it resemble a macabre set piece from a horror film.

"This must have been the original main building," I surmised.

"Then why the hell do they have Admissions in that other building?"

I shook my head. "More modern. This is Gothic."

"Is that a nice way of saying spooky, Doc?"

"Spooky is not a scientific term, Teddy."

"Yeah, but it's the right word."

I turned onto this street and we were in a lovely parklike setting, though it looked dark from the overcast sky. There was a sidewalk along the edges with paths leading to other buildings. There were acres of grass and trees. The buildings just beyond the pavement were closed, some of them surrounded by chain-link.

I pulled the vehicle over and parked in a space marked with faded yellow paint. We stepped out of the van and looked at the building.

"That's quite a sight to drive up to," Santos said.

I pointed over at a small building bearing a state insignia. "Is that an office for the state police?"

Teddy shrugged. "They have a building here?"

"It is a state facility. Maybe it saves money on security."

"Yeah, but what does a state cop have to do to end up in a place like this? Not exactly a great assignment," Santos considered as we walked toward the police station. "Should we ask them for help?"

"Sure, I can hear us now: 'Officer, I experienced a vision with a woman being tortured. It might have been here, or it might not. Can you let us into all the buildings and see?'"

Santos pondered my suggestion. "I take it that might not go over too well."

"Not unless we want to end up as patients here."

Santos cast an eye at the imposing main building. "I don't like that idea either."

"I have a better solution," I suggested and pointed at the winding cement pavements that snaked their way through the well-cut lawns. "There are paths and sidewalks leading to all the buildings. Let's walk around, see what we can without going inside."

Santos nodded as we shut the van doors and walked down the paved walkway, past the police office.

"I have to tell you, Doc, the cops being here actually knocks down the theory that this is the place."

"What do you mean?"

"Who would do anything here with the state police right nearby? I mean, this guy, whoever he is, tortured and murdered people right under the cops' noses? You'd have to have balls to pull that off."

"This guy gets off on risk and the ways he outsmarts everyone. This might just be the perfect place. It would be the ultimate thrill to 'pull this off,' as you put it, with the police in proximity."

We walked along and passed what appeared to be an old band shell, probably dating from the fifties. It sat in the middle of a field, with space on the surrounding hill for people to sit and see or hear a show. We passed another building, red brick, with a magnificent arch in the front, also boarded up, which looked more sad and dejected than abandoned.

"Wow!" Santos said. "Get the architecture — so many different styles."

"Yes, it's like they used an original design on each building."

"They look well built!"

"Maybe they had the budget then."

We continued walking. Now there was a series of small houses, each made of brick, with the same slate roof as we'd seen on the larger structures.

"What were these for?" Santos said. "Patients who were in better shape? To get them used to living in the real world?"

"I don't think so. The construction's appearance suggests builders erected these when the major treatments primarily involved drugs and restraint. They used to turn the mentally ill into vegetables. They were a lot easier to take care of that way." I looked across the street. "Let's go look at the bigger ones over there."

Santos and I crossed the roadway, as I felt a drop of water hit my face. After the clouds had threatened for so long, the drops of rain bounced off the full, lush leaves on the nearby trees. Perhaps it would just be a faint drizzle. The smoldering clouds suggested a thunderstorm, though there was neither thunder nor lightning, just the sound of the raindrops.

"Great! I forgot my coat," Santos said.

"And I forgot my umbrella."

"Both of us are going to get wet, Doc."

"The fate of the ill-prepared. It's not like we didn't know it was going to rain. I—"

My voice deserted me as we approached the building. Suddenly, I didn't care about the rain or that my suit might get wet. The oppressive atmosphere struck me, and it wasn't the storm.

It was the building.

Tall and made of yellow brick, it had a magnificent front entrance several stories high with the seal of the State of New Jersey cast in the cement… but it was much more than that. There was an emanation of pure evil surrounding it. My throat closed, as if just being near it endangered my life.

I shivered.

"Doc? What's wrong?"

"Don't you feel it?" I whispered. I doubted he could. Santos knew parapsychological theory. In fact, he knew and researched some of my pet theories in his work as my teaching assistant. But to him, it was all just that: theory. He lacked the actual psychic abilities, and it was one reason it puzzled me that my work inspired him. He didn't know what any of it felt like.

Rain sluiced down Santos' face as he concentrated.

"It seems… heavy. I dunno, Doc… dark?"

I glanced over at him. "Then you do feel it?"

"I guess. It would help if I knew what I'm supposed to be feeling."

"You tell me."

"Whatever it is, it's not nice."

"That's a start," I said. I got a buzz, big time, as I looked up at a boarded-up window on the second floor. There was a small piece of wood, broken away, making a hole someone could see through. I turned around to take in the view it afforded.

"Santos," I croaked as I stared into the distance. "Here are my keys. In the drawer under the passenger seat, you'll find a pair of binoculars. Bring them to me. Hurry."

Santos looked at me for a moment, then grabbed the keys out of my hand and ran off to the van.

I was looking at a building, not too far away. It was red brick — deep red — but there was yellow brick at the corners. I drew nearer to the building behind me, trying to get directly under the window with the hole in the plywood. I saw a white door on the side of the building with writing on it; the rain made it hard to see.

Santos sloshed up through the rain, which fell in a steady drizzle now. I took the binoculars and pulled off the lens caps.

"Call McGee," I said, and handed Teddy my phone.

Santos nodded as I brought the field glasses to my eyes. I heard my cell phone beep as I focused the glasses on the door.

WARDS

39

45

"Lieutenant McGee?" Santos said. "I've got Doctor Wise here."

I lowered the glasses and put the phone to my ear. My mouth was dry, and I felt like I could barely talk. I inhaled deeply and focused.

"Len?" McGee's voice said, tiny inside the phone.

"Bill? I've got our location."

7. WARD OF EVIL

We waited in the rain, though we finally ducked under the large archway of the yellow-brick building. The song, 'Follow the Yellow Brick Road,' from the movie *Wizard of Oz* kept running through my head as I glanced at the bricks in their even formations.

The tawny brick certainly didn't have the bright yellow of Oz.

The hardest part about the waiting was the psychic flashes that kept invading my mind. Snippets of images, like still pictures of scenes.

But such scenes.

They all involved knives and pain — so much pain. I witnessed brief flashes from each point of view. A scalpel moving toward my eye. Me, pushing the scalpel into flesh. Waves of nausea swept over me as the images swirled, almost drowning me in their gore.

Being so close to a place where torture occurred was wreaking havoc with my extra senses. That, combined with the feeling of evil that emanated from this area so intensely. The place wore the aroma of death like an unpleasant odor.

The waiting felt like an eternity, though it was only about half an hour. I fought to erect mental protections in my mind, to wall away what I perceived, but images still slipped past my defenses.

Despite the images, I couldn't get a strong mental picture of the torturer, even when I saw things from his point of view. That was unusual. If I could see what someone else saw, I could usually find my way into that person's mind. Perhaps I didn't want to go there, considering the unbidden horrors I'd already experienced.

Santos was being a good egg, but I could sense that the energy of the place even got under his skin.

A few minutes later, several state police cars pulled up, and a tall, dark-haired man wearing a blue uniform and hat stepped out of the car. He walked toward us huddled in the doorway as the other policemen got out of their cars.

"One of you guys Leonard Wise?" he said in a booming voice.

"That's me!" I replied and limped out to meet him. He watched me shuffle with the cane.

"What happened to your leg?"

"Car accident, eight years ago."

"Tough break," he acknowledged, looking to Santos and also glancing back to check on the positions of his approaching men. "I'm with the state police."

"I passed the building you gentleman use on site," I asserted, not knowing what else to say.

"We only have one man assigned there. If there's trouble, he calls us and we have to come out from Morris Plains. I'm told you have something to do with a missing person's case?"

"Yes, I'm a civilian consultant with the Mountainview Police Department and involved in an on-going investigation." I held out my official ID, which the man took and gave a perfunctory glance.

An odd smile played across his lips. "You don't look like any kind of detective I've ever seen."

"Actually, I'm a college professor."

"Okay, Professor, whatever," he said dismissively. "Anyway, I got a call from Captain Lindstrom — who, by the way, isn't my captain — said we should run up here and assist you any way we can."

It might've been the energy I got from the building, but I couldn't fight the feeling that this man did not care for my being here, but I needed his help until McGee arrived, so I needed to be as nice as possible.

"Actually, Sergeant—?"

"Stant, Sergeant Stant."

"Yes, it might be a matter of life and death. We need to get into this building." I pointed at the specific one.

His face became serious, and he gestured to another officer who was carrying a large key ring with literally dozens of keys on it.

"I got the keys from our man assigned here," he explained, and then gave me a hard look. "Professor, you do know that this place isn't safe."

"I'm sure of it."

"And that I am not responsible if you hurt yourself."

"Of course not, but we need to get in, quickly."

Sergeant Stant walked toward the building, and the officer with the key ring joined us.

"Open that up, will you, Bobby?"

"Yes, sir, Sergeant," the man said and moved toward the padlocked door.

"Who's the kid?" Stant demanded, indicating Santos.

"Hey! I'm probably the same age as your officer," Santos argued, as he looked up through his thick lenses, taken aback by Stant's style.

"That's my associate, Téodore Santos."

"Also works at a college?"

"Same one, actually."

"Figures."

We approached the door as Bobby was going through the keys, one by one, reading the little pieces of paper scotch-taped to each.

"This might take a while, Sergeant."

"Try to hurry, please?" I urged him, feeling anxious. What if this was the place? What if Mary were still alive?

"Oh yeah, it's a matter of life and death, right?" Stant mocked me.

"Actually," I grumbled, feeling heat rise in the back of my neck, "someone may have tortured a young woman who is bleeding to death just a few feet from us."

Officer Bobby looked up from the keys, shocked by my statement. He glanced over to Stant with a troubled look on his face. Stant turned red from suppressed emotion.

"Look, Professor, I don't know why you're here, and I don't know your angle. But if you're suggesting that there is anything improper going on here—"

"All I'm asking, Sergeant, is that you take this seriously," I insisted, my temper flaring. Santos looked concerned, unused to seeing me angry.

"I take everything that happens here seriously, Professor," he shot back.

"Then get the damn door open," I snapped. "And by the way, it's Doctor. I went to medical school, and I have a PhD. I think I've earned the title."

Stant's face turned another shade of red, and I could see he was fighting a desire to tell me off. Instead, he turned to Officer Bobby and barked, "You got that door yet?"

"I think this is the key for the padlock, Sergeant."

"Then open the damn padlock, or break it if we have to," Stant ordered as Bobby jumped to open the door. He turned to the other officers who had drawn near. "Bring flashlights, and let's get ready to move in." He turned to face me and controlled himself very well. "Any particular direction, Professor?"

I nodded. "Yes, upstairs and to that window there, the one with the hole in the plywood."

"Fine. Bobby?"

"I got the padlock, and I think I got the key for the door."

"Then will you open it?"

"It's kind of… rusted, Sergeant," Bobby complained.

"Get out of the way." Stant shoved Bobby aside and stepped up to the door. His arm muscles bulged through his shirt as he twisted the key. The metal made a high-pitched squeal, and the lock shifted with a thud. Sergeant Stant pulled the door open. It creaked loudly on the stiff hinges.

"Let's go in!" Stant yelled and pulled his flashlight from his belt. He switched it on and took the lead. I quickly followed through the door with Santos and several burly officers behind us. The beams from the flashlights went in all different directions.

"What's that smell?" Santos queried.

"Mostly disuse," I said as we stepped forward. But he was right. The combination of smells was unpleasant. Mildew mixed with the ammonia stench of old urine, and possibly a whiff of feces. But also the metallic redolence of blood.

I saw a form ahead of me in the dark, looking like someone lying in wait. I held back, fear whipping through me as the officers approached. They shone their flashlights on the silhouette, revealing a gurney. A broken or folded-down end created the illusion of a crouching man. I exhaled with relief.

Then I really looked at it. It was the same kind as in my vision. Complete with restraining straps.

"I found the stairs," Stant roared a few feet ahead and to my left.

"Please… get up there," I barked, as if I were in charge.

The men bounded up the stairs as I followed, ascending each step one at a time. Santos stayed with me and held a flashlight he'd hastily borrowed from a cop.

"Is this the place, Doc?" Santos questioned as he shone the light on the next stair.

"It feels like it."

"I know what you mean. This place smells bad, but there is something else. Something… evil."

"Intensely evil, I would say."

We reached the top of the stairs and I tried to get my bearings; the climb had turned me around. I could hear the officers down the hall to my left, so I turned and hobbled in that direction. Santos kept up; the light moving in the dark hallway.

I turned into the room, feeling a wave of recognition. I had experienced déjà vu before, yet that feeling intensified tenfold. The hairs stood up on my arms, and my heartbeat hammered loudly in my ears.

It was the room, no doubt about that.

The gurney was there exactly as I saw it: the hole in the window, the broken glass on the floor. There was a strong odor of urine — fresh urine, which also fit my recollection. There was the chair, still bolted down in the middle of the room, and yes… in the center of a pentagram.

It stood empty.

"Doc," Santos gasped as he entered the room. "It's just the way you described it."

"Yes," I snapped, turning to face Santos, but then a shout escaped my lips as I saw a ghostly face from the corner of my eye. I exhaled deeply as I realized it was the drawing of the horned man on the wall, exactly as in my vision. I shook my head. I had been in many places that were haunted, even seen spirits right in front of me. Why did this stupid drawing scare me so much?

"Hey, Professor!" Stant interrupted. "What's he talking about, 'the room is the way you described it?'"

I fought to calm down, to get over the initial shock of the wall illustration. "We had some insight into this case, Sergeant. A... a witness."

It wasn't a lie. I had seen this room, if only in my mind.

"A witness? Where, how?"

"Gentlemen," I said to the three or four policemen in the room with us. I put my hands up. "I would ask you to carefully step out of the room. We need forensics to go over it. There may be valuable trace evidence that we are stepping on. So, please, slowly walk out as carefully as you can."

Stant drew close to me. "What about this damn 'life and death' thing you mentioned?"

"I think we're too late," I murmured. "There was a woman — in this chair. She was being tortured." I grabbed the flashlight from Santos and shone it on the floor around the chair. "See? There's fresh blood on this floor."

"What the hell is this—"

Sirens wailed nearby, cutting Stant off. I peered out the hole in the plywood to see four police cars pulling into the huge circular road in front of the building. Three were state cars and one was McGee's unmarked.

"McGee's here." I turned to Stant and added, "If you have questions, the tall lieutenant in plainclothes can answer them."

Stant grumbled. "He'd better have a damn good explanation. How could you have a witness up here to see the supposedly tortured woman? You saw that door! No one has opened it in years. And exactly what is your 'consultant' position where you get off telling the state police what to do?"

He stormed out of the room and headed downstairs to meet McGee and probably give him a piece of his mind.

I wasn't worried. Bill had shown up with a couple of state police vehicles. I was sure they didn't have to take crap from a sergeant assigned to a mental home. Like Santos said, you couldn't be a crack trooper and end up with this job.

"He sounds angry," Santos worried, as the other officers followed Stant downstairs.

"He was angry when he got here, Santos. Some people don't like to be bothered."

I looked out the window again. McGee stood outside the car and reached in to help someone get out of the passenger seat. I saw a flash of red hair and watched Doctor Yearling step out of the car.

So Kate came with him. That was a good choice. She might be of some help.

Sergeant Stant walked out of the building and up to McGee. I couldn't hear what he said, but he gesticulated toward the window, visibly upset. McGee looked to where Stant pointed and just walked straight for the building, with Kate having to run to catch up. Stant felt shocked at being ignored, but a tall, uniformed, blond man with chiseled features walked over to him and calmed him down. I noticed he wore captain's bars.

I heard footsteps come up the nearby stairs with a heavy tread. A lighter step followed and soon arrived on my floor.

"Here, McGee!" I yelled and carefully stepped back from the window toward the door of the room.

"Len!" McGee said at the doorway. "Hey, Teddy," he added as an afterthought. Kate walked up behind him. They paused and looked around, and they both swept their flashlights through the room.

"My God," Kate exclaimed, her mouth dropping open. She pointed her light at the floor for the pentagram and the blood around the chair. Then turned it to the wall to see the horned man graffiti.

"Pretty amazing match, wouldn't you say so, Doctor Yearling?" McGee boasted. In our work together, McGee had heard me describe a place so dead-on that when he finally arrived, he felt like he'd already been there.

"Astounding is more like it." Kate looked around again and added, "The girl?"

"No sign of her," I said, as I rubbed my face, suddenly exhausted. The evil energy of this place was draining.

"We think that's blood on the floor," Santos said. He walked over to Kate and offered his hand. "I'm Santos. Teddy Santos."

"Kate Yearling," she said, a bit confused who this person was and why he had introduced himself. Santos didn't help the matter, as he gazed at her with puppy-dog eyes, as if she was the last bone on earth.

"Kate, Santos is my TA. Uh, my… assistant."

"Yeah, Doc and I do everything together!" He addressed her with a little too much exuberance.

Kate smiled briefly at Santos with an 'are-you-kidding' glance to me.

McGee stayed in the doorway but looked around the room. "Len, do you think it was Mary? Do you think she might still be alive?"

"Yes and no, Bill. I'm sure it was Mary, and I'm pretty sure she's dead. But I hope the killer didn't clean up too well."

Kate spoke up, "I put in a call to the FBI Evidence Response Team. They're on their way."

"Not your guys, Bill?"

He shook his head. "No, the Feds have better equipment and can get things done faster."

I nodded in agreement. "I'm afraid the cops walked through this room and may have contaminated some of the trace."

"We'll have to take what we've got," Kate interjected. "This is an FBI scene now."

I frowned. "I thought you had to cross state lines to get the FBI involved."

"Not this time, Len," McGee remarked. "New laws. Multiple murders fall under a serial killer law."

Kate said, "Add to that, this murder might represent a violation of Mary Gillian's civil rights."

"Wow," Santos blurted. "That's great!"

"I didn't think people applied that law like that," I pointed out.

Kate shrugged. "We use what we've got."

"Besides, this murder — and the others — have become a situation for all of us together — local, state and federal," McGee added. "We'd better get out of here. We don't want to touch anything else by accident."

"That's a good choice," I decided and gingerly exited the room. I wanted to get away from the smell and the psychic bombardment. I felt an eerie cold that chilled my soul deep into my bones.

We went downstairs and back outside. The rain had been good enough to stop, though the sky threatened more.

Santos followed Kate down and spoke inanities to get her attention. I guess I should have been glad he was interested in something that didn't have a monitor and keyboard attached.

As we walked out, the tall, blond fellow walked over to me with a big smile and a firm handshake.

"Doctor Wise?" he announced. "I'm Captain Lindstrom."

"Ah, yes, Bill mentioned you."

"Yes, he's mentioned you, too. In glowing terms, I might add. Did you have any luck?"

With a glance over my shoulder at the imposing yellow-brick structure, I said, "This seems to be the place where someone held a woman — we believe Mary Gillian — and tortured her."

"If I need you to assist with a case, would it be all right if I called you?"

"Of course, Captain."

Kate touched my shoulder, and I turned.

"Can we talk?" she asked.

"Sure. Excuse me, Captain." I walked with Kate to get out of earshot of the officers, who chatted in small groups.

"Sorry if Santos bothered you," I apologized.

"No bother. It's nice a young man finds me attractive," she said as we sauntered away. She glanced back at the group of officers.

"That was pretty astounding in there. The amount of detail you described—"

"It's how it came to me."

"Look, Len, this is still new to me, like I told you. I only worked with you that one time, and that was an odd situation."

"I agree."

"The level of information — I mean, we would never have found this place without it. How did you know where to look?"

"Someone mentioned this place, and I got a buzz."

"Ah yes, those buzzes of yours," she said, then took a deep breath. "Let me cut to the chase, Doctor."

"Please do."

She smiled. "Have you considered working for the FBI? I mean, a man with your gifts could really—"

"A man with my gifts, or anything else, is happy here."

"But the opportunity—"

"Kate, I appreciate you becoming a fan, but I wouldn't do well under that kind of scrutiny. Besides, I'm a teacher. I have commitments and a wonderful lady. I don't really wish to give either of them up."

"Pity. You could help many people."

"I'm helping people right now. And I want to get this killer."

"So do I."

"Can I ask you a favor?"

"Sure."

"I'm still having trouble trying to see the guy's face. Would it be possible to do another session of hypnotic regression, help me push past whatever is blocking me?"

"Of course." She pulled out a card and handed it to me. "Call me. Perhaps we can do something at my office."

I nodded and glanced at my watch. "I've got to get back to my campus."

"Santos with you?"

"I could leave him."

"He's sweet." She grinned. "Like having a puppy, but I'm afraid he'll get in my way."

"And drool on your shoes?"

"Call me tomorrow. I'll probably be here until late tonight."

We walked back to the group as some black vans pulled up. I assumed it was the FBI guys who would go over every sliver of glass and every speck of dirt in the room. I collected Santos, and we made our goodbyes and headed back to the van.

At my vehicle, Santos looked back at the group by the building's entrance. "That Doctor Yearling is hot! Do you think she noticed me?"

"You made yourself hard to ignore, Teddy."

"Really? Did she say anything about me?"

"She thinks you're sweet."

"She does? Cool. When are we going to see her again?"

"I might see her tomorrow," I said as I opened the passenger door for Santos. "When you will see her again, I have no idea."

8. MENTAL HOME

Ttrue to my word, the next day I drove out to meet Kate. We met at the FBI office she was using in Morris Plains.

I was grateful that I didn't have any nightmares that could ruin another night's rest. In fact, I went to bed about nine-thirty the previous evening, downing a melatonin tablet to help me sleep.

Which I did, deeply, although I still felt that fragments of the horrors I tapped into yesterday were flying around during my slumber, just beneath the point of nightmare.

It was Friday, an easy day with only one afternoon class for me. I would actually spend some time with my lady this evening where we could catch up and share some long-neglected intimacy.

The address Kate gave me was for a series of buildings diagonally across from the train station in the center of town. I found parking and walked into the building with the correct number, and up a flight of stairs to the second-floor offices.

As I opened the door at the top of the stairs, I stopped for a moment, stunned. There were two people, a man and a woman, working at a large machine behind a plexiglass wall. They were both in white lab coats, and for a moment I hearkened back to the vision of the man with the scalpel.

He walked into the room in that stained lab coat, with rubber gloves and holding that scalpel. I can see his feet, his coat, his arm, and the face—

It was gone again. Every time I tried to focus on the face, I lost it, even in my memory.

"Leonard?" a female voice spoke up. I jumped and turned to see Kate. She held a mug that had cock-eyed lettering that read, 'I'm NOT crazy — I just work for people who are.'

I attempted to recover. "Hi, Kate. Thanks for making time for me."

"No problem. I didn't mean to startle you."

I flushed. "This case is affecting my nerves. I would appreciate anything you could do…"

"I imagine so." She walked toward the back of the large, open space. I followed her as she took a sip from her mug. "What do you think of our offices?"

"Pretty nice."

"That's not all. Look at this." We turned a corner and into a private room with a large desk and one of those 'psychiatrist' divans, like you see in the movies.

"I even have a couch for patients," she said with a grin.

"Pretty classy."

"Yes, elves or something set it up overnight."

I moved to the nearby window with a view of the train station and Speedwell Avenue. The carpeting was an ugly old brown rug, but the impressive desk had a laptop computer open on it. I sat on the divan, which was covered in red leather and made a 'squelch' noise as I sat.

"The couch is only here because I told them I was going to work with you again."

"I don't see how that would get you the time of day."

"Ah, you underestimate yourself, Doctor Wise," she said as she went to the computer and shut the lid. "When I told the FBI you were the one who found the place, and how you did it, they gave me complete autonomy to help you any way I can."

"Our government at work."

"Don't sneer, Leonard. Both the USA and the Soviet Union spent a lot of money on psychic research in the 1960s and 1970s, with some rather incredible results. If you talked about psychics helping police twenty years ago, they'd laugh. No one's laughing now."

"By the way, any word on what they found at Blackshale? I haven't heard from McGee."

"I'm afraid McGee is out of the loop for right now."

I bolted up. "What? He was the one who received the map. He put it all together—"

"Yes, and the FBI is grateful, but we have to take it from here. Bill is… was… an experienced agent. He understands. This is not a job for a small-town cop."

"I think highly of that small-town cop. He's—"

"Leonard, the forensics people can find trace even the state police could miss. Plus, the FBI can track leads faster and make an arrest quicker. Isn't stopping this guy before he does it again the number-one priority?"

"I guess," I muttered.

"Believe me, Bill's a big help, and I am keeping him up-to-date with info. Containment is important now. We don't want this guy to know we're close to him."

He already does…

The buzz in my head hit me like a revelation, and I immediately knew it to be true.

"Leonard?" she said, and gazed at me, but I didn't really see her.

"Sorry." I shook myself to get back to the present moment. "What if he knows we're after him?"

"Then we have to work even faster." She gestured toward the couch. "Shall we begin?"

We spent the next hour in frustration. Because of my programming, she didn't have any trouble hypnotizing and returning me to my vision of Mary Gillian, tied and bleeding to the chair at Blackshale, but when the man came into the room, it was always the same. I could see his body; I could even focus on parts of him — his shoes, the blue of the nitrile on his gloved hands, even the silver glittering scalpel — with no problem. As soon as I moved to the face, it was gone.

"And you are awake, fully awake, and you feel refreshed," Kate told me as she pulled me all the way out of the hypnotic state.

I sighed. "Not anything new, I'm afraid."

"I don't know, Leonard. You could see as high as his shoulders. I just wish I knew what stopped you. Can I get you a cup of coffee?" Kate said, as she stood and moved to the door.

"If you're having one."

"Sure, cream and sugar?"

"Just cream, no sugar."

"Shaken, not stirred."

I smiled at the *James Bond* reference. "Of course."

Kate came back into the room two minutes later with her mug refilled and a Styrofoam cup for me. I took mine and carefully sipped.

"Not bad, for government issue."

"This line of work requires a lot of coffee," she explained, taking a file out of her desk drawer. "You asked about what we found."

"Yes."

She opened the folder. "I've got some preliminary information. First, there was indeed fresh human blood and urine on the floor."

"Mary Gillian's?"

"It is her blood type. We can't run DNA yet. We're trying to get a sample."

"The hair."

"What?"

"Bill had her purse. Inside, there is a brush with hair on it."

She jotted herself a note. "Good. Now, there were also drops of several other blood types, but they were older."

"Suggesting our perp committed other murders there."

"Perhaps, and we also found traces from an animal. We're still checking out what kind. There wasn't a lot, indicating that someone cleaned it up or—

"Collected it somehow?" I considered, as an odd feeling came over me.

"Do you have many vampires in northern New Jersey?"

"Hmm? No. Most of the vampires live in the south."

Kate's eyebrows went up. "You're kidding, I hope."

"I could be. Were any of the bodies the police found drained of blood?"

Kate opened another file and pulled out pages she reviewed. "Considering each of the found ones were missing their head—"

"So, the answer is that someone killed them somewhere else and dumped them where the police found them."

Kate nodded. "I would have to concur."

There was a knock at the open doorway. A man leaned on the doorjamb. He was about five-foot-eight with a receding hairline, though not too bad; it gave him an amazing widow's peak. He was in a gray suit, powerfully built, and he seemed to crackle with energy.

"Kate, can I speak to you a minute?"

"Sure, Gabe," she said and stood up. I stood too, following her lead.

"This is Doctor Leonard Wise, Gabe."

"Hi, Doctor. Gabe Petrie. I'm the head of this little party." He offered his hand, which I took.

Something's wrong…

I pulled my hand away, which broke the contact quickly as the buzz passed through my mind. I felt an unusual awareness of this man. There was something cold in him, in his eyes. Agent Petrie didn't seem to notice my reaction, which was just as well.

"You're the one who has taken over for Stan Frazier," I realized. I had collaborated with Stan on several cases, but a few months prior, he sustained a severe injury prompting his early retirement.

"The very one," Gabe beamed.

"I just realized I never went to the offices of the New Jersey Task Force before."

"This is it, such as they are," Gabe declared. "Kate was telling me about your — what do you call it, talent? Skills?"

"Hunches would probably be the best word," I suggested, and noted that my hand felt as if an electric shock had passed through it from my contact with him.

"Let me tell you, we're impressed. I would love to have hunches like yours. It would save a lot of time pounding the pavement."

Kate turned to me. "Gabe now runs the Task Force office." She looked up at him with admiration. "He's also an expert on serial killers."

"Yeah. When Stan retired, he was foolish enough to request I take over for him," Gabe mused with a smile on his face. "He went on and on about you."

What was it about his smile that bothered me?

"Come on, Gabe, you've been working in New Jersey for years. You earned it," Kate praised him.

"Thanks, Kate," he said and faced me. "But, Doctor, you're the one who found the location. I can't tell you what a surprise that was."

I'll bet.

"I'm glad I could help."

Gabe nodded. "My theory is that you have to think like a killer, know their motivation, understand their way of life."

"Within reason, I hope," I surmised.

"Of course, but how else can we stop them?"

Kate gushed, "Gabe is also the man who arranged for me to join this office and set me up overnight."

Gabe continued. "If you're going to do an investigation, you need the tools. Am I right, Doctor?"

"Of course."

He turned his attention to Kate. "So, I just came from the site —"

"How is it going, Gabe?"

"Good. I mean, there's so much there. But others certainly haven't left it alone. There must be at least a thousand sets of fingerprints from all the people who went in over the years. So far, no body or any kind of scalpel. Some blood, but it looks like our guy cleaned up. I have a couple of field agents looking to see if there is any loose dirt nearby."

"Loose dirt?" I questioned.

He looked back at me and nodded. "Shallow graves, that sort of thing. These guys are up from DC and have worked several multiple-murder cases, so they know where to look and what to look for."

"Grisly work at best." I shuddered.

"At best," Gabe repeated.

"What did you want to see me about?" Kate asked.

"I heard you might work with Doctor Wise today and… we found something pretty strange," Gabe said, reaching into his pocket and pulling out a plastic bag with a folded piece of paper in it.

"What's that?" I asked.

"To the best of my understanding it's a message," Gabe answered.

"What do you mean?" Kate scrunched up her face and took the bag from him.

Gabe reached into the plastic bag and pulled out the note. "Don't worry, we already checked for fingerprints — it's clean. Now, look here on the front. It has the letters L-E-W."

"L-E-W?" Kate queried. "I wonder what that is?"

I cleared my throat, which made them look at me. "Those are my initials. Leonard Ethan Wise."

Petrie's jaw tightened. "Really? Could you look at this? We couldn't make any sense of it."

I took the small piece of paper from Agent Petrie and turned it over in my hand. It had an energy all its own, like holding a small ball of fire. I brushed my fingers across my initials neatly printed on the outside.

I gently opened it, my mind screaming a quick warning as I did, but I was determined to see what was there. As I read the words, pins and needles flared up my spine to the back of my brain.

You have to be careful

what you conjure, boy!

The room shifted around me as the writing touched a long-held memory. My vision spun in bright-white spots all around me.

"Leonard?" Kate barked, seemingly far away. "Are you all right?"

"It's my fault," I heard myself saying. "It's all my fault."

The room began to dim, and the world faded away.

"Doctor Wise, do you need—"

"Leonard—"

The room reeled as I fell to the ground, but I was beyond caring, beyond feeling. I fainted dead away into the darkness with the desire to never wake again.

9. MEMORY RETREAT

I floated, blissfully unaware. There was a smell — an unpleasant smell, like mothballs. I hate the smell of camphor. My grandmother's closets always had that odor, like the smell that clings to a dirty dog in summer. It stung my nose and made my eyes water, reminding me of old clothes and confined spaces.

I was lying somewhere... actually, somewhere very comfortable, but the scent made me cough and wave my hands as I tried to fan the stench away.

"Leonard!" a woman's voice insisted. "Wake up."

I was in a dream — I guess it was a dream — in my grandmother's house. She stood over me and attempted to rouse me, her thin, time-worn face close to mine, her breath smelling of age.

"No, Grandma," I heard myself say. "I wanna sleep—"

A male voice spoke. "I think he's too far gone."

"Leonard?" the woman chided me.

I coughed again, and all at once, I was looking at a drop ceiling, some tiles discolored in patches, and a large fluorescent light panel. I started.

"Easy, there," a man said, and his firm hands grabbed me. I knew this man who spoke to me rather like a farmer would to an animal. Why couldn't I place his name?

"Leonard?" the woman repeated, a small bottle in her hand.

"Kate?" I said, her name finding its way to my tongue. I brought my hands up to rub my eyes. "What happened?"

"You tell us," the man grunted. He had a name — Gabe something.

I closed my eyes, a dull throb in the back of my head. I reached back to massage a growing lump.

"Yeah, go easy there," Gabe warned. "You gave yourself quite a lump. Fell pretty hard, right out on the floor."

"I did?" I tried to concentrate, but it all seemed lost in a mist.

"He probably doesn't remember, Gabe." Kate sat in front of me and held a small penlight, which she flashed into my eyes. My hand went out to ward off the light. "Let me look, Leonard."

I put my hand down and stared straight ahead, as the light flickered and danced in my eyes once, then again.

"Is he okay?" Gabe asked.

"Doesn't seem to have a concussion." She looked at me carefully. "Do you know what happened, Leonard?"

"I, uh, fell down." I struggled to reconnect the spliced tape of my memory. "I read something."

"Yeah, you were saying it was all your fault. What was that about?" Gabe moved closer.

"Gabe," Kate advised, "could you come over here for a moment?"

As I lay back on the leather divan, they wandered out of my focus a few feet away. They talked in low tones. Gabe sounded frustrated and displeased with the situation.

I caught snatches of the conversation.

"He knows something," Gabe confirmed, his voice rising in volume.

"—It to me, he's gotten a shock," Kate's voice faded in and out.

"Okay!" Gabe finally accepted, and his lumbering form headed toward the door. "Doctor, I'll catch you some other time," he said loudly in my direction, and was gone.

Kate approached me carefully and gave me the impression that I was a jungle cat that she didn't want to spook.

I suddenly saw a mental picture of an old professor I had when I was part of a psychiatry fellowship. "Always approach a person with a psychological disorder carefully," he'd said in his whiny, nasal voice. "You don't want to do anything that will alarm them."

I endeavored to pull together all the thin strands of my consciousness to retrace my last few minutes of sentience when I was upright.

"Leonard, do you remember what happened?" Kate inquired as she helped me to sit up.

I tried to collect my thoughts. "I was just wondering about that. Gabe showed me something—"

I leaned forward, which made my headache worse.

"Lay back," she said. "You need to rest."

I nodded, which also hurt.

"Gabe showed you a note," she explained in a steady voice, then raised her hand to show the folded, yellowing piece of paper now back in its plastic evidence bag. "This note."

I put up a hand to ward her off. "You hold it. I really don't want to repeat the experience."

She raised her eyebrows. "You said something about it all being your fault. Do you remember what that was about?"

It flashed into my mind all at once, an overwhelming flood of memories.

"Oh God!" I moaned, tears stinging my eyes, as I sat up again.

"Leonard?" Kate took my hand in hers. "If you want, I can put you in a light trance. You can detach from whatever this is and experience it as an observer."

"No, no!" I barked, a little stronger than I intended. I strove to get up, felt light-headed, so I returned to a sitting position. "I can talk about it. Have you got a Kleenex?"

She rose and grabbed a tissue from the nearby box. It made no difference where a therapist set up shop, even if it was a temporary location. There was always an open box of tissues near the couch. I wiped my eyes, blew my nose, and realized I couldn't tell her all I knew. She would never believe it.

I glanced at my watch. It was past one o'clock.

"My God, I have a two o'clock class," I announced and attempted to get up again, with much more success. "Can you give me my cane?"

Kate went to where I had collapsed and returned with my cobra-headed cane in her hand. "Leonard, you're in no condition to drive."

"I'll be fine. Look, I can go over more of the story with you later. May I borrow that note?"

She held out the evidence bag. "I don't see why not." She offered it to me, then pulled it back. "Are you sure your TA... uh... Teddy can't cover your class? I mean, that's why he's there."

I gently took the bag and the note and placed them in my pocket. "You need to look over a case that Stan Frazier and I worked on. McGee has a copy of the file. It involved a group, the *Following of Astarte*. I'll answer questions you might have tomorrow."

"You're being very cryptic."

"I'm sorry, I need to go."

I lunged for the door — lunged being the right word, as I was still unstable. But getting downstairs and into the afternoon air quickly cleared my head, and by the time I reached my van, I was in my right mind.

I drove away knowing that I would have to tell Kate the story — the entire story.

But I realized there was someone else I had to tell first.

"That was a lovely dinner, Margery," Jyanette said as I picked up our three plates and brought them to the dishwasher.

"Oh, now dear, it's noice to have a chance to just sit and share a meal after a tryin' day," Mrs. Higgins said. She glanced over at me with the suggestion that I had indeed had a trying day. She rose from the table and went on, "Now then, ye young folk have things to talk aboot."

Jyanette looked over at me as well. "I hope so. He hasn't said five words yet tonight."

"Sorry," I sighed as I put in the last dish and closed the metal door of the dishwasher.

"You should probably stay, Margery," Jyanette suggested. "If he's in one of his moods, I could use the support."

Mrs. Higgins grabbed Jyanette's hand. "If anyone can get him to open up, it will be you, dearie." She wandered out of the kitchen as I packed away the leftovers and loaded more dishes.

Jyanette went to the large industrial refrigerator, opened it, took out a bottle of Chardonnay, and refilled the wineglass she'd nursed through dinner. She walked to the table and leaned against it.

"You mad at me?" she challenged.

I turned to look at her, and suddenly I felt guilty. "No, not at all."

"Well, you're not your usual bubbly self," she pointed out and put the glass down. "I know I've been distant lately, but so much is happening in the office right now…"

Forcing a smile, I said, "I know, I'm sorry. I've had a bad day."

I walked up to her. At five-feet-eleven, she was so striking and fit against me so well. I pulled her close and kissed her with all the passion I had in my heart. Then I gently pulled away.

She opened her eyes slowly as if she savored the kiss. "Mm. That was nice."

I held her hand and smiled. "I need to tell you something. It's going to sound crazy, but you need to know."

She pulled me close and ran her fingers through my hair. "Our life — and your job — is pretty crazy. You mean, this is worse?"

I lowered my eyes. "It's how it all began."

Her expression changed and her eyes grew wide. "What's this?" Her hand had found the bump on the back of my head.

"Nothing."

"Nothing? It's the size of an egg."

"I fainted during a session. I'll be okay."

"You fainted — Len?" she worried and pulled me closer.

"Jyanette." I withdrew to create space between us. "I really need to tell you this. It's important."

She looked deeply into my eyes, let me go, and returned to the table and her glass of wine.

"Okay," she affirmed. "Should we talk here or in your room?"

I looked around the kitchen. When Jyanette was over for dinner, we sometimes ate in the dining room, but I preferred the bright, cheery kitchen.

"This would be better," I decided.

She nodded and perched on the table's edge.

"Jyanette," I started, and stared at my hands, as the courage to look into her eyes suddenly failed me. "You know about my dead fiancée."

She nodded. "Cathy."

"Catherine Cynthia Garber." I felt a slight smile at the memory. There she was in my mind: pale skin, dirty blond hair, and beautiful.

Jyanette interrupted my reverie. "I know what you've told me. She died in the car accident that ruined your leg and messed with your mind."

"There's more to it than that. There are things I've never told you, told no one."

"If you're comfortable telling me, Len."

"No, I'm not, but I have to. For you, for us. Let me set the scene for you." I told her about that night, recalling as much detail as I could. After all, I had worked very hard for eight years to drive it from my mind. It felt a lifetime ago, when Cathy and I graduated from medical school.

The night started harmlessly enough, a party that Jon Baines threw to celebrate my graduating summa cum laude from Johns Hopkins. He insisted on a party in New Jersey for Cathy and me since we were all New Jersey natives. Cathy had grown up in Mountainview, and Jon and I in Copeland.

My clever fiancée had also graduated magna cum laude, and we had a lot to celebrate with an upcoming wedding and the start of our residency at Rutgers Medical Center in the fall.

The party was uneventful at the beginning: there was drinking, loud music, some pot smoking; the usual college stuff. I imbibed one beer slowly and spent the night reflecting on the fact that this gorgeous woman was going to marry me.

I explained that during the night, someone pulled out a box with a Ouija board, the kind you buy at toy stores. He set it up on a card table, and a group formed to play with it. They were asking pretty tame questions, and the shuttle moved around to answer, to the group's amazement. Not that it's hard to amuse drunken college kids.

Cathy and I joined them and added our hands to the shuttle as it moved about the board. A small crowd gathered and, instead of the 'smartass' questions, asked some very personal ones.

That's when the shuttle spelled out names, dates, and words that were quite astounding. One girl, who was standing, not touching the board at all, asked her mother's birthday. The shuttle flew about the board to answer the day, date, and even the year correctly.

However, as soon as I removed my fingers, the shuttle slowed down; the answers stopped coming. I would put my hands back and it would fly around the board again, always going to the correct place.

"You were discovering your gift," Jyanette interjected.

I shook my head. "I didn't know what it was. I thought it was a joke, a lark — does anyone use that term anymore?"

She smiled at me. "Some lawyers do. Go on."

"That's when it got bad," I said, lost in the reminiscence again. "One of the other students suggested, of all things, that we conjure a demon. It sounded like a game, a diversion, a trip into the imagination, so I said, 'What the hell?'"

"Conjure a demon?" Jyanette responded, and her eyebrows went up.

"Yeah. Hanley, Jeff Hanley," I said as the realization struck me. "Gosh, I'd forgotten who it was until right now. Jon and I knew him from high school, and he was always trying to impress people."

"You didn't remember it was him?"

"I guess not," I replied with a sad smile. "Anyway, he claimed he knew an incantation. We all sat around in a circle and joined hands. Someone turned off the lights and lit candles. I listened to this guy's voice as he spoke words from some foreign language."

"Did they mean anything to you?"

"At the time, no," I explained, and suddenly I froze in place.

"What is it?" Jyanette asked, concerned.

"I just realized that I've heard those words again, recently."

"When?"

"Just a few months ago when I faced that chemist — Claude? It was the very words being chanted in that abandoned church."

"I remember, you showed up with a black eye on my birthday," Jyanette muttered, and took a large swig of wine to push away the unpleasant memory.

"But years ago at the party, I tried to help Jeff Hanley to accomplish whatever it was he was trying to do. Then I suddenly felt the hairs on the back of my neck stand up. The room closed in around me. I had the strangest feeling, like somehow I was giving him the power to actually bring something to where we were… to actually conjure something."

Jyanette stared at me, her mouth a tight line. "Go on."

"We sat there, and I wanted to pull loose, break the circle, but I just couldn't move. Then all at once, there was this flash of light all around us. We let go of each other's hands as if an electric charge went through us. The others started laughing and stuff, thought it was a big joke — 'hey, look what we did' — but I couldn't shake that fear. It was as if I knew I'd done something I shouldn't have. I quickly grabbed Cathy, and we left soon after that."

"How did she react?"

She felt puzzled. She sensed a shift in my mood and marveled that such a trivial matter could impact me so profoundly. We drove back to her parents' house in an old VW Beetle we owned then, which I barely fit in. As I drove, I talked about what it was, that I felt a force — something evil — I wanted to get away from it. In that patient way of hers, she just accepted it and spoke to calm me down."

"Do you remember anything else about that drive — I mean, before the accident?" Jyanette inquired.

"Clearly. Cathy talked briefly about our upcoming wedding, which was only two months away. She still maintained her position that since we were both about to start our residency, getting married was going to be rough."

"I've heard that a residency is very stressful."

I smiled at the recollection. "She was always the reasonable one. I said I didn't care, I knew something good when I found it, and she would not talk me out of it. She beamed with that smile that could light up a room."

"Uh-huh," Jyanette took a sip of wine.

"We were driving in the rain, up in the hills. I pulled the car around that big curve on Schooley's Mountain, a route I'd driven a hundred times. I smiled at her and when I glanced back to the road, something was in the middle of it. We were driving straight toward it, right at it. My brain could not accept what I saw."

"What was it?" Jyanette asked, her eyes wide.

I hesitated. I knew the next part wouldn't make sense to her. It barely made sense to me all these years later.

She insisted. "You can tell me, Len. Don't hold back."

I nodded. "A tall, blood-red demon stood there."

"A… demon?"

I exhaled heavily. "I can still remember every detail from the horns on the head down to the cloven hooves."

"A *demon*… was… in the road?"

"I know, it's insane. I could see its tall, muscled body covered only with a piece of cloth — like a loincloth or something — and it was staring right at me. I screamed and pulled at the wheel to swerve the car, to try not to hit it. Cathy was yelling, 'What are you doing, what's wrong?' The car screeched as it slipped from my control, and we careened over the edge of the mountain and spun through the air."

"Oh God," Jyanette blurted, her hand to her mouth.

"It was the oddest feeling in the world," I told her. "Everything shifted into slow motion. We were in the air, we flipped over, like on one of those big roller coasters that turn you upside down."

I went silent, totally lost in the recollection.

"Go on," Jyanette's voice was barely above a whisper.

"Inside, even with my seat belt, Cathy and I were being thrown against each other as I saw the ground rising to meet us. I remember the moan of metal as we hit the ground, roof first, followed by an explosion as the windshield shattered in our faces, and the car spun over and over."

Jyanette handed me a paper napkin. I suddenly realized I had been crying.

I touched my eyes with the soft paper. "I could hear Cathy scream, and a male voice yelling that I knew was mine, yet it seemed detached from me. We rolled, the roof crushed in closer and closer."

Jyanette took another gulp of wine.

"We hit the bottom of the ravine, the steering wheel smashed against my chest, and the front of the car crushed beneath us."

"You remember all of this?" Jyanette marveled.

"Clearly, and more. My vision was clouded with flashes of light. I was fighting to stay cognizant, to stay awake. We landed upside down. I tried to push my body upright, away from the steering wheel, but there was a terrible pain in my legs, especially my right one. I could barely move my head, but I looked over to see Cathy's head dangling upside down in her seat, and she was bleeding from her head."

"But you were awake?"

I nodded. "Yes. Then, all at once, in the state I was in, not quite dreaming and not quite conscious, I had my first true psychic vision. I saw a life — the life Cathy and I were supposed to lead."

"Your life together?"

I nodded. "I saw her give birth to one of our children, and each of us sacrificing to help the other. I saw us pull together but also drift apart. I saw resentment over minor disagreements and forgiveness for others. I saw us holding hands into our old age."

I dabbed my eyes again; the tears flowing freely at this point. Jyanette grabbed a napkin, as she was crying as well.

"Then, it changed and grew dim. Life was leaving her body; the image faded with her existence. I cried out, 'Cathy, don't leave me!' But her body trembled, and she didn't draw a new breath."

I sighed heavily, leaned against the kitchen counter for support, and put the tissue to my eyes to absorb the moisture, and went on. "She was gone. We would never have that life."

I blew my nose, and Jyanette handed me a fresh napkin.

"Len, in your condition… I mean, semiconscious, in shock—"

"The story doesn't end there, Jyanette. Because I heard — felt — something or someone outside the remains of my window. I thought maybe somebody saw us crash and there was an ambulance nearby. The blood was in my eyes that turned everything crimson. I shifted — to look… to see… that red face staring at me, the horns rising out of his head."

"What?" Jyanette burst out.

I stood up, agitated, even though it was just a memory. "I drew back, wanted to scream. My heart felt like it would burst through my chest, but I couldn't make a sound. He — it — knelt inches away from me. Its long, narrow face twisted into a smile, the white teeth shining against the deep-red of its skin, as it leaned against our broken car and watched me."

The fear in Jyanette's eyes concerned me. Was she afraid for me… or of me?

"The… thing… opened its mouth, which had — I saw it — a forked tongue inside, and it said…" My voice died away.

"What did it say, Len?"

I reached into my pocket and pulled out the slip of paper from my meeting with Kate, and handed it to her. She opened it and read:

You have to be careful
what you conjure, boy!

I stared straight ahead and smashed the napkin in my hands. I finally raised my eyes to look at Jyanette.

"The demon said this to you?" she whispered.

"Those exact words. I'm telling you, Jyanette, no living person could know that phrase—"

"Are you sure you didn't tell it to someone? The police? Could it be in a file somewhere? Maybe that guy you pursued for the case you worked on in Staten Island?"

I shook my head. "No, no. I told the police a deer ran onto the road, and it caused the crash. What else could I say? A demon crashed my car?"

"Maybe you told a doctor?"

"Jyanette, I woke up in the hospital in intensive care with both legs damaged, one knee gone, and the knowledge that Cathy was dead. I was in such terrible shape, I had to attend her funeral in a wheelchair. Where, by the way, I saw my first ghost."

"Perhaps you mentioned it to a therapist? You went into therapy after the accident, right?"

"Yes, after going through nightmares for three months, with that face at the window in every one of them. I went back to school instead of residency, switched to a psychiatry fellowship, and moved to California. I got into therapy and fought the depression that made me want to fall into the darkness and join my dead fiancée. But I never mentioned what happened to me that night. Not to anyone — ever."

She sipped her wine and looked at the small piece of paper. "Where did you get this note?"

"It was at a crime scene. Where a woman suffered torture and murder."

Jyanette dropped the note as if it were on fire. "Oh God! Did you—"

"They tested, photographed, and checked it for trace before they showed it to me."

Jyanette looked at the note on the table and then at me. As an Assistant District Attorney, her job had taught her the importance of all evidence. "How did this note get to the scene?"

"You want to know my theory?"

She sighed. "We've gone this far."

"Forensics found it in a place that I saw in a vision. It had my initials on the outside and a phrase only two beings in all existence could know."

"So what's your point?"

"The only logical answer is that this… entity that I helped release eight years ago is our serial killer. It's what I missed when I helped the FBI take down the *Following*. They left a painting on a wall that claimed 'the demon is made flesh'."

Jyanette took the glass and gulped down the last of the wine. She walked around the table and sat down without taking her eyes off me.

"You don't believe me?" I fretted, cowed by her stare.

Jyanette took a deep breath and let it out slowly. "Len, I don't know what to believe."

I moved to the opposite end of the table. "But don't you see? This explains it! In my vision, I can't see the face of the murderer —"

"Because it's a demon?"

"Its true face is a demon. The form it moves in is just a shell."

"The form it moves in?" she repeated.

"Yes, an entity can't really do things in the physical world unless it has a physical form. It's what crazy Claude kept telling me, 'The demon is made flesh—'"

"Oh, I see," she said, and her attitude had changed. "So now it's possession! Welcome to The Exorcist Part Seven: Leonard Meets a Demon."

I exhaled heavily. "I know it sounds crazy, which is the reason I never told you. In my defense, there's a ton of historic documentation that suggests that demonic possession is possible. This… thing took over a human body, and then—"

"All right!" Jyanette set her jaw. "This is crazy—"

"Please," I gasped, and gently reached out my hand to grip her arm. "I am sure of this."

She looked at me, and her expression softened. "It's a lot for me to take in."

I let her go, nodded sadly, and sat in a chair. She came over to touch my hair, to reconnect, and I was grateful for it.

"And I guess it doesn't matter if I believe in demons or if this was all in your head. You believe it and you have to do what you think is best."

"Good, then you'll understand what I am going to ask of you."

She rubbed my head and pulled me close. "What?"

"Watch yourself."

"What?" she repeated and pulled back.

"If this is the entity I released, then I'm involved, and the people I love are in danger," I said as I rose to take her in my arms in earnest.

She hugged back half-heartedly. "I'm an Assistant DA. I know how to handle myself."

I let her go. "Okay, but be aware. Carry your handgun. If you go to your car at night from court, have a bailiff escort you."

She spoke calmly. "I'll be careful, but I am not becoming paranoid."

"Sorry, sorry." I sat as my eyes became wet again. "It's just if anything happened to you, I—"

She pulled my head to her bosom. "Sh, nothing's going to happen to me. We'll be fine. We'll work through this."

She lifted my face and brought her lips to mine.

I kissed her delicately at first, then with more passion. I stood and pulled her close and tasted the Chardonnay on her tongue. She moaned during the kiss.

She pushed me gently away, and we both were breathing hard.

"It's been so long since we've made love," I breathed, totally aroused.

She looked at the floor. "I'm afraid it will have to be longer."

"What? But I thought you had the night off—"

"I do, Len. But I have an early morning meeting in the office with the entire District Attorney staff, and then I have to train a new intern."

I forced myself to step back, the heat of the kiss still stinging my lips.

"Are you mad?" I asked, my voice sounding thin even to me."I mean, it's been months since anyone's actually tried to kill me."

Jyanette didn't laugh. She stared at the space where I'd just been standing, her eyes tracking something invisible. "I'm not mad. But a demon? It's a lot, Len."

I looked at the floor, the shadows there suddenly feeling long and jagged. "I get it."

"I should go," she murmured. She leaned in, pressing a chaste, dry kiss to my cheek—a polite gesture for a stranger, not a girlfriend.

"Are you okay to drive?" I asked.

"I'm fine. I just… I need to wrap my head around this."

I wanted to tell her that I'd been trying to wrap my head around it for eight years. Instead, I followed her as she headed into the hall towards the front door.

"It's okay," she said, her hand on the knob. She gave me a small, sad smile that didn't reach her eyes. "I'm the one with the boyfriend who sees monsters."

The click of the lock as she left was the loudest thing in the room.

10. NOWHERE SAFE

K ate Yearling paced her Morris Plains office as I sat in front of her desk.

I'd spent the morning writing out the story I had told Jyanette before heading off to Morris Plains to bring my hypothesis to the FBI team.

I had texted Kate, asking her to read the *Following of Astarte* file before I got there. Then, upon my arrival, I gave her a one-page explanation of my theory that the cult did it to empower the demon that they claimed existed in a human form.

Then I handed her the neatly printed pages which told my entire story: the Ouija board, the ritual led by Jeff Hanley, the drive home and the demon in the roadway, and finally at the car. I watched her face as she read it. She frowned in several places.

I returned the note to her and told her that only two beings could know what was said that night... myself and the demon.

Kate stood up from behind her desk to pace back and forth while she read.

I opened my mouth to add to my conclusions, and she held her hand up, silencing me.

Finally, she looked up at me. "I'm sorry, Doctor. I read the *Following of Astarte* file, and it is interesting from a psychological point of view—"

"You don't believe my story?"

"I am here to catch a serial killer, a flesh-and-blood man. Okay, perhaps he believes a demon possesses him, but he is just a person. Your experience in the car — and this note — notwithstanding. I must say, this speculation is ridiculous. 'The demon is now flesh?' How does that help us?"

"Look, Kate, how about a compromise? You use your techniques to solve this, and I'll use mine based on what I believe."

She stopped and glared at me. She slowly sat down as she considered my words.

"Leonard, are you suggesting that I continue to profile the case, gather evidence, etc? Meanwhile, you'll… what? Burn incense and light candles?"

"All I'm asking you to do is keep an open mind."

"An open mind I can give you. Gullibility is another thing altogether." Her temper flared. "You're a parapsychologist — God, I thought you were a scientist. You actually believe this medieval crap? I mean, historic demonic possession is just people who were schizophrenic or suffered from some other mental disorder."

"What we individually believe, Kate, is unimportant. We can do better if we work together — share our information."

"But you believe in a demon!"

"I saw it!"

"You were at a party with a Ouija board and did some kind of ritual, and then you had a traumatic accident. Your brain was not getting enough oxygen, and you had a dead fiancée beside you. Your mind took the events and turned them into an image of a demon. If you'd been at a UFO party, you would've seen aliens."

I looked down and muttered, "I know what I saw."

She exhaled deeply, frustrated by my response. "Okay. You have my phone number. Stay in touch if you get a lead. And I'll let you know if we need your talents. Do me a favor, don't mention this 'demon thing' to anyone else."

"Of course."

"If my colleagues discover we discussed a horned figure with a pitchfork, my career will be over."

"I understand. I know it's not a normal line of investigation," I frowned and stood as I held out my hand. "Still friends?"

She gave it a light shake and forced a tight smile. "Sure. But I have to tell you, if you were anyone else right now, you'd be off the case. Finding that scene was pretty remarkable, so I have to admit there is something to your techniques."

"You helped me recall the room."

She shook her head. "I don't understand your whole 'vision' thing, but I respect the fact that you can do it. But then you have to drop this in my lap."

"This will not be a normal case."

"Yes, it is. It's only this perp's unique psychology that's different."

"Very different," I asserted as I retrieved my cane and headed for the door.

"Not reassuring," she muttered as I left.

I drove back to GSU to do some research and reread my copy of the file about Claude Vandersteen and the *Following of Astarte*, the 'group' he created. I wanted to see if there was anything I had missed or forgotten in the months since I confronted him.

I felt troubled — deeply troubled. The clan and its drugged and psychotic leader had been dangerous — in fact, deadly. One abducted girl died, and another almost did. If a demon possessed the killer we sought and inspired that cult, he might be impossible to catch.

And yet, during my pursuit of that case, Claude had touched my mind, communicating with me mentally. In fact, the image he'd sent me of the Astarte he worshipped had been a beautiful woman.

Could our serial killer be a woman? That certainly would mean that other women might be less on guard.

It didn't fit the profile.

Whoever left the note there did it for one purpose: to taunt me, just like the map they sent to McGee.

Over the last year, I had built a reputation for solving situations other people couldn't. This note was a slap in the face of that work. It was basically telling me he was out there and there wasn't a damn thing I could do about it.

Also, he, she, or it caused the event that killed Cathy. I always blamed myself for that night, always feeling that if I'd kept control of the car, the accident never would have happened.

But I might be wrong.

That thing followed us from the party and manifested in a place that led to our destruction. It could sense my dormant abilities when I was still unaware of them, so it pursued me.

That thing killed Cathy.

My Cathy.

I wanted to send it back to whatever hell it came from. I wanted to make him suffer for the way I had suffered. This was not just another case to me.

This was personal.

I got back to the university and found Santos, which wasn't hard; he was in the computer room down the hall from my office.

"Teddy?" I called out.

He jumped and grabbed his chest. "Doc! You gotta cut that out."

It was a bright spring Saturday afternoon. I didn't see how I could have surprised him. "I have a couple of jobs for you, Teddy. They're important."

"Sounds great."

"How's the thesis?"

"Not ready to show yet, but I'd like it if you could proofread it for me."

"I can only correct your spelling and guide you if you're off-base."

"I know that, Doc!" he said, a bit insulted that I would demean his integrity. "What do you need?"

"Two things. Get on the net and download any information you can about serial killers. Specifically, any references to demons or satanism. Print me up what you find — only the good stuff."

Santos jotted down notes. "Yeah, what else?"

"See if you can find me any information about a guy I went to high school with: Jeffrey Hanley."

He fell silent as he wrote. "Got it, Doc. And don't tell me, you want it all done by this afternoon."

"Teddy, you know me too well."

"You don't ask for a lot, Doc, but whenever you do, it's always in a hurry."

"Thanks," I said, going back into my office. I organized my papers and looked over my computer file marked '*Following*.'

I recalled when I walked into the basement of the abandoned church, in the cells set aside for monks when the building had long ago been a monastery.

I went with Private Detective Darren Ward, who had insisted I join him because of the strange things he'd found.

We'd come down a spiral stone staircase into an underground passage that smelled of death and neglect and entered a small room where Darren pointed to a dimensional sculpture on the wall.

"Is that a fresco?" I'd asked him.

"Plaster and paint combined to push it out from the wall," he responded.

It was a portrait of a woman, totally naked with surprising detail. She was beautiful, and whoever had done the fresco had made her flesh smooth in the plaster. In one hand she held an ankh and a Kris knife in the other. Her feet became claws like a bird of prey at the bottom of the portrait. Above it were the words '*The Following of Astarte*' and below it was written 'The Goddess is made flesh.'

"Who did this?" I had asked him.

"Claude, while he was drugged out," Darren told me. "But that's not the one that bothers me."

He turned his light and shone it on the wall opposite the woman's portrait, and I gasped.

"That's something, isn't it, Doc?" he said.

But I could not reply.

It was an artful fresco, and there, though not fully three-dimensional, was the red body and face I had known so well. Even though it was only about three feet tall, I recognized the large horns on the head, the crimson skin, the yellow eyes, and the muscled body of the demon from outside the car the night Cathy died.

Under this figure were the words, 'And walks among us.'

This was startling enough, but then under that, written with what appeared to be nothing more than a marker, were words that haunted my dreams and filled me with dread.

"Sacrifices must be made."

I closed the folder. That phrase and the other, 'You have to be careful what you conjure, boy' were the ones that made me terribly afraid.

I returned to Santos, who handed me a sheaf of papers. "I guess you had some luck, Teddy?"

"Luck? No, Doc, the hard part was finding what not to print up. I found a site that lists the most famous serial killers of the last thousand years."

"Sounds thorough."

"More than that, it gives a bio on each one, and a body count."

"Nice, light reading."

"Yeah, but, Doc, you told me to match the killers and satanism? There were more matches than not. You'll see as you read it over."

"Thanks, Santos." I took the pages. "Any luck on Hanley?"

"I'm just getting started on that. Give me a few minutes."

I nodded and went back to my office. Santos had given me information on killers listed in order of body count, starting with the largest number of murders (300+). They even included Jack Kevorkian.

What was most stunning was the repeated mentions by many of them of 'satanic cults,' 'voices in the head,' and 'an urge I couldn't resist'. One of the more famous Russian killers, Andrei Chikatilo, claimed to have telepathic and hypnotic powers at a level higher than ordinary people. Then again, he once told a reporter he was being 'groomed to serve Satan.'

The more I read, the more my hypothesis held water. People who were ordinary in so many ways allowed a dark power to work through them, committing murders on a level that stunned the imagination.

In a way, it was like what I did, where I allowed images and information to flow through me, but I'd always tried to act as a positive influence in the world. Once I'd learned to focus my abilities, I knew that was what Cathy would want me to do — help people.

What if someone like me only wanted to act out on his own baser instincts? What if this person only wanted to do evil? I had some experience with people on the evil side of the paranormal, but the thought still surprised me.

I sat back, put the pages down, and shook my head. It was certainly a visit into the darker recesses of human existence and only depressed me.

I had a few minutes, so I decided to meditate. I focused on my breath, tried to bring myself down, down to calm myself and quiet the rampant thoughts which crowded my brain.

It was said by the mathematician and philosopher, Pascal, that 'all of humanity's problems stem from man's inability to sit quietly in a room alone.' I wanted to sit quietly and be at peace.

Little thoughts came through while meditating — 'cloud thoughts.' I let them just breeze through my mind, no importance given to them. I saw them and moved back to focus on my breath.

I always liked to picture myself in a green field, one that was filled with peace and love, and I could watch my cloud thoughts literally float by.

This time, it felt like something else was there. Something just beyond my consciousness that I was suddenly aware of.

My beautiful sunlit meadow was darkening, as if thunderclouds rolled in. I gazed around my imagined safe place, puzzled. This had never happened to me before. Then the answer came to me.

He was there in my meditation place.

Definitely a he. The masculine energy was powerful, but twisted viciously. I gazed about the meadow, expecting to see the tall demon standing out there.

"You have to be careful what you conjure, boy."

I could feel him inside my mind, like the announcer's voice in a baseball stadium echoing over and over.

"Get out of my head!" I whispered.

I've been here for a while, boy. You just didn't notice…

I didn't understand for a moment, but it suddenly became clear. Since I'd brought down the *Following of Astarte*, I had been on edge without knowing why.

This was why. This creature had touched my mind back then, and now I realized he'd taken up residence.

"Why?" I murmured. "Why me, why now?"

It was only a matter of time, boy. Sooner or later, we had to meet again…

"What do you want with me?"

There was a chuckle, a deep, throaty one. Then, all at once, I heard a feminine voice in my head.

I have need of you…

These were the words I had received when Claude had forced the image of the woman he worshipped, Astarte, into my mind.

I pushed myself out of my meditation and jumped up, my eyes open, sweat flowing from every pore, as my heart pounded in my chest.

He can find me. I'm not safe anywhere, even meditating.

I stood in my office and felt every bit the fool. He'd been waiting for me, waiting for me to discover it was him, so he could play the next move in his game. He'd been the female voice of Astarte when I had taken on the *Following.*

To him... her... it was just a game.

For me, this would be a matter of life or death.

11. LOONY BIN

At the Jazz Club Restaurant with the most beautiful woman I could imagine, I put on a brave face. My fear and insecurity would not lead to a pleasant evening, and I owed so many to Jyanette. Cancelled dates, out-of-town emergencies. I even missed last New Year's, which led to our first fight.

And yet, as Jyanette and I made small talk and stuck to recent events in the world, I could not help but look nervously around the restaurant at the other patrons.

He could be here, right in this room, in human form. I was sure he could block me sensing him, and I could look right at him or her and never know. There was no safe place .

"She'll be here next week," Jyanette said, as she forked a loop of her pasta into her mouth.

"Hm? Who?"

"My sister, Shanika," she chided and glared at me. "Honestly, Len, have you heard anything I've said?"

I gave my best smile. "I just love the sound of your voice."

She grinned. "Nice attempt. I'm sure that worked with the dumb girls you used to date."

"I can't fool you. I should know better."

"You should. She wants to meet you."

"Who?"

"My sister, Shanika!" She slammed her fork down. "I know you're working on a case, but I looked forward to this all week. You don't see me thinking about my caseload, do you?"

I gave her a sheepish look. "I'm sorry. I'll try to pay attention."

"Please do." She took a sip of wine. "I expect you to make an effort."

I reached over, took her dark hand in mine, and brought it to my lips. "Forgive me, my Nubian princess."

"Don't start with that stuff," she whispered, but I could see the delighted twinkle in her eyes.

We went back to our meal, and I made sure to be involved. She did everything with such grace and beauty that watching her eat was a pleasure. She took delicate bites and had such amazing table manners, while being relaxed and fun at the same time.

After my frightening meditation, I'd had a quick talk with Santos who had located Jeff Hanley.

It was very disconcerting to come out of that frightening mental encounter in my office to have Santos thrust an index card at me with information about Jeff.

"I got what you wanted about that Hanley guy," Santos had told me.

"Is this his address?"

"That's not an address. That's his location. He's in prison."

"For what?"

"Murder."

If my disturbing meditation hadn't shaken me up enough, this would have pushed all my buttons. My mouth fell open.

"You okay, Doc?" he asked, as he seldom saw me surprised. I had a reliable poker face. A psychic showing visible shock didn't look good.

"No, I'm fine." Though at that moment I felt like crap.

Santos dismissed it. After all, he didn't know about my possession theory. It was not a sound parapsychological concept I'd expounded to my students. He'd probably think I was crazy, concurring with Kate Yearling's hypothesis, as well as Jyanette's.

But no, it was more than that. I was involved. In the end, this was going to be a private party — this demon and me, our battle, our conflict.

It wasn't about just tracking down a killer. That I'd done before. This was about coming to grips with exactly what happened to Cathy and precisely what I was about.

As I tried to decide what to do with that information, I went home to get ready for the date.

I had worked to protect the home I shared with Mrs. Higgins, using visualization and energy manipulation techniques to make it a haven.

Despite Kate Yearling's snide remark earlier in the day, I was also not above the use of incense and candles, as these affected the mind through the senses. That's why they were part of all religions — they help us focus the abilities within.

It was necessary to make the house a place shielded from all the mental energy that flew around. It was annoying, like static on a radio, and it was relentless. Everyone needed an asylum where they felt protected.

But the house was undisturbed.

As we finished dinner, the band came back from a break and played some wonderful classic jazz.

I stood up and put my cane aside. This got Jyanette's attention. I held out my hands and said, "Dance with me?"

"You? *Dance?*" she said, surprised.

"I can hobble about," I assured her, and gestured for her to come to me. She got up and into my arms. We stood close and rocked together, as I enjoyed the smell of her hair and stared lovingly into her marvelous brown eyes.

"You have all my attention," I murmured.

"Very rare, indeed. Okay, I'll give it to you; you saved the date."

"You can yell at me anytime I neglect you."

She pulled into my shoulder. "You don't neglect. You just let your mind wander somewhere else." She pulled back and smiled up at me. "Now and then, I want to be all you think about. Not every day, not all the time, but every now and then."

I bent and kissed her. Even at five-eleven, I had to bend a little to reach her lips.

I touched her back, caressing the firm muscles.

"I really need to be alone with you," I sighed.

"That's just because you're horny," she whispered in my ear.

"It's been over two weeks," I whined quietly.

She chuckled. "Poor baby. And it's going to be longer, I'm afraid."

"But I'm buying dinner," I expressed with mock indignation.

"And I have a girlfriend who just went through a big breakup. I promised I'd meet her for breakfast."

"Weren't you the one complaining that I hadn't taken care of your needs a few days ago?"

"Guilty as charged," she sighed. "But you dumped a big thing on me last night. I'm still processing."

I held her at arm's length. "I didn't know it would bother you so much."

She pulled me close and whispered just loud enough for me to hear, "I'm dealing with it, and I still want you. I've just got to be certain how I feel about all of it."

I sighed. "Another night with an empty bed."

The song ended; we parted, clapped our hands, then she returned to our table as I limped over and retrieved my cane.

"To make you feel better, I'm buying tonight," she said, and picked up our check from the table.

The next morning, I drove to Rahway State Prison to visit an old friend: Jeff Hanley.

I drove a circuitous route heading south on Route One and Nine, then taking a service road past the 'Airport Sheraton,' a tall and impressive part of that chain, which was fairly convenient to Newark Airport. Its only drawback was the nearby prison, where the state caged its most vicious criminals.

I passed a large sign, cheaply made, with plain black letters on a white background reading:

RAHWAY STATE PRISON ONLY
BEYOND THIS POINT

As soon as I passed the sign, a large chain-link fence crowned with barbed wire appeared around me. I felt immediately intimidated, which I supposed was the intent.

I pulled the van into a small lot marked with 'VISITOR' signs. I walked to the only doorway accessible from the lot.

A large building with an impressive facade loomed ahead of me; I could see the metal detector standing behind the door. That made sense. You didn't want people bringing weapons into a prison. The stainless steel pins permanently embedded in my leg made such detectors a time-consuming experience.

Of course, I left my preferred cobra-head cane — which contained a handy twenty-four-inch sword — in my van. Instead, I used a metal cane that folded down, but because of an internal elastic cord, pulled together into a full-size walking stick.

It took about twenty minutes to get into the visitor's meeting area, while guards patted me down and waved a handheld device over me. I finally had to roll up my pant leg and show my scars. That made the guard, a rather burly fellow with a buzz cut, wince.

"That must've been a mess," he stated with a whistle.

"I could've ended up permanently in a wheelchair, so I consider myself lucky."

He waved me on, and I walked into a small room that was remarkably reminiscent of the Division of Motor Vehicles: cramped, with dirty walls and faded linoleum. I joined a line of visitors moving slowly toward a guard behind bulletproof glass, like at a bank. They were waiting to be approved, to have their loved one located, and then perhaps to have ten minutes of visitation.

It was a slow process.

I stood in line and pulled out a notebook. I wrote things out while I waited.

Possible connections:

Jeff Hanley convicted of murder.

Could it have possessed him?

If so, how could he commit other murders?

What is the connection to Blackshale?

I decided some sensible questions would be in order. I wondered how I should approach Jeff. After all, the last time I had seen him had been that night.

That night…

A buzz went off. There was something, a detail in my memory that was there, and yet not immediately in my consciousness, that needed my attention. But what was it? I approached the window and decided I would have to let it wait.

"Good morning," I said to the bored woman behind the window. She was middle-aged, white, and had her hair up in a bun. She had the look of a smoker: too thin with heavy bags under her eyes.

"ID please," she demanded.

I handed her my driver's license, and she wrote my name and the number.

"Who'd ya wanna see?" she said with a Staten Island accent as she returned the laminated card.

"Jeff Hanley, please."

"Really? You wanna see the Reverend?" she asked, without her expression changing at all. "What, you was a con here? The only guys ever visit him useta be cons."

"No, I'm an old friend," I said.

"Okay, we'll call you when you can go in."

"Thank you."

I sat on one chair; the vinyl ripped and stained. Looking around the room, I realized how out of place I was. I was in a suit jacket and slacks, but most of the other people wore jeans. One young woman with dirty-blonde hair stood with a fussy baby on her hip in a plain cotton sundress. She watched me disapprovingly. The baby had a vacant look on his chubby face. I finally realized my attire resembled that of a lawyer, likely an unpopular figure among the families of men admitted here.

Eventually my name was called, and I followed a uniformed guard into another room. There was a row of glass-enclosed openings, again looking like the ones in banks for tellers. But these were closer to the ground, with chairs against the wall between them. The guard led me to the third window, and I sat in the chair with some difficulty.

On the other side of the glass sat a thin man — I might even say gaunt. He was in an orange jumpsuit, sported a short beard trimmed unevenly, and around his neck was a black priest's collar. His eyes told me who it was: Jeff Hanley.

I picked up the phone, as Jeff picked up the one on his side of the thick glass.

"My goodness, Leonard Wise!" he said jovially, like he used to when we'd run into each other between classes.

"Hi, Jeff," I greeted him as I struggled to decide the right way to act. I knew he might have the answers I needed, but seeing him here made me feel clumsy and unsure of the right way to approach him.

"This sure is a surprise, I have to tell you," Jeff said.

"Not as big a surprise as that collar."

"Oh, that," he said, his fingers moving to his throat. "That's a bit of a story. After I got here, I worked with the man who was the priest, Reverend Talbot, a Presbyterian. He was trying to help the prisoners with their spiritual needs."

"Tough place to do that."

"You're telling me! Brilliant man, though. He helped me work through a lot of things, and I started helping him in the little chapel we have here on the 'campus', as we call it. He had me study with him, and I became a layman, and then he had me ordained. Me, can you believe it? He retired about a year ago, and he recommended me as his replacement."

As Jeff spoke, I reached out with my mind, trying to get impressions from him. That was difficult because any attempt to do a reading with all the emotions flying about in this location created a hotbed of negative energy. Yet from Jeff, I couldn't sense anything bad or out of place at all.

"How do you like the job?" I asked, as I wanted to keep him talking.

"It's difficult. But that I'm just a Joe like them, stuck here? It opens doors. I lead services every Sunday, and even have some of the more hard-boiled cases show up."

"Quite an accomplishment."

"It's gratifying. But I'm sure you didn't come here just to talk about my current vocation."

"Jeff, I'm hesitant to bother you with this—"

"Don't worry, Len. I've made peace with God. I've kept up with you in the news. You're the 'Super Psychic of Scudder House.'"

"Thanks, Jeff, but don't say that too loudly in here."

He glanced around and smiled. "Good point."

"I want to ask you about that party. Do you remember? The night I had the accident."

His eyes glazed over for a moment as he recaptured the long-ago memory. "Jeez, Len, that was eight years ago."

"It's important. Do you remember the Ouija board?"

"Most of that night is a blur. I wasn't a full-blown alcoholic then, but I was getting a good start."

"I never knew you drank all that much," I considered, surprised at his confession. Everyone at that party drank, some of them quite a lot.

"I didn't let people see me drunk, except at parties. I was mostly a closet drinker." He rubbed his eyes. "I kind of recall that board — yeah, you were real good with it, too."

"Yes, and then you suggested we conjure a demon."

He looked up at me. "I did… what?"

"You suggested we conjure a demon. You had us all join hands, and you said words — I think they were Latin or something."

His brow wrinkled. "I don't have any memory of that—"

"You had us sit in a circle, and you said some words — Latin or Hebrew, I'm not sure."

Jeff closed his eyes as if to track down the memory. Finally, he opened them and shook his head. "I honestly remember nothing like that."

"Are you sure? Can you think of anything you might have read that would contain such words?"

Jeff looked at me sadly. "I really don't know what you're talking about. Conjure a demon? Why would I do that?" He eyed me suspiciously. "Leonard, why do you ask?"

I sat back in the chair, trying to think of anywhere else I could go with him. If I told him my idea, it might make him not want to help me at all. He was now a priest, and demons were definitely medieval.

"Actually Jeff, anything you recall from that night would be a great help. I'm trying to find someone who is killing young women."

"How could anything from that party help?" he said, puzzled, watching me.

I shrugged, trying to look trustworthy. "Whatever you can think of."

He sat stock-still, and the words tumbled out of his mouth, but his face remained emotionless. "That night, that's when things went wrong for me. I mean, it's as if I were under a curse. My drinking got out of hand. I just kept getting angrier and angrier. I was living with a girl, Betty. She was a cute little thing. Then, one night when I was so drunk I should've been unconscious—"

"What happened?" I said, my attention riveted as his face contorted.

"I still don't really know." His voice trembled, a raw quiver slicing through the air. "She was sleeping, and this overwhelming surge of rage just consumed me, for no good reason at all. I felt caught in a storm, drowning in my own fury. I got up, my heart pounding like a drum in my chest, and I went to the kitchen... I got a knife."

He closed his eyes, and for a fleeting moment, I thought I saw a flicker of a shadow cross his face as he fought to suppress the horror of that memory.

"Did you—" I stammered, my voice barely a whisper, the words getting stuck in my throat as dread clutched at my chest.

He nodded slowly. "I killed her. But it was worse than that. I, like... tortured her first."

His confession hung heavily in the air, and I felt ice seeping into my veins.

"I slit her wrists while she slept, and as she woke, she was already bleeding to death." He squeezed his eyes shut, as if trying to block out the images that haunted him. "It took me so long to accept that I did it. To come to grips with the fact that this kind of evil… it was inside me. I felt like some dark entity had taken over."

My throat constricted, and the world around me faded into a blur. I was grappling with the reality of his words, and panic rose within me. The image of that red-skinned demon I'd seen on the rainy road flashed in my mind; it was all too real, and now I understood. Somehow, that creature had burrowed its way into him, feeding on his pain, twisting his thoughts until he was no longer himself.

"Jeff, did you ever visit Blackshale?"

He frowned. "The state place? Yeah, my lawyer tried to pull a 'not guilty by reason of insanity' defense, so the state had me go there for two days of testing and therapy." He shifted in his chair. "That's when it changed for me. I accepted the fact of what I did, that I was accountable. That's why when I got here I sought Reverend Talbot and took full responsibility and asked God to forgive me."

"Do you know which psychiatrist talked with you? His name?"

He frowned, lost in concentration. "Yeah, give me a minute. It was a heavyset guy. Dr… Banner… Bailey… no, Brice. His name was Doctor Richard Brice," Jeff said with a nod of his head. "I tell you, after I left Blackshale, I felt much lighter, like a weight was gone. Even though I was going to prison, I still felt better."

Because someone else took that weight.

He went on, "I still don't see—"

"Look, Jeff, I'm grasping for straws." I looked into Jeff's eyes through the glass and decided I needed to level with him. "I think we unleashed something. Some kind of entity that enjoys hurting people."

His hand rose to a small gold cross on a chain around his neck. His lips moved in a quick prayer.

I waited until he raised his eyes. "I need you to think about where you found those words you said that night. Or if you know anyone else who might know where you got them."

Jeff shook his head. "It was so long ago. I can't think of where I would have read something—"

"Was anyone you knew interested in the occult? Perhaps a book—"

Jeff just shook his head.

"Okay, Jeff, I'll tell you what. Can I leave you my number? If you think of something, call me — collect or any other way you have to."

Jeff nodded. "Give it to the guard and tell him it's for me. I'm pretty well-liked here, so they'll get it to me."

"I can't tell you how important this is, Jeff."

"Do you honestly think that the words used make any difference? I mean, this all sounds — how do I put it — outside the accepted tenets of my church."

"Jeff, you yourself said that your luck seemed to change, that you did things you can't explain. Could that possibly result from something that pushed you to do it?"

Jeff pondered for a moment. "Are you suggesting possession?"

I nodded. "And if I am?"

He frowned and considered the idea. This was the Jeff Hanley I knew, a man with a fine mind, confronted with a problem, as he sought an answer. "It was an accepted concept, even a hundred years ago. But modern psychiatry and even the Catholic Church don't accept it now." His eyes lit up. "I could do some research on it. Reverend Talbot left me an entire library of books when he retired."

"If you have the time."

Jeff grinned at me. "Time I got, Len."

"Anything like that would be a big help."

"I'll be in touch if I get anything you can use."

"Thanks, Jeff."

We both hung up the phone, and with a little wave, we both got up to leave. I went to the guard with one of my business cards. It had all my major numbers, even my email address, if he had access to a computer. I muttered to the guard that it was for Jeff Hanley, and he nodded and took it.

Getting out of there was a great relief, especially on a psychic level. Claustrophobia didn't trouble me, but other minds heavily affected me, and a prison was confining in more than just the physical sense. Invisibly, I could feel those vast walls and sharp wires, even when I couldn't see them. Anger and hopelessness filled the very air, and going outside into the light was like stepping out of a smoke-filled room. I let the stale energy fall off me, like you would air out a suit after a night at a cigar bar.

On my way back to GSU, I tried to decide my next course of action. Demons were not my field of expertise.

I was an active member of the American Board of Parapsychology. The organization works to establish scientific principles for the work I did. Unfortunately, members ranged from researchers to out-and-out frauds.

I recalled at one national meeting having a fascinating conversation with a man with a gray beard who claimed to be a 'demonologist.' I normally found such people complete flakes, but he wrote a book that was quite scholarly, and he spoke to me intelligently on the subject, and I could use the help.

I still felt the fear in the pit of my stomach from the encounter in my mind the previous night. I was apprehensive about how it could taunt me. Was it reading my mind? After all, if I were part of bringing it into this plane of existence, there had to be a connection. And if we had one, why was I only learning of it now?

With these questions and far more that I didn't even want to consider, I pulled into my parking space at the university. Students were enjoying themselves outside in the beautiful Sunday weather. Some sat on the grass, enjoying the lovely May day, sunny, with hardly a cloud in the sky.

As I walked up the stairs and toward my office, Jon Baines nearly knocked me over.

"Hey, Len!" my large friend bellowed in his booming voice. "I was just looking for you!"

I'd known Jonathan Baines since high school, then we both studied the physical sciences here at Garden State University, preparing for medical studies. Even then he possessed a sense of organization and leadership, but absolutely no talent as a doctor.

He could have run a health insurance company. But he felt his talents were in education, and at only thirty-one, he was one of the youngest college associate deans I'd ever heard of. He did his job well, raising funds, getting the best teachers he could find and afford. Also, he made the tough choice to open a Parapsychology Department and put me in charge. Which made him not only my boss, but the creator of my job.

"Hi, Jon, what are you doing here on a Sunday?"

"Len, you think I have a schedule?" he barked. He had one of those big voices that made you think of a radio deejay or an announcer. It was great when he had to give a speech; I just sometimes wished he had a volume knob. "I'm glad you're here, I've been meaning to phone you."

I took a deep breath, concern tightening my gut. "Are you going to tell me I need to find a new job?"

"What, no! Why would you think that?"

"I haven't been told that I'm renewed, and my contract—"

"Oh, that! Mere formality, buddy. When we don't rush to tell you, we assume you know we've extended you for another year.

I sighed in relief as he engulfed me with his big right arm, just like he always did in college, practically swallowing me up and spinning me around. "I was looking for you because I need a favor."

"What is it, Jon?" I always got the feeling he was trying to sell me insurance when he did this, even though I knew better. He's one of those guys who likes to shake hands and hug. I just would never get used to that kind of demonstrative behavior, gregarious though it may be.

"I need you to come to an event I'm doing this week—"

I exhaled air with a big 'whoosh'. "Another one of those 'wine-and-cheese-and-we're-all-so-upper-crusty' things?"

"Len, I gotta tell you, I raise a lot of money from those."

"I know, and I've done my share of them. But they're all dreary —"

"It's your own damn fault." He gave me a look that was almost sincere.

"My fault?"

"You're the 'Super Psychic of Scudder House.' Then your paper on the Mishan case got you a book deal. That stuff generated a lot of interest. Len, I'm telling you, you come to this soiree, and it'll get the college a hundred grand more in donations. You'll come, say a few words—"

"Oh great, a speech," I whined.

"Not a speech, just a few kudos. Len, you're terrific at this sort of thing." He gazed at me, a beseeching look in his eyes.

"I guess I have to," I replied sullenly. "It helps pay my salary, now that I know I still have a job."

"That's the spirit," he cheered, and slapped me on the back with enough gusto to leave a mark. "Bring Jyanette!"

"I'll try," I groaned.

"Do it. She's perfect to make you look good."

"What do you mean?"

"Does the phrase 'eye candy' mean anything to you?" he added suggestively.

I felt the flush of embarrassment pass over my face. "Jon, I don't know. Her schedule—"

Jon let loose one of his huge, blaring laughs. "Please ask her. She will help charm the donors."

"Okay, okay."

"By the way, Jenny wants to know when you're coming for dinner."

"I'm free tonight."

"Tonight's not good," he said, his voice again lowering to a dull roar. "Jenny's fertile."

"That's more than I want to know. But I thought you two had luck a couple of months ago."

"False alarm. But it's fun to try. We've been working on it since last January. I know Jenny's cycle better than she does."

"Have you had any tests?"

"Any tests? We've had every test. The doctors say we're fine. We just have to keep trying."

"There are worse things," I grinned.

"Maybe, but a thermometer isn't exactly my idea of a sex toy."

"It'll happen, just be patient."

"Yeah, I suppose." He moved again. "So, tomorrow, with that beautiful woman on your arm."

"Okay, Jon." I headed back to my office, then went farther to enter the computer room and found Santos at his usual machine.

"Hey, Doc," Santos reported, "heard you coming down the hall. I guess Dean Baines caught up to you."

"He did." I pulled out the note I had written and held it out to Santos. His eyes brightened behind his lenses.

"What's this?" he said, suspicion creeping into his voice.

"I need you to get me some information on this doctor. His name is Brice. Richard Brice."

"Psychiatrist?"

"Yeah, he might work at Blackshale."

"Ah-ha!"

I looked at him questioningly. "Ah-ha?"

"He must be a suspect in the murders."

"No, he isn't. Just get me what you can dig up about him, if there is anything."

"What else is this you wrote... demon — ologist?" he asked. "American Board of Parapsychology, annual meeting, and a date?"

"I need you to go check online and see who was giving a lecture on demonology at that meeting. I had a fascinating conversation with the man, and I need to call him, so if you can also track down a current number—"

"Doc, you know this isn't very fair."

"What do you mean?"

"I'm doing the grunt work, and you're not even telling me what's going on. Psychiatrists? Demonologists? Are you looking for a guy that's crazy, or possessed?"

I felt a slight tingle from the hairs on the back of my neck standing up. In dismissing Santos's non-existent psychic abilities, I forgot he was good at putting clues together.

I exhaled deeply. So much for not telling anyone. So far, I had shot my theory past Jyanette, Kate Yearling, Jeff Hanley, and now it looked like Santos as well. "Okay, what do you want to know?"

"What's your current theory?"

"Possession might be involved. And there is a catch — it might be a demonic force that I helped release."

Santos sat up in his chair. "Really? Cool!"

"No, it's not cool," I fumed, my voice raised in anger despite myself. "It was dangerous and juvenile, the work of a damn fool who didn't know he could do things. Now, seventeen people or more are dead, and I might be to blame."

Tears stung my eyes as the realization hit home.

It was my fault.

I should be the one in jail, just as surely as Jeff Hanley. I also killed a woman I loved, just like him. Only I used a car instead of a knife.

Santos sat there, wide-eyed, surprised at my sudden outburst of emotion, maybe more than I was.

"Just check on those guys, please," I pleaded and headed up the hall to my office where I closed the door. I sat in my big chair, grabbed a tissue from an open box, and dabbed my eyes.

"I'm going to get this thing," I said in a low tone, which pushed me over the edge. I wept for Cathy again, as I had done all these years.

I also wept for Mary Gillian and the others still unknown and unmourned.

12. DEMONIC DEN

After about twenty minutes, I could compose myself and went to the men's room to wash my face. When I got back to the office, my cell phone made its musical tone.

"Leonard, it's Kate Yearling."

"I'm glad to see we're still in communication."

"Of course, but ever since we talked about that demon stuff — it's just that, there's some evidence—"

"Evidence?"

"Leonard, I'll tell you what we've found, but you can't repeat it to a soul."

"Of course." My surprise continued, as Kate sounded so unsure of herself.

"I really wouldn't have even thought of it, except all that stuff you said about demons…"

"I don't have a clue what you're talking about."

"It's that room at Blackshale. We've disassembled it, going over each piece one fragment at a time: DNA on everything, stains, bits of food. Anything and everything," she said, and a deep, short chuckle burst from the back of her throat. "They're even digging up the basement looking for graves."

"And you found something that doesn't quite fit your original theories."

"Yes, as we cleaned up the debris — with tweezers, I'll have you know—"

"The FBI is nothing if not meticulous."

"I suppose that's true. But as they cleaned away the glass and dirt, all over the floor they found these — what are they called?" The line went silent for a moment as she thought. "Symbols? Hex Signs? Cartouches?"

I held the phone to my shoulder as I booted up my computer. "Demonic graffiti?"

"Very funny. They were odd circles with all kinds of little shapes and writing in them. Some contained, I guess, Latin, but not modern Latin—"

"There's modern Latin?" I wondered and realized I was asking the wrong question.

"I mean modern letters. This alphabet was… different."

"You think it might be too sophisticated to be the artwork of some winos."

"Exactly. I looked it over myself and had one agent photograph them all. I downloaded them onto my computer and compared them. They seem to be very slight variations of the same symbol over and over."

"Can you e-mail them to me?"

"I was hoping you'd ask that. I've just sent you the one that is the clearest. Perhaps you can make heads or tails out of it."

"I'm working to track down someone who might be an expert," I told her, with a pause for effect. "Are you reconsidering my theory?"

There was a heavy exhale into the receiver. She went on with a tone of patience one saves for a child. "Leonard, satanism is an interest of many serial killers. It's part of the sickness, a focus on morbidity." She then hesitated and said, almost as an afterthought, "I thought this was… an interesting coincidence."

"That's a start. I'll get back to you once I see the photos."

I ended the call and hit the button to call Jyanette.

"Hello, lover," came the answer.

"Not recently. You're in a mood."

"Not yet, but you could convince me."

"I need a favor—"

"I'll be right over—"

"Not that kind of favor." I chuckled. "Besides, I'm at the office. I'm wondering if you're doing anything tomorrow night?"

She considered it. "I have court in the morning on Tuesday. What do you have in mind?"

"Jon stuck me into speaking at a fundraiser tomorrow for the college. He said I should bring you to the event."

"You didn't think of asking me yourself?"

"Jyanette, I love you, and those things are awfully dull. I didn't want to subject you to it. But Jon suggested I needed some eye candy."

This made her laugh. "I make you look good. Doctor Wise, are you asking me out on a date?" She said brightly, a mocking tone in her voice.

"Every chance I get," I told her. "I'm trying to convince you to have sex with me again, too."

"Hmm. Duly noted. So you want your 'Nubian Princess' to help you pull money out of the drunk patrons?"

"You got it."

"How romantic." Her tone shifted to sarcasm. "What girl couldn't resist such an invitation?"

"Okay," I said. "My darling ADA Emery, also known as Nubian Royalty—"

"Ooh, I like that—"

"It would honor me to escort your beautiful persona to this event and be the envy of every man there."

"In that case," she said, a tone of admiration now coloring her speech, "I'd be delighted. Nice save."

"Thank you. I'll pick you up at seven."

"Wow, you'll even pick me up. Hoping to get lucky?"

"Hoping very hard. And tomorrow… please wear something slinky."

"Of course, how else can we strike envy everywhere we go?" A giggle rose in her throat. "Talk to you later."

She hung up the phone and I exhaled. Now, if only I could get rid of the feeling of impending doom. But what was I afraid of?

One simple fact: the women I found attractive ended up dead.

Was that why I was on this case with such fixation? If I could find this thing and, I don't know, exorcise it, then maybe I could make amends to the past and live a normal life? Maybe Jyanette and I could get it together, get married, raise children?

Our children would be beautiful.

I smiled to myself, surprised by my pleasure in the thought.

Teddy's entrance startled me out of my reverie. Teddy never actually just walked into a room. He sort of stumbled and burst like fireworks in the sky on July Fourth.

"Doc, I think I've got your men."

I smiled. "Great! What did you find?"

"I'll give it to you in order. Doctor Richard Brice was at Blackshale. In fact, he's still there. He's in charge."

I raised my eyebrows. Brice's being there was a good sign. It meant he was accessible. "Did you note anything unusual in his biography?"

"No, but then again, the bio I got looks like he wrote it. It lists his accomplishments without too many citations. According to it, he's a pretty established therapist, well respected. I got his e-mail address."

"Good, any luck with the demonologist?"

"I found what I could at the organization's website. I went through the listed speakers trying to track him down."

"Logical place to start," I encouraged him.

"I hit pay dirt with listings from two years ago and found Doctor Dennis MacAdam. He's the head of the Literary Department at the University of Arizona."

"That seems familiar." I tried to attach a name to the dim memory of the man I spoke with.

"He claims he's an expert on demons. He gave one of the lectures," he reported, watching my response. "Does any of this ring a bell? He was hyping a book — a modern translation from Latin of a book called *Demoniality* written in the seventeenth century by…" He checked a slip of paper in his hand. "Sinistrari?"

"Right!" I exulted. "A limited edition, but very well received in scholarly and historical circles."

"I guess you don't pick that up at Amazon?" Teddy joked, his eyes flickering behind his magnifying glass lenses.

"You might. I wish I'd read it," I divulged, feeling a tad guilty for not getting a copy of the book — it was part of my field. But looking back, I realized demons were something I had avoided since the night of the accident. "It would come in handy right about now."

"Try going to the horse's mouth," suggested Santos, never one to let a cliché get by if he could avoid it. "Here's his office number." He looked at the paper again. "And his alternate number. Might be his house or his cell."

"Teddy," I mused, smiling in admiration. "How do you do it?"

Santos shrugged his shoulders. "I just look for as much info as I can get. On the net there's always five or six ways to do something. I use them all."

"Teddy, I rarely take time to tell you how much of a help you are to me—"

"It's okay, Doc, I know," he replied with a smile as he put the slip of paper on my desk. It was a computer printout with all of

MacAdam's information on it. "I'm downloading information about demons right now. I'll work my way through it and show you anything that looks promising."

"Thanks, Teddy. How's your paper?"

"Done. Just needs a rewrite!" he said as he dashed out of the room.

I looked at the printout.

"I'll try his office first," I muttered to myself as I picked up my cell phone and input the numbers. I opened my e-mail program on my laptop so I could download Kate's image of the Blackshale floor.

"You've reached the Literary Department of Arizona State University, and this is the voicemail system," a whiny female voice told me disinterestedly. "Please stay on the line for a complete listing. If you know your party's extension, you may press it at any time—"

I saw the number 122 next to the phone number and quickly punched it in.

"This is Doctor Dennis MacAdam, the head of the department. I can't answer your call at this time—"

I listened to the deep bass voice, which indeed sounded familiar. It appeared Santos got his research right. I heard the beep.

"Doctor MacAdam, this is Doctor Leonard Wise. We spoke two years ago at a convention. I have a... situation that might be up your alley." I left my office number.

I ended the call and looked over at my computer. Twenty-two new emails faced me. I went quickly through them, eliminating the ones that offered to make me rich in a week, told me how I could get Viagra without a doctor, or create a fake college degree for under fifty dollars. One was from Jon Baines — the formal invitation to the party tomorrow night. I shook my head. He certainly did that quickly.

I immediately opened the one from Kate. It had a brief message, basically "Hi, here it is" and contained a JPEG. I clicked on the attachment, and the image appeared on my screen. I sucked in the air through tight lips, though I couldn't figure out why it disturbed me.

The overall design was a circle-in-a-circle. Within the second circle were three odd line-drawings, each one resembling what a child could make with a crayon.

The top one was a cross with tiny circles at the four corners, which took a ninety-degree turn at the bottom. Next was a diagram of a sword with three U's imposed over the line that would be the blade. The last one looked like a German Iron Cross, except the bottom looped in a semicircle and attached to an Egyptian ankh lying on its side. Between the two circles were letters — they looked like astrological symbols, but none I had ever seen.

The closest thing I could relate them to was Hebrew, but I would recognize that from my Jewish upbringing and going to Hebrew school at the synagogue once a week.

I could see why Kate suggested the word cartouche, which was usually reserved for Egyptian symbols. This circle contained the unusual letters and designs in a curious combination, suggesting hieroglyphics — or perhaps something even older.

Old and evil.

I pondered it for a few more minutes, then finally called it a night and headed home.

I walked in the door to a fantastic meal Mrs. Higgins had made — her own variation of Eggplant Parmesan. As I ate the hot casserole with a Caesar salad, I wondered how my nice Irish housekeeper became such an expert at Italian dishes.

We spoke of local events, philosophy, and even played a game of chess after dinner over tea. I had a much-needed night away from serial killers, demons, and even school.

Although during the chess game, where she trounced me, Mrs. Higgins observed me when she thought I didn't notice. She looked concerned, as if she knew I felt I was in over my head.

It wasn't until the next morning that I was able to get MacAdam on the phone. I called him from my cell at about nine on Monday morning.

"Leonard Wise? Yes, I remember you," the boisterous voice announced over the phone. "Read some good stuff attributed to you. You wrote that paper about that pyrokinetic?"

"You read it?" I asked, flattered.

"Some of it. You write well. Let's see if I have this right: we had a very enjoyable discussion over dinner at a convention, and then three years later you call me out of the blue. What can I do for you, Leonard?"

"Doctor MacAdam—"

"Dennis, please. Let's not be formal," he threw in good-naturedly.

"Very well, Dennis. It's… about a demon."

"I would hope so!" I could hear the excitement in his voice. "Do tell!"

I quickly and carefully brought him into the information I had. I didn't mention Cathy and me, but I touched on Jeff Hanley and the symbols the FBI found. He listened intently and grunted in places.

"You mentioned finding symbols. What did they look like?"

I briefly described them.

"Sounds like a sigil."

The term inspired a vague recollection. "I've studied those myself, but this was unusual."

"There are many variations, possibly more than you could have found in most research material," he urged. "Most people in the field are familiar with *The Key of Solomon the King,* where he calls them Pentacles. Some of the more obscure are in the *Grimorium Verum.* Do you own a copy of either of those?"

I thought for a minute. I was familiar with both volumes. *Grimorium* was written in 1517, a book of black magic. *The Key,* a book of ritual magic, traced its lineage to antiquity, where legends say King Solomon of Israel wrote it over three thousand years ago. The founder of the Golden Dawn, a ritual magic cult in England in the 1800s, translated it into English.

I cleared my throat. "I believe I have a copy of *The Key* somewhere. It was required reading in Doctor Kohl's class."

He chuckled. "Fritz Kohl. That's right, you told me you were one of his. He definitely would've made you read that — if only to refute it as unscientific."

"That's exactly what he did." I chuckled, the memory firm in my mind. I meandered through the archaic and often unreadable book, only to have Doctor Kohl use it as a demonstration of how not to do research. He pointed out how the tools the book listed, like candles, incense, and wands, helped focus the mind to achieve desired results.

"Now, about those sigils," MacAdam pulled me back to the problem at hand. "Do you have a photo of any of them?"

"The FBI agent e-mailed me a copy."

"Excellent. Can you send it on to me? I might open some dusty tomes and find out what you've got there."

He rattled off his e-mail address.

"Dennis, the strangest thing is the lettering. They look more like astrological symbols than any kind of alphabet."

"Hmm!" he said, taking a moment. "Could be what some call the Mystic Alphabet. If you can find The Key, they have some samples in the back."

"You know a lot more about this than I do. Is it possible that this could be a possession situation?"

I heard an exhale over the earpiece. "I'm not one to avoid going out on a limb, but I don't want to speculate until I have more information. I don't have to tell you that in parapsychology circles, a lot of far-out things are acceptable: spirit photography, automatic writing, and the like. But you and I are also college professors, and I don't need to tell you what would happen if our universities heard us talking about demons and possession."

"Good point," I agreed. I couldn't help but like the man, as I did at our last meeting. For someone who studied demons, he was incredibly down-to-earth.

"Demonic possession is a possibility, considering your friend, Mr. Hanley. But a serial killer? It could be someone interested in satanic ritual."

"I've been told that's common among such killers."

"Yes, and then the situation with Hanley might be merely a coincidence. Remember, even if this is a sigil, it might not appear in the sources I mentioned. There is another possibility. Someone might try to make you think it is a possession."

I was dumbstruck but mumbled, "Why?"

"If there was a person who wanted to discredit you, perhaps?" he proposed, with the tone of a man who had been through this in the past.

"Can't think of anyone. Besides, I had a very clear vision of the scene, but I can't see the man's face—"

"I see," he said. "I actually might have an explanation for that. If it's someone close to you, your own mind might block you."

"You're suggesting some kind of subconscious resistance?"

"Yes." Then he added, almost as an afterthought, "Then again, I'm not a psychic."

"Great." I smiled more at his delivery than at his information. "I'm blocking myself. Something else to worry about. I'll send you that photo. Get back to me with what you can."

"Very well, Leonard. Nice talking to you. Don't make it another three years."

"Thank you, Dennis, I won't."

I hung up the phone and sat in the chair at my desk. I forwarded the photo from the e-mail over to Dennis MacAdam.

So here I was on Monday morning with no class, as I tried to decide my next course of action. I could try to call Doctor Brice at Blackshale, see if he was in—

Just go there…

The thought flashed into my head with the strength of one of my buzzes. But then again, I might get a little more information if I waited a day or two. Additionally, I could find myself wandering where people didn't want me.

JUST GO…

When the voice in my head got loud, I listened. I quickly got ready and bid Mrs. Higgins goodbye.

"But, Doctor, ye were goin' to talk to me about getting the gutter cleaned—"

"I promise, we'll talk tomorrow and set up a time to do it. Really, Mrs. Higgins, we have the entire summer to figure out this stuff," I said as I walked toward the door.

"Ye'll have excuses then as well. Ye've been puttin' it off—"

"Tomorrow, I promise," I said, walking out to my car.

Mrs. Higgins followed me into the driveway. "Make sure ye do!"

I waved, jumped into the van, and drove off before she could say another word.

Of course, I didn't discuss the gutters with her on Tuesday.

I was not going to be able to.

13. THE HORNED MAN

After a forty-minute drive I was at the psychiatric facility, grateful that I could look around without it being dark or raining. It was sunny and warm, and I drove through the entrance that led me straight to the tower, which seemed much less imposing on a fine spring day.

I wondered if I should call Kate and let her know I was at the site. A good idea, except I didn't know what I was up to, other than trying to meet with Doctor Brice. However, her office wasn't far away, and I could call or visit her if I had anything to report.

I parked the van once again near the police building, positioning myself for a clear view of the 'crime scene' structure, as well as the towering edifice that loomed beyond.

Stepping out, I followed the winding path leading toward the tower, certain it was one of the primary entrances. The smell of growing things permeated the air. Nearby, the trees stood tall and proud, their branches draped in rich, verdant leaves, as if preparing to welcome the summer just around the corner.

My first impression today was correct. Blackshale didn't look nearly so intimidating on such a beautiful day. Even the buildings of dark-gray stone weren't as menacing as they had seemed on my last visit.

I decided a frontal assault was my best choice. I would go right in and ask for Doctor Brice. My mind made up, I pushed forward with decisive energy. I walked in the front door and, much to my surprise, into a very modern-looking reception area. This was totally unexpected from the archaic facade. The walls were clean with nice paintings; the floor was modern vinyl and bright white. I walked to the glass window of the admissions desk, but there was no one there.

This took me aback. I was all set to ask for Doctor Brice, and there was no one to urge me into action. Since there wasn't anyone trying to stop me, I continued, unencumbered.

I headed down the hall, my pace speeding up, when I hit a wet patch of floor and slipped. I put my cane against the floor, but even the rubber tip skidded on the wet floor, and I half-fell, half-tumbled into a bench that was safely bolted to the ground.

I caught my breath and tried to get back up as a familiar figure approached me from down the hall, a mop in his hand.

"Jim?" I called out, puzzled.

The tall figure looked up in response to my voice and broke into a wide grin.

"Doc Wise? Is that you?"

"Sure is, Jim," I said and pulled myself up carefully so that I didn't sprawl out on the floor. Jim came closer and took my hand in a firm handshake. "What the hell are you doing here? They ain't committin' you, are they?"

I laughed. "Not yet, Jim. I'm researching a case."

His smile shrank, and he furrowed his brow. "Here? A case? Like the ones you do with the police?"

"Seems like there's been some murders nearby. I can't really talk about it."

"Damn!" Jim said, nodding. "I saw the cops over at Building 'B'. I just figured they found another wino in there."

"Do they get many homeless here?"

Jim glanced around to make sure the two of us were alone. "Frankly, Doc, they got people going into those old buildings all the time. Kids the most, 'specially when the weather gets nice. They sneak in and get drunk, maybe smoke some weed, and scare the piss out of each other." He glanced around again. "Always leave a mess, not that anybody cleans them deserted buildings." He looked down the hall as if to glimpse Building B. "Well, at least you explained why those guys with the suits are there."

"Yeah, they're FBI. Are they a problem?"

He frowned. "They got a bad attitude, talkin' to you like you work for them. There's one, about five foot eight, with muscles. He's just nasty."

"Is his name Gabe Petrie?"

He chewed it over for a moment. "Yeah, I think that's it."

"I've already met him."

"I don't want to meet him again," Jim complained, punctuating with a quick nod. "That would be fine with me. It's funny, though. I thought I'd seen him here before."

I turned to Jim. "What do you mean?"

"He's been here visitin' somebody, I think." He shrugged his shoulders. "Makes no never mind. None of my business."

"Jim, can you tell me if Doctor Brice is here today?"

He looked at the ceiling and thought for a moment. "Brice? He should be in his office. I didn't get to it yet."

I asked him where Brice's office was, and he gave me directions that included going up a nearby stairway.

"But whatever you do, don't go up or down the 'E' staircase. That'll take you into the wards, and you don't wanna deal with the crazies."

I felt surprised by his insensitive expression. "I doubt the patients here will bother me."

"Depends on which ward. I ain't talkin' about the regulars — they're okay. But you go into Ward 18, that's the ward with the crazies. They're trouble. You best avoid that."

I shook my head and assured him of how careful I would be. "Thanks, Jim." I tried to cross the floor he had wet down so well. "So, how is it — I mean, working here?"

He made a quick snorting noise. "As bad as I remember."

"Take care, Jim."

"You too, Doc."

I walked down the hall, and using my cane and the handrail, slowly climbed a set of stairs into an older part of the building. The transition was jarring. Layers of blistered, leaden paint clung to the walls like molting skin, while the tiles beneath my feet were dirty and discolored. Round spherical lights hung on metal poles from the ceiling, but half of them were unlit. Brilliant shafts of sunlight pierced through the few windows, but they did little to warm the space; the light only illuminated the stagnant dust, failing to lift the heavy, dismal weight.

I followed Jim's instructions, up a staircase to the second floor, then around a corner, through a door that looked two hundred years old, and into a hallway carpeted with that kind of cheap indoor/outdoor carpeting that was popular in the early sixties. I continued down the hall and saw a door with a plastic plaque that announced:

"Doctor Richard Brice, Chief Administrator."

I knocked gently.

"Come in?" a deep voice answered.

I opened the door and stepped in. Behind the desk, a man glanced up. He was balding and large without being fat. He wore a white lab coat that had seen better days, a tie that was frayed, fraying, or both, and the look of a harried administrator.

"Doctor Brice?" I asked.

"How can I help you?" he demanded, looking at me as if he were a gem cutter and I was interrupting a delicate procedure on the Hope Diamond.

"My name is Doctor Leonard Wise. I'm part of the team that is investigating the... uh... incident here at Blackshale."

He visibly stiffened, his face turning red. "Look, I have tried to cooperate with you people, but I want to assert that there has been no murder." His voice raised in volume, not as loud as Jon Baines, but probably very loud for him. "Any blood found there is merely from some vagrant who cut himself getting into the building."

I held up my hands, trying to calm him. It was also a chance to focus my energy and reach out to read anything from him on a psychic level. "I understand, Doctor. But actually I'm more interested in a patient of yours."

"A patient?" He calmed down, his face returning to its natural shade. "What does a patient have to do with any of this? I was told the police suspected an abduction—"

"Yes, I know, sir. But I have a personal interest in this man. I knew him in high school: Jeff Hanley."

"Hanley?" he grumbled and grabbed a folder as he rose heavily from the desk with a quizzical look. "I vaguely recall the name—"

"He was here for a psychological evaluation. A murder trial about seven years ago? He killed a young woman."

"Oh yes," he said and put on his psychiatrist demeanor. He opened the folder to read the top paper. It was a very dismissive gesture designed to suggest I go away, as he was so very busy.

He went on without looking up from the paper. "Now that you mention it, I do recall... the man who sliced his girlfriend like a London broil." He closed the folder. "He ended up in Rahway State Prison. I don't see what this has to do with—"

"I'll be frank, Doctor Brice. I'm trying to locate anyone here who might have come in contact with Mister Hanley."

He put the folder down and went to a filing cabinet and opened a metal drawer. "For what purpose?" he added, his back to me as he put the folder in its proper place.

"It's part of the investigation."

He turned to gaze at me carefully. "Jeff Hanley was here for two days, years ago. How could he possibly have anything to do with this incident?"

I could see this wouldn't be easy. "Anything at all would help. Psychological evaluations — perhaps you could tell me what ward he was in?"

He closed the drawer with a bang and turned to face me. "This is very unorthodox and might be unethical. Doctor Wise, are you a practicing psychiatrist?"

Glancing at the floor, I said, "I've studied psychiatry, but my PhD is in parapsychology. I teach at GSU."

"Parapsychology?" he repeated, as if he needed to remember the term. "Why are you here? Is the FBI looking for ghosts now?"

"Doctor Brice, I work with the police and the FBI. I'm following up on information that came to me, and I'm trying to make sense out of it. I would appreciate any details you could give me about Mister Hanley. Even if it is just your own recollections."

He returned to his haven behind the desk and parked himself in the chair, the padded seat groaning under his weight. "I'm not in the habit of helping gypsies, mediums, or parapsychologists. You'll have to leave, sir!" He picked up the next folder and returned to his work at hand.

I didn't move. "Very well, Doctor," I agreed. Then I tried to play my ace in the hole. "But that will mean that Agent Petrie will have to get the files for me."

"Gabe… Petrie?" Brice stammered, dropping the folder, his head up, and his attitude crestfallen.

I had said the right name.

"Yes, sir. He gets the job done. Of course, he is pushy—"

Brice leaned back into his chair and glared at me. "Pushy? The man is impossible. In two days, he and that group of jackbooted thugs have turned this place upside down. He's been a problem to me for years."

"Years?" I asked, as I remembered Jim mentioned he'd seen him before.

"Yes, his sister's been here for, I don't know, six years?" he said, pulling a thick file from his desk. "Severe cognitive delay, used to be at home, but the parents died and he moved her here. The first year was fine; she fit in well and was in our newer wing where we help guide such patients, and was very independent. But then he moves to New Jersey and visits and makes complaints every chance he gets. 'This is wrong', 'she should have these medications', 'her treatment isn't right', and the like. The state reduced our budget, and we have some patients who require a lot of care. I tell you, he's been waiting for something like this."

"I understand," I sympathized. I had seen Brice's metamorphosis into his 'harried administrator' act, so I shifted into 'understanding colleague' for him. "I didn't even want to bother you, but I felt I might be a little easier for you to deal with —"

"Deal with? You don't know what I have to deal with. The state is trying to shut us down, they've cut our budget, and now the damn FBI..." His sentence petered out and his energy faded.

I clucked encouragingly. Brice didn't consider me the same bad guy I was a moment earlier.

"If I could see his file, it might —"

"Oh, what does it matter?" he grumbled and rose to his full height. "Come with me."

Grabbing a huge ring of keys, he led me directly across the hall, studying the keys as he went. Extracting one, he opened the door and flicked on a light. Metal file cabinets lined the room, leaving tight aisles between them.

"Wait here," he ordered, and went in. I could hear him opening and closing several file cabinets, and the sound of papers rustling. He strode back into the hall with a file and a large manila envelope in his hands.

"Here, take. The Hanley file. This is everything I've got."

"That's very kind," I told him, remaining solicitous.

"Just bring it back!" he directed as he handed me the file and the large envelope. "Put it in the envelope and leave it with the front desk." He had recovered some of his venom and was trying to maintain what little dignity he had left. "I personally would prefer you don't see me again."

"I'll do my best," I said, and tried not to push my luck. "I can't thank you enough for your time, Doctor Brice."

He returned to his office and waved at me with a 'go away' gesture and shut the door behind him. I headed for the stairs. I'd found out three very important things: first, an authority figure could easily intimidate Doctor Brice; second, that even I could get him to give up patient files with the right amount of pressure; third, that he definitely was not being used as a host for any kind of demon.

Although our time together was short, I had used my abilities to read him, his energy, and anything else I could think of. His personality was purely his own, unpleasant though it was. I had also subtly reached out and influenced him to give me the folder.

I glanced at the file while I tapped my way down the stairs. I hoped there might be some small tidbit of information that would save me taking the file away at all. I reached the bottom of the stairs and turned down a hallway to read the report. I put my cane under my arm as I read and limped along.

I felt annoyed by how little there was.

"Patient Hanley demonstrates typical anti-social personality disorder…" along with far more technical assessments. It appeared to be a pretty fair report, but it lacked details or treatment suggestions.

I forced myself to remember that it was only a competency evaluation, nothing more. They assigned him here to determine his competence to stand trial.

I walked down another staircase as I mulled it over.

There was nothing here to help or hurt my case. The report listed Doctor Brice, but Jeff could have come into contact with anyone: a nurse, another patient, or even a visitor. There was no way to follow his interactions the night his 'unseen guest' moved out for better hunting.

As I walked, I pulled out my phone, opened an app, and made notes of the dates Hanley was here. It was probably the only useful information in the file.

I stopped at the bottom of the steps to input the data and heard a dull sound. It was a moan — definitely a moan, the cry of someone in pain.

A mental picture of Mary Gillian popped into my head unbidden. I put the papers into the envelope and slipped it under my arm and hurried toward the sound. I pulled open the door in the stairwell, not really certain what floor I was on. The moaning grew louder, then the door shut solidly behind me. The click of the door made me realize I had locked myself in.

I turned back and pushed the door. My intuition was correct; I couldn't open it from this side. I was not sure where I was. The moan was not someone being tortured, and it was clearly a man, not a woman. I turned down the hall, and it opened into a spacious room.

The room had been white once, and I was sure that every year they repainted it, but the dirt and scuff marks on the walls probably reappeared quickly.

The room was busy with wheelchairs, slow-moving bodies of men, doped and twitching as they walked, with a few sitting in chairs in different states of awareness. One man huddled in the corner near a wall and would occasionally gently slam his head against it, while he made a noise. He was my moaner.

I'd been to private psychiatric facilities — it was part of my research when I was in the psychiatry fellowship — and the conditions often depressed me. But this place, a state-run facility, was much worse.

There were people with severe disabilities strapped into their wheelchairs, and the room carried an air of industrial cleaner and drugged disinterest.

Also, it exhausted me on a psychic level, as their mental energy was not only twisted and vacant, it was like a black hole that sucked at my energy.

It was very similar to my experience in a haunted house, where the spirits needed to use my mental energy to manifest. I could sense the attraction this place would have for my demonic opponent. There was a feeling of helplessness and death all around. I felt more paranoid with each step.

Some of the more aware patients watched me.

The most surprising thing was that I didn't see any nurses, doctors, or orderlies. Here was a stranger who walked into a ward, and no one accosted him.

A sudden fear gripped me. Had I wandered into the place where they kept what Jim had called, 'the crazies'?

"Excuse me," a voice said behind me, and I nearly jumped out of my skin. I rotated to see a nurse, only five feet tall, looking at me. She was a plump, efficient-looking woman, with hair dyed an auburn color, and her face showed strong laugh lines.

"Are you here to visit someone?" she asked politely enough, but her eyes were watching me with suspicion.

"No, I… uh… just met with Doctor Brice. I must have taken the wrong stairs." I tried to sound convincing.

"Oh, yes. Which way did you come in?"

"From the tower?" I told her, realizing that although I called the huge facade 'the tower' it might have another name altogether.

She nodded and turned her head. "William!"

A tall, black man came into the room. I looked up at his six-foot ten-inch frame and my jaw came loose. He looked like a basketball player and moved with natural grace. He wore green scrubs, though I had no idea where he found them big enough for him.

"This gentleman got a bit lost. Can you take him out to Exit B4?" she insisted. William nodded solemnly. She looked back at me with a smile on her face that appeared harmless enough. "The fastest way is past the cell block. It would be better if someone accompanied you."

I nodded, grateful to have an escort. "Thank you." My voice sounded much quieter than I had intended.

William gave a slight nod of his head, and I followed. He unlocked a different door with a set of keys connected to a reel, and they flipped back to a box on his belt. I tapped along with my cane to catch up with his elongated stride.

"We have to go by the cell block?" I asked the tall man.

"Yeah," he answered in a deep voice. He didn't turn to look at me, but his eyes roamed to make sure everything was all right. "That's where they keep 'the crazies.'"

I wanted to stop and absorb this, but William moved with such long legs, I dared not slow down if I wanted to keep up. "Do they have anyone dangerous here?" I asked.

"In the cell block? Sure. Most everyone else here is just too far gone for their families to take care of — and they're too poor to put them anywhere else. So here they sit, yours and my tax dollars at work." As he said the last line, he turned to me with a knowing smile.

I returned his grin and tried to push the matter. "So, 'the crazies,' what did they do?"

"They are the ones that are 'not guilty by reason of insanity'. I dunno, murder, most of them. I help with them sometimes, being big and all. Some of them are pretty far gone."

I remembered seeing a chain-link fence with barbed wire surrounding a basketball court. It occurred to me that this was a place 'the crazies' went. The people I had seen in the ward were certainly in no shape to play basketball.

We came to a new hallway, much narrower than the one we were leaving. On the right side were doors — heavy doors that I could tell were quite solid. Each one had a small opening at about eye-level that was covered with crossbars of thick wire.

"Speaking of which." William nodded toward the doors. That simple gesture told me that the gentlemen we had been talking about were behind those substantial portals.

As we passed, I peeked in a window where, in the room's dim light, I could see a figure on the bed. He remained motionless.

"William," a voice just above a whisper sputtered in the next cell.

The tall man stopped, stooped a bit, and peered in. "What is it, Reuben?" he said impatiently, as if he'd done this a hundred times already today.

"William, c-can I go outside and p-play b-ball? It's nice out."

"Reuben, we got a short staff today. It'll have to wait until tomorrow."

I approached and could see a bearded man looking through the wire hole in the door. His pale blue eyes turned to me. He seemed to peer right through me.

Reuben glanced questioningly at William.

"He's a guest. I'm showing him out," he said, as a way of explanation.

"You're l-looking for him, aren't you?" Reuben babbled, his attention returned to me.

"Looking for who?" I asked.

His lips quivered as he tried to form the words. "The horned man," he blurted, straightforward and without a stutter or hesitation.

I stood stock-still, frozen in place.

William exhaled, almost a sigh. "Reuben, this guy doesn't care about—"

"No, wait." My tone probably sounded desperate because William stopped talking. I drew closer, making my voice quiet, conspiratorial. "The horned man?"

Reuben nodded nervously. "He gets inside you," he said, his face twitching as if he remembered something that he didn't want to. "He m-makes you do b-bad things."

"Reuben, nobody believes in your horned man!" William mocked. "There ain't a devil man walking these hallways!"

Reuben nodded frantically and turned back to me, as I didn't argue with him.

"He's here!" he hissed. "Still here! I see him some nights, when he walks the halls. Sometimes, he's c-carrying b-bodies."

William looked at me. "We'd better go. This will only upset him."

"You know." His finger pointed in my direction through the crisscrossing restraining wire. "You know he's here." His voice had become agitated, but he lowered it, just in case. "And he's still killing."

He leaned back from the door and stared at me, unblinking. A gob of drool rolled down his chin, but he didn't seem to notice or care. His eyes stared at me with a depth that was chilling.

William snorted and walked again. Reuben crept away from the door, back to the safety of his cell. His eyes never left my face. Although I couldn't see inside his room, I was sure it was padded.

I moved on, tapping with my cane to catch up to William. "What did he do?" I asked.

William stopped and glanced back at the cell. "It's an old story. About ten years ago, from what I hear, he was a patient here, with depression or something. This place was a real psychiatric hospital then, not a dumping place for retards like it is now."

I cringed at his word choice.

"Then one night, he goes nuts. Finds himself a scalpel and hacks up a nurse. Got her in the stairway and cut her up pretty badly. The state said he was nuts, and he's been in with 'the crazies' ever since." William shook his head. "It was crazy, too. The nurse was pregnant, and he sliced the kid right out of her."

William walked again. "He says the 'horned man' made him do it, that he's still here, and Reuben can see him sometimes." He glanced over his shoulder and looked down on me, his eyes a good six inches above my own. "You know, crazy stuff."

We turned down another hallway, went through a door, and walked into the modern entrance, belying the secured cells just a few yards behind us.

"Well, here you go," William announced. "You can find your way from here?"

I nodded and thanked him. William turned and passed back through the door, which locked sturdily behind him. He had to duck as he went through.

I still held the file in the envelope. I jotted 'DR. BRICE' on the front with a pen and walked toward the front desk. Although empty when I arrived, there was now a nurse who sat behind the glass partition. The floor was dry, and Jim was gone.

I stopped at the desk and gave the nurse the envelope, thanked her, and walked out.

It had been an educational experience.

The horned man, I thought, and the image of the wall drawing from the murder room returned to my mind.

14. PSYCHOLOGICAL PREPARATION

T hinking of the drawing and the horned man, I walked toward what Jim had called 'Building B' and the police now called the crime scene.

Two black vans were now across from the yellow-brick facade. No one was in sight, but I wanted to go in. Perhaps Kate was there.

As I walked over, I experienced the same feelings as the last time, despite the warm sunlight and the smell of blossoms.

I could focus my mind and wall myself away from the effect, but that would shut out any other second-level impressions. I just had to endure it.

I peeked cautiously through the open front door, my eyes adjusting to the stunning difference between shadow and brightness. The agents had pried open several boarded windows, stripping the hallway of some of its darkness.

Rather than offering comfort, the light only amplified the building's skeletal wrongness. Great, slanted beams of brilliance lanced through the air that caught every swirling dust mote they had stirred up. This harsh exposure revealed the floor's carpet of rotting rags and the fuzzy, black spread of mildew across the walls in all their neglected glory.

I trudged upstairs and toward the door of the room, which I now thought of as 'Mary's room.' The door was open, and I could hear voices as I got closer.

Something's wrong…

The buzz hit me, and I froze to the spot. What was wrong? I glanced around the hallway in the dim light, looking for a shape, a form, something that would spell trouble.

There was a sudden noise as someone burst out of the room all in one movement.

"Freeze!" he shouted as I realized I was staring at the receiving end of a rather large handgun.

I threw my hands in the air, hoping not to lose my balance or fall in a direction that could get me shot.

"It's Doctor Wise!" I babbled. I didn't want to upset the nice FBI man with the enormous gun. A flashlight flared in my face.

"Wise?" the voice asked. "Jeez, what're you doing here?"

"I was doing follow-up, and I saw your vans," I babbled, as I sought a better excuse than wanting to see some graffiti. "I thought I could help."

"Clear! Guns down," he stated, his silhouette turning to speak over his left shoulder. "Get that damn light out of his eyes."

I recognized Gabe Petrie's voice.

The flashlight fell away, and other lights came on in the room. I made out Petrie's form, as well as several other men. They wore rubber surgical gloves, and I guessed they were still doing forensic examinations.

"That was one bonehead move, Wise," Petrie observed, turning to me. "We heard you coming up the stairs—"

"I would hope the perp could be quieter than I am." I had come up the stairs with no thought of trying to be silent. I was sure the clip-clop of my cane and my slow ascent were easily distinguishable.

"I wish you were louder." He holstered his weapon in the harness hidden by his jacket. "We can't be too careful. We're here to catch a killer, if there is one."

I stepped closer to Agent Petrie, not sure I had heard correctly. "If there is one? But the blood — what I saw."

"Look, Wise, I know you're supposed to be good at what you do and all that, but I'll be honest with you. I don't know what you saw. Now, Doctor Yearling said she found some of these symbols, but that isn't what I'm looking for."

"What do you mean?"

"Wise, I'm looking for a large amount of blood, enough for someone to be dead. Or a body. If all we have to go on is some vision, that isn't enough."

"I understand, evidence first," I agreed, though I felt like I was about to fall into an open chasm. "But the disappearances, and the map McGee received—"

"Look, people run away, and not just when they're kids. Most of those seventeen women are probably living in another state with a married name, worrying about how much weight they're gaining."

"I don't—"

"As far as that map? McGee put a lot more value into it than what's actually there. We went over it, and between you and me, it could've just been someone trying to yank his chain." He took my arm and turned me around to walk me farther down the dim hall, out of earshot of the other agents. "Look, Wise, you seem to have something personal in this. That note we found and all. But I have to tell you, unless we uncover remains of a body, we're out of here as of Wednesday."

"But you can't," I gasped, and felt the chasm open wider under me.

"We can't keep this amount of manpower on this site. We have other cases to work on. Some with actual dead bodies." He walked back toward the stairwell, his grip on my arm bringing me along. "In the meantime, Doctor, this is an FBI crime scene, and it is off-limits to visitors."

I thought for a moment of asking him about his sister, but I was alone with him down a dark hall, and the memory of his gun in my face was fresh.

He dismissed me with a slight push toward the stairs, turned, and walked back into the room.

I followed him with my eyes. I wanted to tell him how wrong he was, how important it could be to keep going, to find the clues to stop the 'horned man.'

Anger bit at the pit of my stomach, but I decided I should get to Kate and let her know what I'd found out, to get a second opinion.

"That's ridiculous!" Kate said, smacking her desk with her open hand for extra emphasis. "Petrie is new in his position, but I decide when we pull out."

I sat and nodded. I found her in the Morris Plains office and had just spent the last fifteen minutes bringing her up to speed on my call to the demonologist, Brice, Reuben, and the confrontation with Petrie.

Kate paced. It was wonderful to see her angry. She usually reigned in her emotions so tightly. "And what is he doing, pulling out his weapon like that? I'm lucky you're not shot! Oh! That frosts me."

"In his defense, if he caught the killer, it would have been quite a coup."

"It was stupid and unnecessary. If he wanted the place secure, he should have put an agent at the front door. There certainly are enough people on his team."

"I want to be honest with you. There's something about Agent Petrie that makes a little buzz go off every time I'm near him. What can you tell me about him?"

Kate sat on the edge of her desk and shrugged. "Not much to tell. The first time I met him was the day after I met you. I know him by reputation. He has specialized in serial killers—"

"He mentioned that."

"And he's had some impressive successes. He stopped a killer in Chicago, and then one who'd been terrorizing the Midwest."

"Is he married?"

"No, he's not. That's all I know about his personal life."

"Anything about his sister? She's a patient at Blackshale."

"Again, I know nothing about it. But it could explain how he ended up seeking a position in New Jersey."

"Yes, but I take it he was a field agent. Is this the first time he's running an investigation?" I queried.

Kate shrugged. "I'm sure he's been the lead in past cases. Otherwise, I would imagine he works the local office on whatever needs to be done. Until now, I thought Gabe knew what he was doing."

"He's made things unpleasant for the staff at Blackshale. All I had to do was mention his name and Doctor Brice went ballistic."

"Still working your possession theory?" She sat down at last.

"Yes, and I believe I may have found the next link in the chain," I said with a nod. "Jeff Hanley was the man who said the words that released it—"

"That dark and stormy night," Kate jibed with a half-smile, then grew serious. "I still think you haven't told me the complete story."

"Be grateful. To support my theory, it turns out he committed a murder — a rather brutal one. In fact, I would suggest that it was similar to our serial killer, though not up to his current level."

"Interesting, and you said he was at Blackshale?"

"He was there for a psych evaluation."

"Coincidence," she said with a shrug.

"If you believe in such things."

Kate stood up again, restarted her pacing. "Oh come on, you're going to tell me that there is no such thing as a coincidence? Even Freud accepted that."

"Yes, but Jung didn't, and for my money, Carl Jung was a far more spiritual man." I turned toward her as she moved. "The next step, if you follow my theory, would be Reuben, a patient at Blackshale. He possibly had contact with Hanley. Reuben kills a pregnant nurse, claiming 'the horned man' made him do it. I already told you that made me think of that drawing on the wall, as well as that fresco I saw in the chapel in Staten Island. This murder somehow connects to the others."

She walked to her desk and pulled out a paper, which I recognized as a copy of McGee's map. She looked at the dots. "I don't see it. These abductions look random." She tossed the map to me. "That's what makes this kind of killer so very dangerous. You never know who he's going to strike or how."

"Not this guy." I rose from my chair as the realization washed over me. "He plans each murder, watches the victim, and takes them from a public place. There must be a reason for each one, including Mary Gillian, which pulled me — us — into the case."

"There you go making it personal again."

"It is personal. You saw the note." I sat back down and gazed at my hands. "The problem is, if my theory is true, this entity could be inside anyone."

She shook her head. "For argument's sake, I'll play along."

"That might help."

"Then let's hypothesize. Let's say you are right, and there is a demon running around. How does it get into people? Is it like the vampire legend, where you have to invite it in? Or does it just leap into your body and, bang, you're under its control?"

"Okay, I'll play," I proposed, standing up. "If I am right, then the person has to have a bit of psychic ability — more than the average person."

She looked at me quizzically.

I went on, "Reuben is a good example. From our brief encounter, I got the impression he has an extraordinary amount of ESP, which could also explain why he ended up in Blackshale. Trust me, I know. Images and insights popping unbidden into your head could make anyone insane."

She seemed to accept this. "Okay, let's say I agree."

"With the right person, the demon might step in at any time. It could take over when needed and lie dormant the rest of the time."

"Like a tapeworm," Kate suggested, then shuddered, grossed out by her own metaphor. "Ick!"

"That's it!" I realized, feeling slightly sick myself. "It's a parasite! It needs psychic energy to live! That's why the murders!"

"Okay, Leonard, now you just lost me."

"The murders, they're more than just killing. It's the torture, the psychological, as well as the physical. That kind of torture doesn't just affect your body, it affects your psyche."

"Of course!" she mocked my triumphant tone. She then shifted to sarcasm. "So what does that mean?"

"Energy! It feeds off the energy the victim releases while in agony." Now I was pacing, which, with my cane, was a slower process than Kate's. "He must start with pure psychological torture first, and then become more violent as the victim gets accustomed to each mistreatment. To get the same reaction!"

"Hold on!" she interjected as she tried to wrap her fine mind around my idea. "You're suggesting that the victims all have ESP ability?"

"Exactly, and that's why he chooses each victim. Do you have the files on the disappearances? Maybe the victims had psychological profiles—"

"Leonard, people don't routinely undergo tests for psychic ability like they do for the SATs or something."

"Pity," I frowned. "But I have the strongest feeling that I'm right—"

"Great, we're going by your 'feelings' again," Kate mumbled, annoyed. "I'm not convinced."

"I thought you were theorizing with me?"

"Right, right," she grudgingly agreed. "So, if he picks on people with psychic power, why is he taunting you?"

The clouds seemed to part, and my awareness was so right on it was like a tidal wave that washed over me. I grabbed the chair and lowered myself into it.

"Because if you get off on psychic energy, wouldn't a trained psychic be a logical victim?"

"You? You think he's after you?" Her eyes widened for a moment, then narrowed as she thought about it. "But why didn't he strike you earlier? According to what you told me, he's known about you since that car accident years ago."

"That night he could get enough power to materialize for me to see him. Maybe he wants that much power again. It could be he's been lying in wait until everything was right. Me, involved with the police, investigating murders. Then the human sacrifice by the *Following of Astarte* giving him all that extra juice. Think about it! If he killed me now, everyone would assume that this serial killer did it to protect himself."

I watched her reaction.

She exhaled heavily. "This is a very involved theory." She sat down across from me. "But that's all it is, Leonard, a theory. As a psychiatrist, I have to tell you how much it sounds like an elaborate self-delusion."

"Just keep helping me. I wrote the dates Hanley was at Blackshale." I opened my smartphone and brought up my memo screen. I grabbed a note from the desk and scribbled the dates down. "Try to find out the names of everybody who was at Blackshale then. Perhaps we can find out where this thing is living."

"Leonard, that is a lot of research, and I might add, ultimately a dead end. If this thing can move from person to person, like a disease, it could be very far from anyone at Blackshale."

I shook my head. "Blackshale is the key! It's the haven, and Reuben says he still sees the horned man walking the hallways. All the murders connect to that site."

Kate looked at the note I'd written and sighed. "Okay, I'll do some digging. We already have a lot of patient and employment information in our database."

"You do?"

"We've been investigating everyone who works there for a history of domestic violence, a police record — you know, like detective work."

"Also look at any visitor logs, and it might not hurt to see how long Petrie has been showing up there."

She glared at me. "So now you think he's the demon?"

"I don't know, Kate. But there's something that makes my little psychic 'buzz' go off every time I see him. Anything you could find out would help," I said as I rose.

She hesitated for a moment and then nodded. "Okay."

"And if you could, have it ready as soon as you can. Like tomorrow."

"Tomorrow? Are you crazy?"

"I thought we'd established that. I'm concerned that if Petrie really can pull the plug as soon as Wednesday—"

"I'll try, no promises. You'll be around tonight?"

"Actually, I'm giving a speech at a fundraiser with my girlfriend."

"Oh yes, the ADA. I read about you two dating in your file. Lucky girl."

"What do you mean?"

She looked at me and smiled. "Who wouldn't want to go to an event with you on their arm?"

I looked down at my feet for a moment and felt my cheeks heat. "I was told Jyanette is my eye candy."

She bit her lower lip, as if to stifle a laugh at my reaction. "You're shy about this, aren't you?"

"I guess."

Kate smiled. "Cute. The shyness thing on a man as tall as you is very sexy."

I turned redder. "Kate—"

"I'll stop. But it's interesting from a psychological point of view to see your weak spot. You usually come off so confident and in control. Anyway, I'll see if comparing the employment records makes something pop. Might go out there myself, oversee the team."

"Call me if something breaks," I urged her as I got up and headed for the door.

"You're really something," she said as I went out, "for a mental patient."

I smiled. Considering how out there on the edge this was to Kate, she rolled with the punches as well as I could've hoped.

I drove home and went into my bedroom, where books lined the walls in a series of built-in white bookcases. In half an hour, I was holding a copy of *The Key of Solomon the King* in my hands. I opened it to see circular shapes — the Pentacles — and I looked at them with my mouth agape.

One had a pentagram in the center, and I remembered why the term was familiar. The tarot deck had numbered pentacles, coin-sized metal circles. Seeing the design on the computer screen, where it was roughly the size of a baseball, I didn't make the connection. Looking at the templates in the book helped me remember.

I moved to the kitchen and put the copper teapot on the stove. I pulled up the design Kate had e-mailed to me on my laptop.

The book's archaic language featured lots of 'thees' and 'thous,' and old King James English. A lot of it was prayers and pleas.

Very few of them had a Hebrew sound to them at all. I reminded myself that the author translated from Latin, even though Hebrew letters covered the line-drawings throughout the book.

It interested me that the basic principles of sympathetic magic, which he spelled 'magick,' were there. They expected the magician to prepare his mind and abstain from sex. It would have to be the latter, as I was planning to make love with Jyanette that night.

A momentary image flashed of Jyanette in my bed, stark naked as she focused on me with her 'special' look, filled with desire.

I gave myself a momentary shake and refocused. Although alone, my face felt flushed, and I felt embarrassed that the image had jumped unbidden into my mind.

I certainly was in a mood.

I heard the whistle of the kettle and poured the water into a mug with a tea bag, the book with me. There were pages of illustrations showing the different tools of the magician, how the participant should prepare each one, and what symbols were to be used.

But the Hebrew letters reminded me of something else.

I brought up the design that Kate sent me again on my phone. I looked at the odd letters. MacAdam had said something about the letters in the book.

I flipped to the back and found a chart that started with Hebrew and then showed several variations. None of those distinct alphabets was a dead-on match for the one on the sigil, but the letters from the 'Alphabet of the Magi' were close.

Very close.

Apparently, whoever designed the shape at Blackshale was familiar with this material.

Or lived it.

I went through the book with a new interest, as I tried to find anything that could help me.

Each of the 'seals' had explanations of their magical use. One was to protect from evil, another to stop the evil eye. I gazed deeply at each design and studied each explanation of its function and use.

One design struck me.

If I could reproduce it, it might be useful if any of these things worked. To make the design, the book told me I would have to draw it on parchment with an exorcised pen.

My better judgment suggested it was all ridiculous; there was no point in following these meaningless rituals. Despite it, I drove into town and went to a stationery shop to seek parchment.

The lady behind the counter, gray-haired and matronly, looked up at me as I asked for lambskin parchment.

"You don't look like the usual type," she prattled.

"Really? How do you mean?"

"They dress in black and look — well, unwashed. They also usually buy one of these pen sets." She indicated a box which was decorated with plump floating cherubs and read Magickal Cherub, Inscribing Pen.

I bought both without even a glance at the price and thanked the lady heartily. She eyed me with suspicion as I made my way out of the shop.

After about two hours, my hand was fighting a combination of severe cramps and a mild numbing similar to carpel-tunnel syndrome. I had drawn the symbol on two small squares of parchment I'd cut from the sheet. I was pleased with myself, as it was a complicated drawing. After several attempts on plain paper and two attempts on the parchment, I did a fine job.

I had used a compass to make the circles, and the pen truly was a joy, a ballpoint that flowed evenly on the page in red ink, the color of blood.

I also re-created the sigil Kate sent me, making it about the same size as the other.

I decided I might need it as well.

After sitting for so long, I wanted to get out, so I spent the rest of the afternoon at my dojo, where one learns martial arts.

Since becoming a 'man of action,' I discovered after getting my head handed to me a few times, that I needed to learn some fighting skills.

I took up the study of Aikido, an Asian form of self-defense that was the best workout I'd ever done. It was also devastatingly effective, and you could overpower people well-versed in *karate* or even *tae kwon do*.

I was lucky enough to get some personal time with my *sensei*, or teacher. Agent Petrie pulling his gun on me unnerved me. I felt I should've done something, but I was too slow to react.

Ashwan, my friend and teacher, looked up at me as I told him the story of facing the gun, and he assured me I conducted myself appropriately.

"You misunderstand, Leonard," Ashwan consoled me. "The only proper thing to do when confronted with a gun is… nothing. Shall we begin?"

We went over my *kata*, my fighting routine, as well as some practice confrontations. I felt sluggish and wanted to make sure my reflexes were sharp. We spent an hour together, by the end of which I panted, my uniform soggy and glued to my skin. Ashwan had not even broken a sweat.

"You're out of shape, Leonard," he complained as he watched each of my movements through his alert, almond-shaped eyes. "You must be getting old."

My jaw tensed, as Ashwan must have at least thirty-five years on me.

I apologized. "No, I just shouldn't let it be two weeks between lessons."

Ashwan smiled, turned quickly, stepped into my routine, and I flew through the air and onto the mat. I gasped as I hit and fought to inhale my next breath.

"Too slow, Len, too slow." He shook his head.

I rolled over and leapt up, moving close as he countered my every move. Finally, he made a quick attack that I countered, and I threw him to the mat.

He sat up, laughing. "That's better. Enough for today, but come to practice next week. You must hone your skills, or like a knife, you will loose your edge."

I bowed, went to the locker room, showered, and headed out, feeling stronger, with all my senses heightened.

Driving back toward the house, I noticed the clouds beginning to thicken. It was time to get dressed for my date and speech at GSU. I spent the afternoon readying myself, physically and mentally, in case I had to confront demons or FBI agents.

I needed to be prepared.

15. CARNAL CONCEALMENT

At six-forty, I pulled my van out of the circular driveway and onto the main road. I wore a tuxedo, the curse of being the speaker at a formal party. With it I had a festive cummerbund and tie, each appearing to have falling confetti on the black satin, which made them colorful, yet tasteful.

Mrs. Higgins 'oohed' and 'aahed' about how handsome I looked, what a dashing figure I cut, and a collection of other clichés, which I had to admit were really quite complimentary. I decided Mrs. Higgins, as well as Jon Baines, wanted to make sure I kept going out and didn't wall myself up all week in my classroom or office. A worrisome thought struck me: What if they're working together?

I ignored the conspiracy theory and drove off to Jyanette's place on the other side of town. It was a lovely townhouse in a complex that was mostly new construction. It was convenient to her office in town and the Essex County court in Newark.

At seven, I stood outside Jyanette's apartment and rang her doorbell, like a suitor to take her to the prom — minus the corsage. I felt an overwhelming need to double-check my zipper.

The door opened and Jyanette strode out. To see this woman emerge on heels that made her over six feet tall was breathtaking.

She wore a baby-blue strapless dress with a beaded embellishment that went over one shoulder, then snaked around her body. It possessed a pleated bodice, as did the panel over her stomach, and flared out to hug her hips in a way that made my mouth water. Her hair, often in a bun in court, was loose and hung to her shoulders in all its kinks and curls. I stared and hoped my eyes didn't bug out.

A smile emerged as she drew closer. "I can tell by your expression that you like."

"Wow!" I blurted as I walked around her to take in her appearance from every angle.

"I've heard more erudite comments, but that was the effect I sought."

"Jyanette," I effused, grinning like an idiot. "You always look great, but — wow!"

She stepped to my left to slip her arm in mine. "Do you think this will create the level of envy you sought?"

"Even from professors long deceased. Really, Jyanette, you're amazing!"

"Don't act too surprised." She walked close enough so I could smell her perfume, a light floral aroma that went perfectly with her natural scent. "You'll make me feel like I'm frumpy the rest of the time."

I laughed and escorted her to the car, as I reassured her she was indeed lovely every time I'd ever seen her.

I helped her into the van. Tonight, she moved like a dancer, and I enjoyed watching her. I got in and swiftly moved the vehicle into traffic on our way to GSU.

"I suppose you want me to update you on the case?" I suggested.

"I wouldn't mind knowing what you're doing," she said. "Since you often leave me out of the loop."

"Yeah, I know. Sorry."

"But not tonight. Look, we're out, dressed up, and I'd like to spend a night hearing how beautiful I am, instead of talking about murder."

My eyebrows went up. "Very unlike you, Ms. Emery."

"I know," she added, then hesitated. "I'm thinking about the future."

"Uh-oh."

"A couple talking about the future isn't immediately an 'uh-oh', Len."

I chose my words carefully. "I just recall the fight we had about that very subject a few short months ago. You made it very clear, you wanted to focus on the now. And combined with the fact that you haven't been intimate with me in a while, I don't want to push my luck."

She leaned over and put her head on my shoulder. "I am planning to rectify that tonight."

"I'm so glad."

"But I'm thinking we should attempt to be, I don't know, a normal couple. This is normal, going to a party, even with you giving a speech. It feels more right than going over trace evidence and dealing with visions."

"It feels right," I agreed. "At least with you by my side."

"Then how about we actually talk about the future after the party?"

I couldn't suppress the smile on my face. "I'm happy to. This is real growth for you, Jyanette."

"Yes, maybe it is," she agreed, as she kissed my cheek and gave me another dazzling smile.

We pulled into the lot at the university, and I drove to my parking space out of force of habit, and then realized that the event was on the other side of Williams Hall.

"It's a warm night," Jyanette suggested. "We can walk."

"You're the one on the stilts," I taunted.

"They're high heels, not stilts."

"You're tall, but I've never seen you at perfect eye level."

"That's what I was going for," a teasing tone in her voice as we got out of the van. "Can I leave my purse? It's one less thing to carry, and it might rain."

"Bite your tongue! Is there anything you really need?"

"Just my phone, but I think I can ignore it for one night."

We got out of the car, and the night was warm, not too humid, and the air was ripe with the scent of spring. The smell and the warmth of Jyanette on my arm was a heady mixture.

"It's a lovely night," Jyanette sighed, and then inhaled deeply.

"I was just thinking that. Are you sure you aren't a psychic as well?"

"You're just worried that every day I get more and more inside that head of yours."

"I welcome it."

We had parked next to a large building that loomed over us.

"What is this building, again?" Jyanette asked.

"Williams Hall. They built it in the 1930s, just after the campus ceased to be an estate."

"Nice."

"Want to see the inside?"

"I don't know." She glanced at me with a wicked look. "Can we?"

"I have the keys as my classes take place in here," I explained as I walked up to the heavy door, inserted a key, and opened it. "Also, my good friend is the Associate Dean."

We entered and walked down the darkened hallway. Jyanette admired the marble floors and the woodwork on the doorways.

She spoke with her voice echoing in the empty hall. "You know, being psychic would be a useful skill. I mean, do you know who it's going to be when you hear a knock on the door or the phone ring?"

"Sometimes. But you can do that—"

"Oh?" She gave me a 'you must be kidding' face.

"Sure, get a closed-circuit camera for your door and 'Caller ID' for your phone."

"Isn't that cheating?" she laughed.

"Not if it works."

She gazed up at the intricate woodwork along the ceiling. "I love the architecture."

"I'm glad," I admitted.

"I've always been a sucker for Edwardian," she chimed in, and walked a little ahead of me to touch the walls and doors.

"And you know your time periods as well."

"You know my father does restorations. I grew up around woodwork and flooring. It was always interesting to go into a place my father brought back. To see how he restored old, dilapidated buildings into renewed, functional beauty."

"That's more art than craft."

"Both actually. When we were young, my sisters and I went with Dad to building sites. We were all tomboys."

"Yet you became a lawyer."

"My second choice. I worked construction throughout college."

"I liked the story your father told about how you struggled with a load of bricks."

"I estimated wrong, but I did what I had to." She made a muscle. "I was in pretty good shape."

I touched the muscle. "You could do it now, if you set your mind to it."

"Damn straight."

We stepped out through the entrance hall, which was on the opposite side of the building from where we had entered. We were on the second level, hidden in the shadows.

Our view looked down at the quad and faced the front of College Hall, which was three stories tall with its built-out glass-front addition. Beyond the glass wall, we could see the pair of huge, curved marble stairs.

At the bottom of the numerous stone steps before us, and about one hundred feet into the quad, there was a large white tent sparkling with festive lights. The waitstaff scurried in and out of the tent in black vests and pants. We saw women dressed in flowing gowns and men in traditional black and white formal attire.

We stood at the top of several flights of granite steps, which stopped at landings every twelve steps with short walls at each level.

"Oh my!" Jyanette said as she took everything in.

"Ah, now you're impressed."

"This is magnificent! Did you bring me this way for the view?"

"I have to tell you the truth, it was a shortcut. And I knew you liked architecture."

She looked out as I moved my palm to her hip. The soft, slinky fabric slid under my hand. She looked at me as if something primal and needy seemed to pass between us.

"Hmm," she hummed and turned her body toward me to press her warm lips to mine, and gently pushed us deeper into the shadows. "I think you brought me up here to have your way with me," she told me with lust in her eyes.

This immediately aroused me. "Another kiss like that, and I won't be able to stop myself. I don't want to muss you up, though."

She pulled me to her firm chest and kissed me again with even more passion. Her tongue explored my mouth as her breasts squeezed against me.

"What if I want to be mussed?" she said breathlessly when she pulled back. Her eyes sparkled like a thousand jewels, and I felt lasciviousness emanate from her like a force of nature. "It might inspire your speech."

She took my hand and guided me down the first flight of stairs. I had to do it one step at a time, but she waited for me. She then pulled me into the unlit area near one of the low stone walls.

"Do you think they can see us?" Jyanette's voice was a low murmur, barely audible over the pulse of the music drifting up from the party below.

I looked around quickly. The building behind us and the lighting cast a deep, jagged shadow over us, shielding us from the glow of the gala tents in the quad.

"No," I whispered, my heart hammering against my ribs. "We're invisible up here."

She turned to face me, a wicked, defiant grin playing on her lips. Slowly, deliberately, she gathered the hem of her dress, pulling it upwards.

"What are you doing?" The words came out hoarse.

"You complained that I've been neglecting you," she said, her eyes dark and hungry as the fabric rose. "And I feel the ache of it, too. I'm simply acting on my urges."

"Here?" I was stunned, my gaze darting toward the edge of the wall. ""Jyanette, we can't."

"Oh, yes we can," she giggled as the edge of the dress reached her waist, which exposed her matching panties, pale blue against her dark-chocolate skin.

"But this is where I *work*."

"Then we'd better be quiet," she whispered.

With a fluid, catlike grace, she stepped out of her lace undergarments and placed them on top of the stone wall. She turned away from me, leaning her elbows against the rough-cut masonry, looking out over the sea of guests below. The contrast was dizzying—the sophisticated party just yards away, and the raw, breathless reality of her dark skin against the moonlight.

I moved toward her, overcome by a sudden, sharp desperation. "I don't have a condom," I managed to croak, remembering her usual rule.

She looked back over her shoulder, her expression one of wild abandon. The caution that usually defined her had vanished. "I don't care."

"I still have to give the speech," I reminded her, even as my hands found her waist.

"Then make it count," she growled, a teasing challenge in her voice. She gave her rump a shake, which made me gasp.

My pants and underwear fell to my ankles. I moved with frantic haste, the cool spring air biting at my skin as I entered her, drawing her back against me.

Jyanette let out a sharp, jagged gasp, quickly stifling the sound by pressing a fist against her mouth.

The world outside the shadows ceased to exist.

We fell into a rhythmic, urgent heat. Every nerve ending felt set ablaze, amplified by the terror of being caught and the sheer intensity of her response. I could hear the distant clinking of champagne glasses and the swell of the orchestra, but my entire universe had shrunk to the space where we met—a frantic, pulsing friction that blurred the line between us.

She leaned into the stone, her breath hitching in a series of low, sensual growls.

"Yes," she urged, her voice a ragged thread. "Just like that…"

The tension built like a rising tide, impossible to hold back. A sudden, overwhelming wave of heat crashed through me, and I felt her body shudder in tandem—a silent, rhythmic release that left us both trembling.

I pressed my forehead against the back of her neck, my teeth clenched to keep from shouting into the night air.

For a long minute, the only sound was our synchronized, ragged breathing.

"Oh, God," she exhaled, her voice trembling as she slowly straightened up.

"I… agree," I panted, my lungs burning as if I'd run a mile.

Jyanette gave another moan as we separated and she looked down upon the party.

I stepped back and hurriedly adjusted my clothes, while Jyanette reclaimed her composure with a quiet, triumphant smile. She restored her panties to their appropriate place then turned and wrapped her arms around my neck, pulling me into a kiss that tasted of salt and moonlight.

"What came over us?" I asked, still dazed by the audacity of it.

"I don't know," she murmured, leaning her head against my chest as she looked down at the unsuspecting crowd. "But it was worth every second."

"Shall we join the party?" I suggested.

"Yes," she chuckled. "Only now, I'm going to smell like sex all night."

She took my arm and we stepped to the stairs, which we descended. A shape moved in the darkness about ten feet away.

Something's wrong…

"Wait!" I grabbed her arm before she stepped down the next step.

"What is it?"

"I thought I saw a shadow," I explained, and limped up a couple steps to observe the spot where the movement caught my eye.

"Do you think someone saw us?" Jyanette hissed, her hand to her mouth to stifle an embarrassed giggle.

"Nothing there," I decided, but I couldn't shake the feeling that something was not right. I walked back down to Jyanette, who exhaled deeply.

"You're jumpy," she teased as we continued down the granite steps. "I mean, for a guy who just got laid."

I glanced back over my shoulder and smiled. "Yeah. Sorry that didn't last long."

"It wasn't supposed to," she confessed and hugged my arm. "And trust me, you did fine. Oh yeah, just fine."

We reached ground level and started across the quad. The large party tent was a common end-of-the-year maneuver by Jon Baines. This way, they could cater everything much more easily than indoors, and if the guests ruined the grass, the grounds crew had the entire summer to repair the damage.

There was an impressive crowd; not all the guests had arrived. The men sported tuxedos, and the women wore formal gowns that resembled those seen at the Oscars. In the middle of the tent was a wooden dance floor, and a deejay set up a small booth at the edge. A collection of lights projected different colors onto the wooden floor.

Currently, the music filling the air was Mozart, played by a string quartet sitting in the middle of the space.

"A string quartet!" Jyanette bubbled as the flashing lights made her eyes twinkle. "How lovely."

"They're students here. I recognize some of them. Jon must have coerced them to play."

"Isn't that his job, coercing people to show up at these things? Like you?"

"I guess that makes me the equal of the musicians," I said with a a a grin.

"You look much better in a tuxedo," she said as she adjusted my tie. "Hm, I guess I mussed you a little."

An arm around my shoulder nearly lifted me off my feet.

"Len! You made it. I was getting worried."

"I said I'd be here, Jon," I told him as I extricated myself from his grip.

"Hi, Jon." Jyanette smiled.

"Jyanette." Jon beamed as he let me go and delicately hugged my date. "You look incredible. Wow!"

"That's been the repeated opinion," I added.

"How's Jenny?" she asked. "Any luck with babies yet?"

"Not yet," Jon said with a big grin. "But it isn't from a lack of trying."

Jyanette laughed with Jon.

"I mean it, though," Jon praised. "You look fantastic. It makes me wonder why you're here with Len."

"Well, Jon," she whispered, her face totally innocent. "To tell you the truth, he's a great lay."

I turned beet red as Jon and Jyanette laughed. My girl was certainly in a mood tonight.

Jon turned, and Jenny appeared from behind him. They were the original odd couple. Jon was bigger and wider than me, and Jenny was a tiny woman — five feet and a few inches, with a nicely toned body. But she had a vivaciousness that had charmed donations from more people than Jon's hearty handshakes ever would.

"Jyanette!" Jenny shrieked and excitedly hugged her.

"Hi, Jenn," I greeted her, and bent to give her a peck on the cheek.

"Oh, Lenny, it's good to see you, too!" Jenny paused and looked at my date, puzzled. "My goodness, you're practically glowing."

"Thank you," she replied with a smile.

"We're glad you could make it, and from what I understand, it was short notice." She gave Jon a withering look.

"I'm glad to be here, Jenny," I confirmed.

Jenn stepped back and gazed at my girl. "Really you both look so— so—" Her look changed as an impish grin popped onto her face.

I turned to Jyanette. "Shall I get you a drink?"

"I see that there's champagne." Jyanette pointed at a waiter with a tray of crystal flute glasses filled with sparkling liquid.

I limped over to the man and got a glass of the bubbly.

On the way back, as Jyanette looked at me, I saw Jenn pull Jon down and whisper into his ear. Jon looked up at me, surprised.

"Here you go," I said, as Jyanette gazed lovingly at me.

"Well, time to mix and mingle," Jenny announced. "Jyanette you have to meet some guests."

"All right," she exclaimed as Jenny led her off to meet different couples and groups, where she introduced everyone on a first-name basis.

"Jenn took her off pretty quick," I marveled.

Jon grinned at me. "According to Jenn, you've already gotten what you want."

"What?" I replied, still watching Jyanette.

He plowed an elbow into my ribs and pulled close to my ear. "She thinks you two just had sex."

I was thankful that the subdued light didn't show me flush red from head to foot yet again.

"Did you?" Jon snickered. "Here? I mean, as administrator I would consider it inappropriate, but as your friend — man!"

"I — uh—"

He pointed at me. "She's right! I don't have to be psychic to read you, buddy."

I smiled and shrugged.

"Damn! You're like a freakin' teenager," Jon murmured as he gave my back a slap. "By the way, you go on as soon as I'm done speaking. You have about a half hour. Are you prepared?"

I reached up and touched the pages in my breast pocket. "I've got a speech."

"Were you prepared in other ways?" Jon gave me another elbow to the ribs, and what I believed was a lusty wink. "On your way to a party no less, man!"

"I'd better find my date before Jenn makes her prom queen or something."

Jon nodded, still with the smirk, and I was off. I stopped to shake hands every three steps. I remembered why I hated these things. You had to be 'on' the entire time, shake hands with hundreds of patrons, and stick a plastic smile on your face. I usually ended up nodding my head as they talked inanities. God bless them; their money kept the school open, and one-on-one they were probably lovely people. But as a group, they started to all look and sound the same.

It was also difficult for me, as I had to wall off my abilities so that the leaking mental energy of so many people didn't invade my mind.

I could hear feminine laughter to my right, and I turned to see what was so funny. To my surprise, Jyanette seemed to be the one who garnered the response. She stood in front of the group with a look of triumph on her face and basked in the attention of the others.

I approached warily. Jyanette saw me, excused herself, and came over. The women began speaking in half-whispered tones as we left.

"What was all that about?" I asked.

"You fascinate the women here, did you know that?"

"Really?"

"Yes, they call you 'The Enigmatic Doctor Wise.'"

"Even Jenn?"

"Jenny thinks you walk on water. It's the other ladies. They want to know all about you."

"So what did you tell them?"

"Why absolutely nothing," she expressed, the face of innocence. "But I did it with style."

"I was wondering about—"

"Excuse me, Doc?" a voice said to my right. I whirled around suddenly, my weight shifting so my cane was in my hand, as a buzz flashed through my mind.

Danger...

There, with a bewildered look on his face, was Jim Stevens.

"You okay, Doc?" he asked.

"Oh, Jim — I'm sorry you... surprised me." I fought to control my adrenaline rush.

Jim had on a formal shirt and pants with a black vest. He was carrying a tray with a couple of empty glasses.

"What are you doing here?" I asked, as I noted his uniform.

He shrugged. "Serving drinks. You know, any extra job during the summer."

"Oh?" was all I could think to say. "Jyanette, this is Jim Stevens. He works here during the school year."

"Nice to meet you," Jyanette acknowledged him with a polite smile.

"I'm charmed," Jim replied, and his face lit up. "My, my, Doc, you are one lucky man."

Jyanette beamed at the compliment. "That's what I tell him."

"Look, sorry to bother you, Doc," Jim declared, making sure to balance the glasses on the tray. "But that assistant teacher of yours — Santos? He's lookin' for you. He tol' me to find you."

My smile faded. "Did he say what it was about?"

"Nope. But he said to tell you he'd be in your office. It was somethin' about some phone call?"

"Thanks for your help, Jim."

"Sure, Doc." Jim smiled at Jyanette as he moved off. "Nice meetin' you, Miss."

"Likewise," Jyanette said, and looked at me. "What's that all about?"

"I don't know, but Santos wouldn't be looking for me if it wasn't important."

"Len, I thought the pair of us were going to be normal tonight and leave work behind." There was a distinct tone of disapproval in her voice.

"I know, but it's an active case and things are happening."

She smiled and brought her finger to my chin. "Tell you what, you find Teddy, and that's it. And if you don't talk about cases, or visions or any of it for the rest of the night—"

She put her lips to my ear and whispered a particular sexual preference of mine that was only doled out on special occasions.

"Really?" I gasped, my mouth instantly dry.

She nodded with a smile. "Willingly and happily."

I had been correct; she was in quite a mood tonight.

I glanced at the nearby dance floor and tried to get my mind off my girlfriend's prowess. I focused on the podium that was set in the corner. "I've got to give a speech in a few minutes—"

"Can you call Teddy?"

I shook my head. "If it's the information I had him researching, I'll need to see it. I'd best walk over there."

"Go now, so Jon doesn't worry."

I nodded in agreement. "And I promise, nothing police related for the rest of the night."

"You keep up your end of the deal, and I'll keep up mine," she offered with a wanton look that made my knees weak. "Then later I'll keep up something of yours for a, shall we say, more involved session than we just had?"

"I'll be back in a few minutes," I told her, as imagined pleasures ran dizzily through my mind. Then, for a moment, I felt concerned. "Will you be all right?"

"I'll be fine. I'm actually all grown up and able to be at a party alone."

I nodded. "Yes, of course. If Jon worries, tell him I'll be back in plenty of time."

As I walked away, the cool air did little to quiet the pulse she'd set racing. There was a crowd to face and a role to play, but the weight of her promise and the long night ahead remained heavy in the air.

16. LAMB TO THE SLAUGHTER

I passed through the glass door in the entrance of College Hall on my way to my tiny office. I moved at a pretty good pace, but I didn't want to hurry too fast and be all sweaty when I gave my speech.

"Hey, Doc!" a voice called.

I turned as Santos came galumphing up to me, panting heavily. "Doc! Did somebody find you?"

"Yes. What's up, Teddy? I've got to give a speech."

Santos paused in front of me and leaned forward with his arms against his knees to catch his breath.

"It's that MacAdam guy. He called your office," he explained between pants. "He said it was really important."

"Thanks, Teddy," I said as we went into College Hall and passed waitstaff in black vests carrying hors d'oeuvres from one of the conference rooms. My paralyzed leg gave Santos enough time for his youthful body to recover, and he bounded up after me.

We arrived at my office at about the same time, and I grabbed the phone.

"He left a number to call." Santos pulled a note from next to the phone.

I cursed myself for not adding his number to my cell phone after our last talk. I quickly input the digits, heard the phone ring, and MacAdam's voice said, "Hello?"

"Dennis? It's Leonard Wise. You were trying to reach me?"

"Leonard! Thank God you called. I received your email and... I mean I wasn't sure... but then I thought... and once I checked —"

"Dennis, slow down, you're not making any sense."

"Oh, I'm sorry, Leonard. That symbol you sent me? You say it was from a murder site?"

"A possible murder site, yes."

"I think actually... it might have been a sacrificial altar."

"Sacrificial?" I sat down in my padded chair quickly as my one good knee gave out from under me. "Human sacrifice?"

Just like the *Following of Astarte* was doing when I stopped them.

"Yes! You see, that symbol is ancient, and it took me a while to track it down, but it seems to be the representation of Ashtoreth."

"Ashtoreth?" I worried, as I felt the hairs on the back of my neck stand on end.

"Yes, well, this sort of thing is really up my alley. Ashtoreth, or Astaroth, or sometimes—"

"Astarte," I croaked, and I realized I was sweating.

"Uh, yes, that name as well. People consider her a chief demon, although I'll be honest, I didn't know there was a unique sigil ascribed to her—"

"It's a her. It's definitely a her?"

"Oh yes! You see demonologists ascribe Ashtoreth as the god-pair to Baal. Then again, the word 'Baal' might just mean 'God of' or 'Lord of'. After all, Beelzebub means 'Lord of the Flies', and they have the same root words—"

"But, Dennis, you mentioned a demon—"

"Yes! According to demonology texts from the Middle Ages, she can appear as a male if she wishes. You see, I didn't recognize the symbol right away because it is... was... well, ancient. Ashtoreth was originally a god of the Canaanites. Of course, in the Bible, her most famous priestess was Jezebel. It's one reason they killed Jezebel and gave Ashtoreth demon status."

"Dennis, I'm trying to follow this. What does it have to do with human sacrifice?"

"Hmm? Oh yes, well, those Canaanite sects — they were big practitioners of it. At least twice a year, they'd sacrifice to Baal and Ashtoreth. Usually children. In fact, an archeologist—" his voice went down to a mumble. "Let me check my notes." He resumed his robust timbre. "Ah yes, in 1906, Macalister discovered the remains of an Ashtoreth temple; it was a graveyard for newborns."

"So, this demon seeks sacrifices?"

"I imagine she's used to it. I mean, there are cults to her still around. They hold the view that the masculine God threw out the feminine gods because of sexism."

"Dennis, can you give me something I can use?"

"Oh yes, of course. That's why I had to get in touch with you. I've compiled some data. That sigil was really fascinating; the lettering was a mix of the Alphabet of the Magi and The Alphabet of the Demons with a little Apollonian mixed in. I've never seen them used together, different cultures. I have to warn you, Leonard, we are talking about a very ancient and powerful creature. This is not anything to be treated lightly. If she has taken possession of a physical human being, she will be powerful and have no problem killing."

Instead of sweating, I found I was suddenly freezing. "I appreciate that, Dennis."

"Remember, in dealing with demons, trap them somehow. That's the purpose of the circles on the floor and the pentagrams. Then get them to agree to what you want. It's the only way to get them out of the possessed body and release them only when they agree."

I could feel my face scrunching up. "I've studied nothing like this—"

Dennis sighed like an adult dealing with a foolish child. "You college-taught parapsychologists. Give you a beeping machine, and you're fine. Give you a demon, and you're lost. It wouldn't hurt for you to read my book. It's all in there."

"I definitely will." I felt chastised.

"See that you do, Leonard. It's for your own protection, for God's sake."

I thanked Dennis, and we each said our "good-byes" and hung up. I sighed as well.

"So, what's the word?" Santos asked, seeing I was off the phone.

"The word is Ashtoreth."

"Ashtray — what?"

"Ashtoreth. The symbol left at Blackshale is a representative of a human sacrifice cult from ancient Persia. It's connected with that group, the *Following of Astarte*—"

"Cool. Are we gonna fight demons?"

"No, we are not. I'm going down to give a speech and go be with my girlfriend."

Santos picked up another note. "You also got a collect call from some guy in jail?"

"Jeff Hanley?" I blurted.

Santos nodded and handed me the piece of paper and then pulled several pages from next to the fax machine. "Yeah, and he faxed you. I didn't know anyone used fax anymore."

"They do in prison," I grumbled.

"Oh, uh, yeah," Teddy wondered. "He sent this, I don't know, yesterday."

I grabbed the sheets of paper, listing several biblical quotes, as well as information about controlling demons. I tried to speak calmly, considering how agitated I was. "Why didn't you give this to me earlier?"

"Who looks for faxes? Besides, I thought it was like one of those fundamentalist guys we get spam from—"

"We do?"

"Yeah, Doc. You've seen the stuff some guy sent you that you're going to burn in hell for what you teach—"

"Oh yes, and my PhD won't even buy me a thimble full of water. I remember." I glanced at the paper. Along the top it read

"BIND - AGREE - LOOSE". I scanned it quickly. "This sounds like what Dennis was talking about."

"What, Doc?"

"The way to handle a demon." I folded the paper and put it in my inner jacket pocket. "Sorry if I was short with you. Thanks for staying so late."

Santos grinned. "Sure, Doc, it's not a problem. You should get back to your date."

I looked at my watch. "And my speech."

"Doc, go!"

I nodded and was out the door, heading for the party. I made it back to the quad in only a few minutes, hoping that Baines hadn't started.

As I stepped outside into the night air, I could hear Jon's voice, magnified and echoing. He was talking about the 'tremendous strides' our school had made, his voice becoming clearer as I drew closer.

I went out the glass doorway and ran right into Jenny, stationed to be on guard for me.

"Lenny!" she hissed. "You're supposed to be giving a speech!"

I walked up next to her and whispered, "I know. I thought that was why I was here."

"Hilarious! Why did you wander off? Jon's been frantic looking for you."

"I told Jyanette that I needed to go to my office about the case. Didn't she talk to Jon?"

"No, she didn't. We were worried you two went off to fool around in the bushes." Then she added with a giggle, "Not that we'd blame either of you."

A smile came to my face and froze. A terrible feeling of dread rose within me. I had walled away my abilities to protect myself from the mental chatter of the crowd.

"But I told her to—" I stammered, my tongue becoming numb in my mouth, like something foreign. I knew at that moment, without another word being spoken, that something was wrong — terribly wrong.

I rapidly scanned the guests as they sat at their tables or stood near the bar, as if to tell myself that I was wrong. Jyanette had to be somewhere at this party.

Jenny, in the meantime, had let Jon know I had returned through hand movements or smoke signals or some secret code married people have, and he quickly brought his speech to a close.

"But, ladies and gentlemen, it is not my work that deserves praise, but the work of our fine professors."

I was still observing the crowd, hoping Jyanette was there and had just misunderstood what I asked her to do.

"One of those fine teachers has been getting a lot of attention, and I've put him on the spot to say a few words—"

I could feel that she wasn't there. My heart beat faster, as I felt the sense of foreboding continue to rise up my spine.

"In fact, I'd like to ask Doctor Leonard Wise to come up and speak to us for a minute or two."

The entire group rose to its feet and applauded. Jon stood there with a smile, a triumphant reaction that he could take to the bank. Jenny looked at me and pushed me forward, as if I were just a shy guy.

But I was a lot worse than shy at that moment. I was beyond terrified.

All I could think was that someone, somewhere, had gotten to Jyanette. I tried to open myself up on a psychic level to track her movements, and that was a mistake. Because as Jon turned the focus of the crowd toward me, I was suddenly aware of each individual on a nonphysical level. All of those people were in me, all around me. I could hear their thoughts and desires bombarding my brain.

I focused on my breath and forced up the barriers Doctor Kohl taught me years ago, shut them all out so that all I could hear was their applause as I walked hesitantly toward the podium and Jon.

As I stepped onto the dance floor, I felt drained, and I knew I leaned heavily on my cane. To shut out the crowd had taken enormous strength of will. I felt a little voice in my head yammering, "That's why you shouldn't go to these events. All those minds that leak mental energy like damaged buckets. And you hear every one of them."

I pushed my shoulders back and stepped into the impromptu spotlight. I nodded and forced a smile on my face, all the while trying to limit my impressions to the merely physical. I reached into my pocket, feeling very mechanical, and pulled out my prepared speech.

"Thank you. Welcome to all of you, the staunch friends of Garden State University. It is your friendship that has helped keep us going."

A good opener for a fundraiser, I thought. And the audience applauded its approval. I talked about the school, the unique risks it took, which included classes in parapsychology, as well as other esoteric studies. I praised how innovative it was to offer instruction in these unique fields.

I spoke carefully and followed my notes, but my eyes were scanning the crowd. I hoped that my impressions had been wrong, and at any moment my eye would light upon Jyanette, as she watched me in rapt attention with a look of pure hero worship in her eyes.

I didn't see her.

It was all I could do to keep my attention on my notes, to force down the panic. It's odd. I was someone who had never feared public speaking, which I guessed was why Jon wanted me to 'say a few words', but at that moment, fear gripped me.

And I had to fight that fear just to stand in front of these people and move my mouth, something so natural that I did every day in classes as small as twenty people and as large as two to three hundred.

And all the time in the back of my mind I felt the name: 'Ashtoreth... Ashtoreth...' like an evil mantra, just below my consciousness.

"And so, in closing—" I gave an audible sigh of relief that elicited chuckles from the crowd. "I want to thank Jon Baines, this school, and your helpful donations, which allow teachers like me to be a part of the curriculum. Thank you!"

I felt myself being pulled around and into a big bear hug by Jon, who then made a gesture toward Jenny. I dutifully toddled back over toward her, not really sure where else to go.

"Doctor Leonard Wise," Jon was saying to the group as I wended my way past them. "Now, I think Leonard has said it all. And I will not bore you with any more details—"

I reached Jenny, who watched her husband with such adoration, I almost hated to break the spell. "Jenn!"

She blinked at me. "What, Lenny? That was a brilliant speech."

"It's not my speech that concerns me." I took her arm and pulled her around the corner of the building. "Have you seen Jyanette?"

"What? Oh, yeah, we were meeting people. I think she's over at Miriam Teller's table."

I followed the direction of her pointing finger and walked over toward the suggested table. Miriam Teller's name was familiar, but I couldn't quite place it. As I drew near, I recognized her at once. The slightly heavy, gray-haired lady who ran our campus library. She was a fixture at the school and often invited to these events.

I walked over and Miriam rose as I got closer. I scanned the table, but there was only one older couple sharing it with her.

"Lovely speech, Doctor," Miriam praised, which forced me to plaster a smile back on my face. "May I introduce my friends, the Schroeders—"

"Mrs. Teller, I'm sorry to interrupt, but I'm looking for Jyanette — Ms. Emery—"

"Oh yes, she went to get a drink." She glanced over at the makeshift bar a dozen feet away. A puzzled expression came to her face. "Odd. She said she would be right back—"

The panic in my chest grew stronger, and psychic alarms howled in my head.

"Thank you," I blurted, and I hastened off with my unsteady gait toward the bar. I was aware of the music behind me, and I turned to see the well-dressed patrons of Garden State University shake their collective booties on the makeshift dance floor. Here were the cream of the financial crop, all dining on the college's hors d'oeuvres, being made ready to be hit up for money. And somehow, someone got in and forcibly took a young woman with no one being any the wiser.

"Ashtoreth," I murmured, now sure of the name of my enemy. My eyes scanned the dimly lit tent.

He could be anyone.

In a last-ditch effort, I walked over to the bartender whom Mrs. Teller had pointed out to me. I dutifully stood in line, and when I reached him, asked if he had seen Jyanette, quickly describing her.

The balding man in the cheap vest shrugged. "Look, buddy, I ain't seen nothing but the backs of bottles all night. Unless this lady was naked, I wouldn't have even noticed."

I nodded, thanked him, and did the next logical thing: went over and talked to Jon Baines.

I found him with a group of matrons, where he was busily promoting his plans for an expanded course of study. I guess I must have looked awful, because Jon took one look at me and excused himself. He stepped over to me, put his big bear's arm around me, and asked, "You okay?"

"It's Jyanette. She's not here."

"You say something stupid?"

"No, no, nothing like that. I asked her to tell you where I was."

"Maybe she forgot?"

"Jon," I cut to the chase. "I think someone… took her."

"Took her?" Jon fretted with a deep frown. "What do you mean, took her?"

As if called by a silent signal, Jenny Baines joined us as I talked. I needed to increase my volume over the music, which grew louder with each passing moment.

"I mean, I'm after a serial killer, a brilliant one who has a grudge against me."

"What?" Jenny sputtered. "When did all this happen?"

I offered my best explanation. "It's a part of that cult I broke up."

"Len is worried," Jon chattered. "He thinks someone abducted Jyanette."

They exchanged a look. What I would call 'an old married' look, where they each knew what the other thought without a word.

A wave of envy hit me. Jon and Jenn were my friends and a great couple; I'd stayed with them long enough to know they weren't perfect, but their bond was undeniable. For a moment, I craved that level of connection—the kind where a single glance says everything. Jyanette and I were working toward that, but we weren't even close.

"What can we do to help?" Jon offered.

"I don't know," I snapped. "Ask people. See if anyone saw her go off somewhere."

Jenny drew close so I could hear her. "Can't you use — I mean, you know, your… special skills?"

I shook my head. "There's too much going on. Maybe if I was holding something she owned in a quiet place—" I stopped talking as the realization hit me, like a computer that opened a new program.

"Lenny, what is it?" Jenny asked.

"I've got an idea. You ask around." I turned, leaning into my cane as I hobbled away. I needed a quiet place and something of hers—her purse was still in the van. I could—

A hand clamped onto my arm. My thoughts scattered as the grip tightened, jerking me backward.

But my afternoon with Ashwan had left me wired for this.

I seized the intruder's wrist and pivoted, abruptly shifting my weight. I heard a nearby guest gasp in surprise as I used the man's own momentum against him, heaving him over my shoulder and slamming him to the ground.

To my surprise, as he fell, he rolled back up to his feet in one movement. I raised my cane, prepared to defend myself.

Only to see Gabe Petrie standing slightly crouched in front of me, looking primed to go into hand-to-hand combat with me.

"Wise!" he bellowed, shocked. "What the hell are you doing?"

The nearby guests came closer to find out why their esteemed speaker flipped people like rag dolls.

"You grabbed me!" I objected, suddenly feeling incredibly stupid holding my cane ready to brain him.

His voice fell into an undertone, what my brother the performer would call a 'stage whisper'.

"We need to go somewhere more private," he demanded, and stood straight, his eyes on the crowd that approached us.

"Of course," I said to him, and then turned to the hastily assembled mob. "Old friend. That's how we say hello." A quick excuse for my odd behavior. I walked around the building and Petrie followed. He smiled lamely at the group as he went.

As we walked around the corner, he spoke, "All right, Wise, you're coming with me."

"What?"

"I have questions for you."

"I can't," I stammered. "I'm looking for Jyanette."

"Jyanette?" Gabe grumbled as he ran his hand through his hair to settle it.

I stared at him. "My girlfriend. She was here with me."

"I know you weren't here alone."

"You know?" I repeated in disbelief.

"Wise, it's my job to know where my team is and with whom."

"Then maybe you can do better than me. She's gone."

In clipped, breathless sentences, I told Agent Petrie about the trip to my office and my inability to locate Jyanette when I returned.

"I see." Petrie reached behind his back for his cuffs before drawing his sidearm in a fluid, practiced motion. "Doctor, you're coming with me."

My mind raced. Jyanette was gone, and now Petrie was here—his ties to Blackshale looming large. Was he the demon sent to finish the job?

"What is this about?" I stepped back, my eyes locked on the barrel of his gun.

Petrie sneered. "Like you don't know."

"Think about how this looks," I countered. "My girlfriend vanishes, and then you show up?"

I could see that his attitude was going from annoyed to furious. "You saying you know nothing about the body?"

"The body?" I asked, my mouth going dry. "Jyanette?" I gasped.

"No, we found Ms. Gillian."

I shut my eyes and said a silent 'thank you.' Opening them, I saw Petrie still staring at me petulantly. "Where? Blackshale?"

He let out a dry, derisive bark. "That's where you wanted us to look, isn't it? No, we found the body here—buried in a fresh grave near the Templeton Library. Tell me, Wise, what did you do with her head?"

I stared at him, my mind scrambling to piece his words into a logical pattern. "What?"

"We found the rest of her. It's her, all right. But the head is missing."

"I don't..." I stammered, the words dissolving in my throat.

"I got a call from Sergeant Stant at Blackshale," Petrie said, clicking the handcuffs open while keeping his pistol leveled at my chest. "Turns out he's been investigating you in his spare time. He told us exactly where to look. It's a hell of a gimmick, Wise— playing the psychic to report the very murders you commit."

I swallowed hard. "Petrie, you're making a mistake. Even if it were true, how could Stant know where the body was?"

"He said he'd explain later, but that I should dig her up before you could move her. Look, I told Kate, and I think she agrees with me. She said it was someone with access to both GSU and Blackshale."

I felt trapped, especially if Kate was against me as well. I had just shifted from police expert to suspect in less than a minute. I needed time to think, but more importantly, I needed to figure out what happened to Jyanette.

"Now turn around and put out your hands."

"Petrie, I don't think you would shoot an unarmed man—"

His jaw tightened. "I will if you don't turn around and put out your hands where I can see them. If you are innocent, you can clear this up—"

"But Jyanette!" I yelled. "Did you ever think while you're wasting time questioning me, the actual killer has abducted her?"

He looked at me, and I knew he didn't like me, but I had a good point.

"I can find her!" I insisted. "Her purse is in my van. If I can just—"

"Oh, that's great! Then you just drive off never to be seen again!" he said, as he stared at me. I looked behind him at the tower of the college building. That huge facade, which rose several stories, just like—

Blackshale...

My mouth fell open, and I knew. I didn't need to reach out or touch an object. There was only one place my girl could be.

"Put out your hands," Petrie insisted, calmer now.

"What's going on?" a voice boomed behind Petrie, who turned, shocked to see Jon Baines as he moved toward him like a freight train.

Petrie turned his body sideways to me, but his eyes were on Jon. I decided this was my only chance and swung my cobra-headed walking stick at his hand. My cane whistled through the air, catching his wrist with a sickening crack that sent the handgun skittering ten feet across the ground.

"Ah!" Petrie bellowed.

I didn't wait for him to recover. I spun on my good leg and threw myself forward in a desperate, lopsided sprint—though "running" was a generous term for the frantic, rhythmic thumping of my cane and the uneven shuffle of my bad leg.

But I was off as fast as I could. I peeked over my shoulder to see Jon Baines with his enormous foot resting on top of the gun, arguing with Petrie.

"What is this all about?" Jon demanded.

"Federal agent!" Petrie yelled. "Get away!"

"Not until you tell me why you're threatening my professor on my campus—"

Their voices faded as I turned past another building and hightailed it to my van. I would never do the four-minute mile, but I made it in record time.

I jumped in, gunned the engine, and drove off, knowing my destination.

Blackshale…

17. BEDLAM

I was pretty damn tired. The workout that afternoon, which had seemed like such a great idea, had now caught up to me. My arms and legs were sore, and throwing Petrie, though emotionally satisfying, had wrenched my back. I now had an annoying lower-back pain, which, combined with my growing fear, made me feel like I had drunk too much coffee and was getting the shakes.

The first thing I needed to do was to calm myself. I had to make sure my next move was smart, so as not to end up under arrest. I needed to clear my head, and so with my eyes open and on the road, I focused on my breath.

In... out, in... out.

It was working. I was letting go of the tension. I used the hands-free system in my van to call McGee's cell.

It was Monday night so he'd be home with his wife and kids, having an undisturbed evening to relax. I was about to ruin that.

"McGee," the familiar voice said.

"Bill, it's Len. I'm in trouble."

"What are you talking about?"

"I just hit a federal agent."

"Len, if you're talking about Kate, I'll knock your lights out myself."

I quickly explained the situation: Jyanette's disappearance, Petrie's arrest attempt, and the body found headless at GSU.

"I'll get this cleared up, Len," McGee told me reassuringly, then he added with a chuckle, "You actually punched the guy?"

"Smacked his hand with my cane, and now I'm going to Blackshale to see if Jyanette is there."

"You want me to meet you there?"

"No," I said, "try to get me out of the hole I've dug for myself. Petrie said Stant, the sergeant at Blackshale, told him where to find the body, so he set me up."

"How did he know?"

"I think because he put it there. See if you can check up on the guy. And listen, if you don't hear from me in an hour, then come to Blackshale and play cavalry."

"You got it, Len."

I ended the call just as I heard Jyanette's phone go off; the noise jangling my nerves once again. I pulled the car to the curb and reached into the purse Jyanette had left on the floor of the passenger seat. My hand touched cold metal, and I jumped, pulling my hand out as I saw a face and heard an explosion.

I looked around, but the noise was only in my head. An impression. But the cold metal?

I put my hand back in and carefully extracted a small pistol. I wasn't very experienced with firearms, but it was a competent piece of equipment. It was small, light, and I felt it fit Jyanette's hand better than mine. I extracted the gun clip and found it fully loaded.

I knew she had a carry permit and trained in using firearms, but this brought the realization home. I guess when I told her to improve her security, she listened to me.

"This will do," I told the empty car. I reached into the purse and pulled out the phone. The call had gone to voicemail. I held the gun, being careful that my finger wasn't on the trigger; I didn't want to shoot myself by accident.

"Blackshale," I murmured as I shoved the pistol into the pocket of my tux and pulled back on the road.

That journey to Route Ten seemed to take forever, though I was driving probably a lot faster than I should have been. As I reached the traffic nightmare we called the Livingston Circle, the clouds opened up and rain fell. No, not fell, but poured, as if bucketfuls of water came from the sky to be thrown on my car.

I slowed down to a crawl because I could barely see the road. My fear grew stronger. Did Ashtoreth have the power to make it rain like this? I quickly put it out of my mind and focused on driving.

I crawled west, trying to increase my speed as much as I could, but it was pointless. I could barely average twenty-five miles an hour. I had an overwhelming desire to curse.

My cell phone shook in my pocket, and I hit the touch screen on the console to answer the call.

"Hello," I yelled, as if I had to speak in a hurricane.

I heard a few crackles. "Where do you think you're going?" came the voice of Agent Petrie over my car speakers. "I want you for questioning!"

"I'm going to Blackshale. That's where Jyanette will be."

"Blackshale! Wise, you don't have the authority to—"

A tremendous flash of lightning lit up the sky, and his voice was gone. I commanded the voice-recognition interface to call Santos, but the Bluetooth connection failed, or the phone wasn't working.

"Great! The lightning got the tower!" I shook my head in disgust.

The phone rang, but the music was different.

I glanced at it, trying to hear the tune. A shudder went down my spine as I recognized it as "Night on Bald Mountain". I had powerful memories of that music from Disney's Fantasia. I remembered being a kid when I watched that movie, listening to that music, as demons and devils flew across the screen. I hid behind my mother's arm.

I centered myself and touched the incoming call button.

"Petrie?"

There was silence.

"Petrie, are you there?" I repeated.

"No," the deep voice intoned, "he's not."

I was suddenly cold, frighteningly cold, as that voice went into my ear. It was him. I fought to keep from driving off the road, as a part of me froze. I pulled out my phone, and the screen read 'Out Of Range'. That meant the phone shouldn't even work, as I was too far from any cellular tower. I put it on the console to my right, where it stayed lit up.

"Still there, boy?" the voice chuckled.

I could see myself, as if I watched a video of me inside my car, with the realization that I somehow could see through his eyes. I focused on the road and clamped my teeth together to stop them from chattering.

"What have you done with Jyanette?" I demanded, making myself spit out the words, when all I wanted to do was panic.

"She's fine. The other bitch, not so much. Sacrifices must be made."

"What's the matter?" I snapped. "No teenage girls to kill?"

The voice chuckled again, deeply. God, that was so annoying, and he knew it.

"I get a more lasting effect with adults. Especially ones like you —all that mental energy, just going to waste."

"I suppose you have a use for it."

"I can use it, boy. And I don't know if your young lady can give me what I need."

"What are you saying?"

"If you give yourself to me, I'll let her go."

I turned the car to avoid a massive puddle, which I'm sure was a crater in which I could have broken an axle.

"I don't make deals with demons."

"It's the best one you'll get." The phone went dead.

I glanced at the cell phone as my hand went to the pistol in my coat pocket. I'd done some shooting in the last few years, but could it work with something that wasn't corporeal?

I shook my head, still sure my first impression was right: that this creature needed a host to stay on the physical plane. A gun would be very effective on that host body.

I took a slightly shorter route through Morris Plains and was surprised to find the town dark. No streetlights, no lights on in businesses or homes. The lightning strike had disabled the electric grid for the entire area.

I plunged and splashed over the back roads, with only my headlights for guidance, until I pulled onto the long road which led to the vast tower at the end of the street. It was past ten; the grounds were deserted, and there was no break in the gloom. The rain slowed, and my windshield wipers worked effectively. My eyes went back and forth between the buildings as I approached.

Where could he be?

I looked straight ahead where the huge facade loomed over the smaller buildings, when I saw it. At the top of the tower, which resembled a bell tower more than anything else, there was a light, just enough to get my attention.

He wants me to find him.

The only thing worse than getting caught in a trap was to walk stupidly into it. I glanced over at the small state police station to see if Sergeant Stant might be there. The building stood dark and empty. I knew about Stant, but what about any other officers?

Called away…

The buzz came right to me. The police had been called away. All of this was Ashtoreth's plan, and I acted just as he expected. I still could feel the sense of being watched in my car by something, and I glimpsed myself doing things from outside of my body. I pulled the car over and closed my eyes.

I focused on Jyanette, trying to locate her. Images flew up from this evening. Santos talking to me; Jim Stevens saying something, I didn't recall just what; Jon and Jenny Baines exchanging that look; Gabe Petrie as he yelled at me — what was it about that guy that bothered me? I controlled my mind, focused on Jyanette, nothing but Jyanette.

Where are you?

I seemed to sense a response.

Then it changed; my entire vision, which so far had been snippets of the people I had seen throughout the evening. I felt as if I were going somewhere I didn't want to. My car was gone, and instead I looked out over a barren red plain that extended like an ocean as far as I could see.

I looked at the soil which appeared to be sand, like a desert, and it was hot. I smelled sulfur.

"Where am I?" I tried to say, projecting the thought into the empty landscape.

"Welcome to my home," a voice bellowed in me, on me, and all around me.

I turned and looked around. I expected to see the figure who appeared on that road so many years ago.

Where are you? If this is your home, where are you?

A murmured chuckle resonated in my head.

"I'm not there, remember? You let me out. I never thanked you. Can you see why I wanted to be out so badly?"

He paused, allowing the reverberations to die down. "What if I left you here?"

I turned again, only to see more red sand and distant mountains. It was desolation as far as the eye could see. My heart raced in my chest.

You can't. This is only a vision — a dream. In a minute, I'll open my eyes and it will all be gone.

"Will it?"

I glanced around, and for a moment all I felt was a rush of panic. This entity was stronger than anything I had ever encountered. It could get in my head, keep me from seeing his face, keep me from knowing he was at the party, and put me in this hellhole.

That's when I got angry.

Why are you wasting my time? I'm on to you, and you know it, Ashtoreth.

A brittle laugh crackled in the air around me, followed by a female shriek — a voice I knew.

Cathy?

I felt as if all the blood had drained out of my body. Was she somewhere being tortured, in some desolate afterlife like this?

No, this is a trick!

But it was a trick that was working. Anger burned within me. I wanted to reach out and wring this damn thing's non-corporeal neck. Then another shriek rang out.

Jyanette.

Leave her alone!

The deep male voice came back. "Find me, boy. Save this one, if you can."

I bolted upright in my car, my head bumping against the roof of the van with a resounding knock. I gulped in air, as if I had gone without oxygen for several minutes. I was light-headed, and the fresh lump on my head brought me back to reality painfully.

The back of the building…

Finally, a buzz that was more than just a feeling of impending doom. I was sure that the front was open, and that Ashtoreth expected me to run right in and go up to the bell tower. Count on Leonard to play the hero. The few times I had approached an adversary that way, I'd had my head handed to me.

No, I needed to attempt stealth. I had a vague recollection from the first time I was here of a part of the building that was empty and in disrepair. If I could approach from that unexpected angle, perhaps I would stand a chance.

I retraced the street that Santos and I had used the first time I was here and pulled over to the abandoned section. It was all part of one huge main building, a wing branching off on its own. I hoped it connected to the main building and that tower.

I pulled the van off the road and into some hanging vines on the outer fence. The rain was now a heavy drizzle, and I knew there was no way I was going to stay dry.

I pulled out the pages that Santos gave me from Hanley, looking for any information I could use. The pages were long and rambling but gave an effective argument, with biblical references, on the stopping of a demon. The author wrote it from a Christian perspective, but they used notations going back to the Old Testament, which I knew as the *Tanach* from my Jewish upbringing.

The biggest reference was the title page with these words: "BIND — AGREE — LOOSE".

"This is what MacAdam was talking about," I said aloud. I folded the papers and put them in my jacket pocket. I checked my pants pockets for the little slips of parchment I had made up earlier, and they were still there. I grabbed my cell phone and a flashlight, put them into various pockets, which were now full and bulging. I left my wallet in the console.

I checked the catch on my cobra-headed cane, and the twenty-four-inch blade within slid out easily. I rammed it back into place.

I double-checked the pocket which contained the gun and stepped out into the wet grass where I fought to maintain my footing, and shone the flashlight ahead of me.

The ferocious rain had been short but very effective. I waded through puddles, as there was very little light on this side of the building. I approached a nearby door imprinted with:

WARDS

22

24

28

A heavy chain and a padlock securely locked the door. I thought of using the gun, but quickly dismissed it. It would call too much attention and might not do the job. I flashed the light around, noticing a small basement window, the plywood loose around the edges. I put my fingers to it and pulled, exhaling as I gave a good yank.

It shuddered and came loose with a slight 'POINK' as the rusted nails came out of the wood frame. I was thankful that it was nails and not screws.

The opening was once a window, but now merely an empty frame. I flashed the light to see how far down the floor was. I turned, putting my stiff right leg through the window first. This entailed lying down on the muddy ground, and I could feel my coat getting wet. I slid carefully in, hoping I didn't rip my one good tuxedo to ribbons. I lowered myself into the room, farther and farther, until I dropped to the floor.

The room possessed the dank smell of an enclosed space sealed far too long. With the flashlight, I could see mildew on the walls, the discoloring fungus making large dark blotches on the old paint.

But that was the least of my worries.

The place was a veritable fountain of psychic impressions; I guessed from the many patients who at one time resided in this building — perhaps even the entire facility. Those tormented souls who lived and died here left a residue far more staining than the mildew. And it wasn't in patches, but everywhere, like I had fallen into a pool of murk.

I could see why a demon would love this place. The sense of despair was in the walls. Just the sort of energy Ashtoreth would feast on.

I steeled myself and moved on, using my cane to push open the door. I came into another basement room with old, deteriorating boxes of files and papers, broken gurneys, chairs, and other furniture no longer useful but considered too precious to discard.

I found the stairs and walked up to the first floor, as I tried to keep my ears open for any unusual sounds. The rain outside was beating steadily on the roof, and there were still occasional flashes of distant lightning.

The smell grew worse as I climbed the steps, urine and feces mixed with ammonia, no doubt used as a cleaner. From the look of disrepair, this wing had long ago become a place for the homeless and squatters to party.

I reached the second floor and carefully went into the hallway, as I worked to make no noise as I stepped on broken glass and fallen plaster. I wanted to find the connection to the main building before I got as high as the fourth floor.

I reached an opening, where the doors had been replaced with two large sheets of plywood held in a wooden frame built of two-by-fours. A drilled hole contained an inserted chain. I pulled on the makeshift door, and it barely budged. I assumed there was a padlock on the other side, which held it secure.

"Shit!" I hissed. This was going to be trouble. I would have to check the next two floors to see if any of the doors were accessible.

I headed back to the stairs, but heard a tapping as I went. I stopped, listening carefully to see if anyone approached, but the sound was gone.

I quickly and quietly got back to the steps and walked up to the third floor, repeated my path down the hallways to reach a similar plywood door. On this one, the chain hung loose, and the egress stood open.

A little too easy.

My heart beat faster. I considered my options, which were few. I could risk going up another floor, but that might lead to a locked door. This door felt like it should have a large sign on it reading, "Leonard Wise, you are heading into a trap."

I reached out with my mind to feel what lay beyond my five senses.

Help me…

I heard a voice, a familiar voice, and I backed away from the door.

"No, it can't be," came out of my mouth.

Len, help me…

Again, like one of my buzzes, it touched me on a level that went straight into my soul. I stood stock-still, fighting to pull breath into my body. The voice was chilling, because it had been moments and years since I'd heard it, but I recognized it at once.

"Cathy," I tried to say, but it came out of my throat as a gargled moan. I closed my eyes and spoke to myself. "No, it isn't her. Cathy's dead. I saw her die. It's him. He knows how to get a reaction from me."

I exhaled deeply, put the flashlight in my pocket, and grabbed the gun to push any limiting thoughts out of my mind. Jyanette. I had to focus on Jyanette. He had her; he could and would slice her up. I couldn't allow that. I couldn't let it be the woman I loved.

Not again.

I stepped through the doorway, depending on my normal senses. My sixth sense was too easy for this entity to toy with, so I did my best to rely on my vision and hearing. I held the pistol in my left hand and pushed myself along with my cane.

Help me...

I looked ahead to see a figure clothed in white. The fabric flew up as if some large fan were blowing on her, her hair moving like waves. I couldn't see the face, but I knew who it was from the silhouette. Her voice cried out to me and echoed in my mind.

Len, help me...

I closed my eyes and focused.

"No, it's a lie," I murmured, my jaw tight.

I opened my eyes to the empty hallway, which, unlike the closed wing, was free of debris. It was just an illusion, one directed at me. There was no doubt about it; despite my circuitous route, Ashtoreth knew I was there.

I started forward when a voice behind me demanded, "Drop the gun and put your hands up!"

Game, set, and match.

I had a sinking feeling in my chest. It was a perfect setup: distract me with a trick, and then sneak up on me. I thought I should quickly turn around, try to out-shoot the bastard, but that wouldn't help Jyanette. The best I could do was buy some time.

I dropped the gun with a clatter as it hit the tile floor and dutifully raised my hands over my head with my cane and leaned on my good leg to maintain my balance as I pivoted around.

A flashlight projected into my eyes, with a large shadow behind it. For a moment, I thought it was the shadow of that demon I saw the night I went off the road, tall and muscular with those huge horns sticking out of his head.

"Oh shit, it's you," the voice spoke. "Put your hands down, Professor."

I lowered my cane and leaned heavily on it and tried again to make sense of the shape. "Who—?"

"It's Sergeant Stant. I got a call from your buddy McGee that you were here and needed help." He flashed the light in his face and holstered his gun.

I exhaled deeply, grateful for my cane beneath me. I seriously needed to lean on it at that moment.

He walked past me and picked up the small pistol. "I saw the gun, and I figured you were the perp." He quickly gave the weapon a quick look with his flashlight. "Nice."

I reached out for the pistol, but he held it back. "You got a permit for this, Professor?"

"N-no," I stammered. "It's Jyanette Emery's. She's got the permit."

"She gave you her gun?"

"Not exactly. The perp abducted her. Her purse was in my van, and the gun was there."

"Professor, you might be fine with English Lit, or whatever the hell you teach, but you have no business walking around with a gun!"

He sounded annoyed, and he shoved the pistol into his pocket. He was also probably right. I had never trained with a gun, and the odds were that if I paraded through dark hallways with illusions clouding my vision, I would blow my own foolish head off.

"McGee didn't tell me much — something about you coming here and needing help. What's this about?"

I watched Stant, trying to feel him out. Just because he didn't shoot me didn't mean he wasn't Ashtoreth.

"You tell me. Agent Petrie said you told him I buried a body at Garden State University."

"I did — what?" Stant puzzled. I could hear the surprise in his voice.

"Petrie tried to arrest me. He thought you called him and told him where a body was and how to find it."

"I've talked to Petrie maybe two times since this thing started. And I sure as hell don't know about a body at some university."

I stood there as the realization hit home. Petrie had lied, blamed Stant. If that were true and Jon Baines hadn't come along, I'd be dead right now.

Then my mind objected. After all, how could he have gotten to Blackshale before me? More likely the clever demon tricked him into thinking that Stant called, like the voice of Cathy I kept hearing.

My mind reeled with questions, so I decided the best thing to do was tell the truth.

"I'm here because of Jyanette Emery. She's the Assistant District Attorney and my girlfriend. The perp has her somewhere in this place. I'm trying to rescue her."

He considered this for a moment. "Professor, you ever thought of letting the guys who do that for a living handle it?"

I considered a snappy retort for a moment, but he was right. In my rush to save Jyanette, I was acting in a foolhardy way. I let my emotions cloud my better judgment. But I sure would not admit that to him. Instead, I changed the subject. "What happened to the lights?" I said, gesturing at the darkened hallway.

"The power lines got knocked out in the storm. The backup generator isn't working."

That explained why I had seen no lights on in the police station. Stant could've been there the entire time.

"I saw lights in the tower," I challenged.

"So did I. Weird, isn't it? When I got the call from McGee, I figured that was a good place to start. I was on my way up there and saw you."

"I'd appreciate your help, Sergeant."

"The best thing is if you just stay behind me and don't get in the way, Professor."

He turned and shone the beam on the hallway and headed for another set of stairs I was sure would take us to the tower.

How gothic. A heroine in a tower, the handsome young hero rushing to rescue her. It has all the makings of a romance novel.

We reached the stairs, and Stant turned toward me with a finger over his lips. He began his ascent, and I pulled myself up behind him.

"It sure was fortuitous you ran into Stant," the voice inside my head told me. "He just happened to be here after noticing the light in the tower? Now he took your gun. Think about it."

I did, and I slowed my climb, and for me, stairs were a climb. I thought perhaps some space between Stant and me was a good choice. After all, Ashtoreth could be inside anyone, hidden from my mental probing by all the psychic disturbances flying around this place. And Stant was here, assigned to Blackshale. He knew the place and all the abandoned buildings. He could've called Petrie and was lying about it now.

The hair on the back of my neck stood up. Ashtoreth set a trap, and could use Stant as a puppet to lead me, so I would walk right into it.

"Are you coming or what?" the man ahead of me said in a half-whisper.

"Keep going," I whispered back, and moved my hand to urge him on. Wanting that distance between Stant and me, just in case.

I was walking up the stairs in the dark, but I could see his flashlight on the top-floor landing. There was a metal ladder bolted to the wall, and he was climbing up it. His beam shone on a small trapdoor in the ceiling. He pushed it open easily and then pivoted to shine the light down for me as I reached the top stair.

"What do you see?" I called out.

"Nothing yet. Are you coming?"

"Stant, there may be a murderer up there. Shouldn't you draw your gun?"

He gave an exasperated hiss, and then said, "I don't need you to tell me how to do my job. Just get up here."

I walked to the ladder and began pulling myself up, my cane in my right hand as I pushed up with my left leg, leaving my right to hang free, catching each rung as I ascended.

Stant disappeared into the trapdoor but left it open for me. I could see light as it flickered above me. I reached the top rung and Stant offered me a hand. I took it and made sure I had a good grip in case he let go. The fall probably wouldn't kill me, but it could certainly incapacitate me.

He didn't let go, and he helped pull me into a small round room. The smell of dust and closed spaces assaulted my nostrils. I kneeled with my good leg on the wooden floor and raised my head to see the source of the light. Around the room, several large candles were burning, set on gothic-looking carved wooden pedestals raising the flames to eye level.

I pulled myself upright from the floor, got my cane under me and in a position to use it as a weapon if I needed to.

"What is this place?" I asked.

"I dunno. It was a clock or a bell tower or something years ago," Stant said.

I walked around the circular room, listening to the rain on the roof, rising up in a high cone overhead. It made an odd plick-plick-plick sound as the droplets hit the slate. The room was larger than it appeared from the outside. I took a step forward and noticed that I didn't hear the rain directly over my head in one section.

"That's odd," I noted.

But before I could think about it, I saw the large pentagram in the center of the room, with the sturdy black metal chair bolted to the floor. It was large and had two huge flat arms with restraining straps on each one.

This is where he did it...

The buzz flashed into my brain, giving me instant clarity. This was where he finished his victims. Right here in the main building. Somehow he brought them here at night.

But how? By that point, he'd tortured them for days, and they would be in bad shape. You couldn't just have them walk up the ladder.

Then it hit me. He would carry them.

Once more, I had limited my mind to the physical. Our man might appear human, or he wore a human form, but he possessed strength far beyond human limits.

I'd better remember that.

"Jeez," came from my right, as Stant took in a sudden intake of air.

I turned to face him, shifted my weight, my cane ready to crack over his head if I needed to.

"What?" I said.

"All around the room. Near the walls. Do you see them?"

I looked at the walls of the room, which were a series of two-by-fours with no plaster to cover them. But there was something between each pair of studs, hiding in the shadows. Something white that seemed to stare back.

I took another step toward the nearest wall and stopped with a whoosh of air pushing out of my mouth. The empty stare belonged to a skull, right at my eye level, about six feet off the ground.

I whipped around, and now I could see them all! There were skulls all around the room. One between each stud, all at the same height, at eye level to me. Most of them were nothing but dried bone, and one still had muscle remains hanging lightly off it. I approached the not-completely-clean skull.

I now knew what had happened to the victims and why the bodies the police had found were headless.

They were here, right here.

Ashtoreth disposed of the corpses, but each head — each skull — had remained here.

I was now right in front of the one with some pink still hanging on it. The eye sockets each had a decaying, shriveled thing in them, like a piece of dried fruit. I realized it was what remained of the eyeball, still drying out.

This one belonged to Mary Gillian.

Now I knew why Petrie didn't find the head with the rest of the body.

I stepped back, looked away from the gore, fighting the need to fall to my knees and vomit my dinner away. I swallowed a few times, fighting to hold on. Stant pulled me upright and pointed at two empty places on the wall, directly facing the chair.

"What are those spots for?" Stant exclaimed. He no longer spoke with the same authority, as if he suddenly realized that my story of the murders was true.

"His next victims," I told him, still working to keep my gorge down.

The last victims before he moves on…

Stant swallowed hard and got closer to the remains of Mary Gillian, looking into her eye sockets as if expecting them to look back.

"Let's get out of here," he said.

He was right. Jyanette was somewhere else, still being held. We had to move on, find her in the labyrinth of buildings. Yet, as I looked over at Stant, I saw he was in front of a huge, opaque yellow-glass window. These windows transformed the candlelight into the beacon I had seen while driving up.

I felt odd. An overwhelming urge ran through me to rush across the room and push Stant through that window. I could see myself doing it in my mind, like a movie. It would take him by surprise; his arms would go up and flail, he would fall against the window, but it would open as he hit. I could see him falling into the dark, rain-filled night; an unholy noise coming from his throat until he hit the pavement six stories down.

"Professor?" Stant declared, and I blinked back to reality.

"Yeah, let's go," I croaked, my throat tight and dry — so dry it felt like I had been sucking on cotton.

"Use of psychic abilities drains moisture from the body," I remembered Doctor Kohl saying in my head. But I hadn't been trying to use my abilities. Something else definitely tried to influence me.

Evil filled this room. Not with a little 'e,' but Evil with a capital letter. Something used this as its lair and sucked the energy from the sad and deranged souls that existed here, past and present.

I understood why Ashtoreth left Jeff Hanley. It must have been a paradise coming into a place that was filled with the insane. Blackshale had been there for one hundred years, and all those souls passed through here, in the days of straightjackets, electroshock, and frontal lobotomies. For a creature that fed on the energy of terror and on the power of insane minds, this looked like a banquet. No wonder he stayed and didn't need Hanley anymore.

Stant went down the ladder and I followed, being sure to close the trapdoor as I went.

"Should we put out the candles?" Stant asked as I reached the bottom rung.

"They'll be fine. Besides, we should let someone know—" I said, with the realization that we now had the evidence to prove the murders.

Stant nodded. He seemed different, smaller. I realized all at once why he took the assignment here. It was a simple job. He dealt with teenage vandals and the occasional insane inmate who needed to be subdued. But the terrible work — decayed bodies in roadside ditches, the need to disarm a man with a knife, or shoot someone with their own gun pointed at you — he didn't have the stomach for it.

Not that I blamed him. I didn't either.

"Yeah," he said, "but those candles — they're a fire hazard." He shimmied up the ladder. "I'll put 'em out."

I watched him go up that metal ladder and into the trapdoor. Now I found the idea that he was Ashtoreth's host laughable. Those skulls threw him, just like they did me, and that didn't seem like the mentality that would attract my non-corporeal adversary.

Besides, if it were Ashtoreth, I would never have had the urge to push him out the window. I knew that urge had come from the demon as he tried to wend his way into my mind.

I could hear Stant blow out a candle, and the room over my head grew a little dimmer.

He's in danger…

I looked up, grabbed at the ladder.

DANGER…

The buzz was much louder, all but a scream that I could feel in my heart and my head. I pulled myself up another rung and called out. "Stant!"

"No — No!" I heard Stant holler, followed by a scream — that same awful scream he yelled in my imagination.

I pulled myself up as fast as I could in my clumsy way, but I could already hear the bone-breaking thud as Stant hit the ground outside.

"Stant!" I yelled again, as I reached the trapdoor and pulled myself through. But I knew it was too late. Without even looking, I knew he was lying outside on the pavement, his body twisted in the same way as I had seen him in my mind just minutes earlier.

The large yellow window was indeed open, and I pulled myself — all but crawled over — and looked out.

Stant lay on the pavement, floors below, like a broken puppet with its strings cut.

I pulled myself into the room and held the window frame. My body shook, and I set my jaw to stop my teeth from chattering.

My glance circled the room, trying to see if someone — in some form — was there. Anything — a shadow, a moving shape. The floor near the window was wet, soaked, more than just from this window. I pushed myself off the floor and pulled the opaque glass closed.

The water was in a large puddle on the floor about three feet away, just as a drip fell from a wooden rafter.

I froze in place as I looked up and realized that when I first entered the aerie, I had noticed that I couldn't hear the rain hit the roof in one spot in the room.

Of course, I couldn't if there was someone on the roof. There was a rectangular door cut into the canopy over my head, probably from when this was a clock tower or had bells that required maintenance. It was so well made you couldn't see it in the dark. Ashtoreth knew that opening. He'd been on top of the roof when Stant and I first came up here. He bided his time to strike, first by an attempt to make me do it, then pushing Stant himself.

I breathed deeply as I tried to figure out what to do. I was sure he wasn't up there now, but I reached out with my mind to sense him.

Jyanette…

I brought myself out of my reverie — or was it pure panic? I had no other desire than to find Jyanette.

I didn't think that he would've taken her back to the building he used to torture Mary Gillian — that would've been obvious. And he'd led me here. He wanted me to see this room, see those drying bones, and see Stant go out the window.

Ashtoreth was toying with me.

This game was what he wanted. He wanted to scare me before he came for the kill. In fact, he wanted me so scared that the kill would be easy. I would stand there, frozen with panic.

That's what he did with the girls: tortured them and cut them until they begged for it to end.

Would I be the one who begged before much longer?

18. MADHOUSE

I pushed the thoughts out of my head and stumbled to the trapdoor. My legs felt like icy stumps that wanted to stay frozen to the spot. I was still shaking, but at least my teeth were silent.

I shone the beam of the flashlight up at the roof, half expecting the door to pop open and Jyanette, Cathy, and my horned demon to all jump through it, like a hellish jack-in-the-box.

The ceiling appeared solid, though I could see the small rectangle and the hinges that made it function. I shook my head in amazement.

Whoever Ashtoreth was using as a host could climb around on a slate roof in the rain. It suggested superhuman abilities that the demonic influence gave the host body.

I breathed deeply and slowly to calm my sense of panic. This wasn't some scholarly interpretation of ancient texts. This was life and death, and every minute I spent being frightened was another minute that Jyanette was at risk.

I shut off the light and went down through the trapdoor, shutting it after me. Climbing down the ladder in the dark, I kept going until I felt the solid floor under my stiff leg. Only then did I take out my flashlight and turn it on.

Where to go?

I shut my eyes to get an impression, but all I could see was Stant's twisted body on the wet, dark pavement. It shifted to the image of Mary Gillian's skull, the remains of the scraped-away muscle, the two dried eyes.

I shook my head to push away those images, and instead forced myself to see Jyanette in her blue dress as she walked out the door of her apartment.

I used the memory of Jyanette to get a clear picture of her. I could even see that smile on her face as she saw my reaction. It was a gorgeous moment, and she moved slowly in my mind's eye.

Where are you, pretty lady?

In my mind, I watched her stride toward me in her high heels. I could hear her approach, the heels making a slight clicking noise on the steps.

I replayed her approach again in my mind. This time, I focused on that sound, that slight tick-tack on the floor, thinking I had heard that sound again recently.

It hit me with such a powerful realization that my eyes burst open. I had heard that sound here, in the closed wing. The sound of her heels against the tile floor, similar to the steps from her apartment.

Without hesitation, I headed out of the stairwell and off toward the closed wing. I moved as fast as I could, my fear forgotten, as I formed a plan of attack.

My adversary wasn't all-knowing, or he wouldn't have been on the roof to wait until Stant was alone. He seemed to possess superhuman strength and agility, which made hand-to-hand combat a losing proposition.

I no longer had Jyanette's gun — it went out the window with Stant. My cane was an efficient weapon, as was the sword within it, but hardly effective against an armed adversary.

This was not looking any better.

I arrived at the fourth-floor entrance to the closed wing. It also had a huge plywood structure that shut it off, with a door cut into it. The door had the same hole as the other floors, but the chain was open and unfettered.

He's inviting me in.

Fear again crept up the back of my throat.

I reached into my pants pocket to extract the two parchments I had drawn that afternoon and took one more look at them.

I slipped them back into my pocket and went in.

I heard the crunch of someone walking on broken glass to my right.

Ducking low, I flashed the light to the end of the hall to see a shape move at the limit of my sight. I stood and walked quickly and quietly toward it. I hit the catch on my cane and pulled the sharpened sword one-quarter of the way out, ready to be used.

I reached the end of the hall and heard a voice.

"L-leave me a-alone. I won't do it. Y-you can't make me."

"Reuben?" I asked, and slid the sword back into the cane.

"L-leave me a-alone."

"I'm not the horned man. I'm the visitor, remember?"

I turned the corner and shone the light on my face. It was a pretty stupid move if this was one of Ashtoreth's tricks. I had given him an easy target.

I shone the light back down the hall to see Reuben crouched in a corner. His clothes were askew, and he had a haunted look on his face. "D-don't hurt m-me."

"Reuben, it's all right. You can come out."

He shook his head. "N-no. He wants me to do b-bad things. He's here, he's here." Then he added with a hoarse whisper, "The horned man."

I flashed the light down the hall to make sure there wasn't anyone sneaking up on us. The corridor was empty.

"How did you get out, Reuben?"

"He l-let me out. He t-told me I had to do it." Reuben shook his head vigorously. "B-but I wouldn't."

"What did he ask you to do?"

"He wanted me to hurt—" He paused, and one crooked finger pointed at me. "You."

"Where is he, Reuben?"

He pointed down the hall and shielded his eyes.

"Go back downstairs to your, uh, room. You'll be safe there, Reuben."

I headed for the main corridor. I wanted to reach the stairs and go down to the floor where I heard Jyanette's shoes. I stopped to listen and there was the sound of glass behind me.

Duck...

I spun and ducked as Reuben swung past me with a baseball bat. I thrust out my cane to block him as he swung again. The wood hit my sword-reinforced cane, which jarred me.

The crazed man breathed heavily and moved back to swing again with a blow aimed at my head. I dodged, and he hit my left arm with a glancing blow, but it hit my funny bone enough to cause a shooting pain to tingle down my arm, and my flashlight fell to the ground to light us from below.

I cried out and grabbed the bat, as Reuben shifted to dislodge it from my grasp. As he moved, I went with him. Expecting resistance, the bat came toward him, and I pushed instead of pulled. The bat smacked him sharply in the face.

Reuben yelped in pain. Blood spurted from his nose. He shook his head, preparing to come at me again, but I brought my cane up with a quick blow between his open legs.

It was certainly not the Marquis of Queensbury rules, but it produced the desired effect. Reuben made a strangled groan and fell to the ground, grasping at his crotch.

I grabbed the bat, threw it down the hall, and picked up my flashlight.

I helped Reuben to his feet and took his arm as I walked down the hall.

"I c-couldn't help it," he moaned. "He m-made me d-do it."

"Reuben, you don't have to do what he tells you!" I roared and took Reuben through the plywood door into the main building, bending down to grab a piece of cloth I saw on the floor. I took Reuben to a stairwell, tore the cloth into strips, and tied him to the metal supports that held the handrail. He didn't offer any resistance, and the job was quickly done.

"Sorry," he moaned dejectedly.

"Just stay here — for your own good," I said, walking back toward the abandoned section as I flexed my left arm.

Reuben believed he had to do what the 'horned man' told him to do. But Jeff and Dennis, independently of each other, both sent me a different message: that demons could be contained and controlled.

Nice idea. So far, this demon has controlled me.

Jeff's papers were religious and disjointed. His major argument was that we "are bound by our words" and that deliverance is open to those of any faith. But the thing that was becoming clear in my mind was the concept that a demon couldn't make you do anything.

You had to agree to it.

He could not make me push Stant out the window, so he had to do it himself. Even now, he couldn't make me run down the hall after Reuben. I took the initiative. That wasn't control; it was a trick. He used the visions and things like a phony phone call. But in the end, they were merely deceptions.

That made sense with what I had learned from my dealings with the realm of the psyche. All of us suffered, not from demons, but from the consequences of what we chose to do. The smoker agreed to accept the health problems in order to get the nicotine hit. Same with a junky or, like myself, an alcoholic. No one forced the bottle into my hand; I picked it up and drank.

That meant on some level Jeff Hanley agreed to take on this demon, and when he gave it up, his life changed.

I passed through the plywood doorway again, snapped on my flashlight into the littered hall, and headed for the stairs.

Going to the other side of that door, I could've been Dorothy as she walked from her house into Oz. The clean floors, old but well-kept walls and ceilings of the used building, were in stark contrast to the abandoned wing: broken plaster, piles of dirt, and that smell again. I tried to stay focused, tapped my cane down the stairs, and tried to remember where I'd heard the noise of Jyanette's shoes.

I was on the third floor when I heard laughter.

At first, there was just the scurrying of vermin. Whether it was rats, mice, or mutated squirrels, I had no idea, but I noticed an odd rumble which was out of place.

I walked into the hallway, trying to identify the sound. It was a deep, throaty laugh, as if someone shared a very droll joke, and sincere but polite chuckling was the response.

It froze me to the spot. I focused on my breath to keep enough oxygen going to my brain.

"Getting close, boy?" the deep, resonant voice echoed through the empty halls. Then he chuckled again.

I clung to the wall in the darkness, following my flashlight's beam and the false sense of safety it gave me. I fought to stay upright as I recognized the voice from the night of the accident.

It was him, there was no doubt, and it made it nearly impossible for me to get my legs to move. My entire body suffered from a sort of paralysis.

He can't make me do anything. I'm not paralyzed. It's all in my mind.

I drew a deep breath, pushed away from the wall, and started toward the voice, as the beam of my flashlight bounced from wall to wall. The voice seemed to reverberate all around me.

"I'm coming for you, you bastard," I murmured under my breath.

This caused another burst of laughter from the disembodied voice.

"Are you, boy?" he announced, as if this were a hilarious concept. "I've been ahead of you each step. If I choose it, you'll end up as dead as your friend Stant."

"Leonard!" a woman's voice yelled out.

I stopped and slid next to the wall, trying to get my bearings in the darkness.

"Jyanette?" I shouted and started forward.

"Len, he's got a knife!"

Again, I froze.

"Now, now," the low baritone voice intoned. "I'm surprised! Even a lawyer should recognize a scalpel."

I started toward the sound again.

"That's right, boy. Come on! I haven't sliced her up yet, but I will soon enough."

I threw myself against the closest wall as I caught my breath. I had to stop myself. He wanted me to come running, probably so he could spring another trap on me.

He led me to that tower with the candlelight. It was a trap — not for me, but to get rid of anyone who might be with me. I swallowed hard with the awareness it could've been Teddy Santos who lay dead on the pavement instead of Stant, if he'd accompanied me.

Or McGee.

It's a trap, I know it. How do I beat it?

I walked as quietly as I could to a nearby door and found it unlocked. Stepping carefully into the empty room, I shut off the flashlight with a click. I shut my eyes and reached out with my mind.

"What's the matter, boy? You give up already?" echoed through the hall.

I heard him but didn't put any emotion into it. Cloud thoughts, nothing but cloud thoughts. He could hide from me. Well, I could hide my mind as well. I still could sense the flashes of madness that gnawed at my unconscious since I arrived here, but I just let them pass through me. I didn't connect to any of it.

I tried to connect to only one thing: my darling Jyanette. I focused on the smell of her perfume and flesh, how she looked in that dress. She was the only thing that was real, the only thing that had weight. All the other images of people or things were meaningless phantoms.

I became aware of her. She was terrified — I could feel her fear as easily as I smelled her perfume. More importantly, she was close. This floor, possibly, but wherever she was, there was a light in that room. She saw the scalpel in his hand. That's what she'd tried to tell me when she called out.

Clever woman.

"Boy!" the voice boomed in the nearby hall. "You'd better get here soon, or I'm going to slice and dice."

I could feel him as well. He was like a three-dimensional shadow. In my mind, he absorbed the light, sucking the life and energy out of it. But I could also sense where he was regarding Jyanette. He was close, but standing near — what was it — a door?

I returned to the hall, the flashlight off and in my pocket. All of my senses were in a heightened state. Everything seemed magnified: sight, hearing, smell. It was like being a tiny insect in a giant mixture of stimuli. I stayed focused on Jyanette and that shadow that I knew was Ashtoreth. They were all that mattered; everything else was just noise.

My body felt light, weightless, as I moved in the complete darkness of the hall. I was going in the opposite direction than a moment ago, but with a sureness that calmed me. I seemed to sense where there was debris, and I stepped around it, still moving silently.

I stopped halfway down the hall and turned to the left. I reached out my hand in the gloom and felt a sheet of plywood. I remembered that I had walked right by it the first time I had come down this passageway. I sensed another corridor was behind it. How to get through it? I couldn't move that large panel of wood without being heard.

"Boy?"

I could sense an unease in that deep voice, as if since I was no longer fixated on him, he couldn't quite get a bead on me.

I heard Jyanette shriek in terror.

In my mind, I could see it all: the shadow moved towards her, grabbing her by the hair and pulling her head back, the scalpel at her throat. The sudden movement frightened her. I was very much aware of her terror, but I still watched only as an observer.

I knew in my gut that the blocked corridor had another way in. I moved slowly, staying focused on Jyanette and how close the cutting implement was to her skin.

In a way, that was when I understood how he had manipulated me to this point. Somehow, a bond existed between us. He was aware of me and could read what I was doing and where I was going, which gave him the advantage. Now, I put my mind to where he was, so all he could read from me was a reflection of himself. To him, this must have felt as if I'd disappeared.

"Please, please…" I heard Jyanette plead in my head.

I was now in another side corridor, and I knew it connected to the blocked one. On instinct alone, I avoided a large pile of fallen plaster and kept close to the wall. I crept swiftly down to the end and turned left.

"Come on, boy! I can't keep her alive all night," the voice echoed in my mind, as well as off the walls.

Where the hallway turned to the left, I stopped and peeked around the corner.

Down the hall was a light, an open door that projected candlelight, like in the tower. I took another step and watched the images in my mind closely, staying focused on them.

I could feel him, just down the hall. He was still close to her, with the weapon at her throat. He knew I wanted to save her, but I could feel he didn't know I was there; that psychic loop I created was annoying and confusing him.

I bent and quietly picked up a chunk of plaster. I flattened against the wall and threw it down the corridor, aimed at the large plywood sheet that I knew was there in the dark.

In my mind, I could see him gleefully react to the sound. He shifted away from Jyanette to prepare for my approach. I slid closer to the open door, picked up another chunk of plaster.

"Is that you, boy?" he challenged. I could perceive him trying to find me with his mind. But he was still too close to Jyanette with that damn scalpel that could slit her throat without her even feeling the cut.

I threw the plaster as hard as I could, shifting my cane quickly back into my right hand. If I got an opening, I would have only one chance. I had to make it good.

I focused on Jyanette, nothing but Jyanette, my mind totally in that room so all he could sense was himself.

He pulled away, let her hair go… and Jyanette's head flopped limply forward as she fought to catch her breath. He moved to the door and looked into the darkness at his plywood wall.

"Come on, boy!" he yelled. "You can do better than that!"

He stepped into the hall directly in front of me. All I could see was his silhouette. But it wasn't the shadow of the monster I saw on that road years ago — it was just the shape of a man.

I focused on Jyanette, lifted my cane, shifted my weight to bring the metal cobra-head down as hard as I could onto the shadowy head.

I stepped on another chunk of plaster, which crunched and slipped just enough to throw me off-balance. The shape moved as I brought my stick down. I missed his head and brought it down hard on his shoulder.

His elbow smashed into my face with a speed and strength I couldn't block, and I heard a 'crack' as it hit me square in the forehead.

My vision exploded with flashes of light. I turned and shifted back, trying to move away. He still had the knife.

I swung the heavy end of my cane, as I tried to connect with a weapon I couldn't see.

There was a sound of metal on metal, and I heard an object, no bigger than a dinner knife, tinkling and clattering as it fell down the tile floor into the darkness.

"Good shot, boy!" the voice praised me.

I dropped back, fought to clear my vision and get into a strong defensive position. I hit the catch on my cane and prepared to pull the sword.

I never got the opportunity.

The shadow leapt toward me, pushing me back into the darkness, and hammered me with fists that seemed to come out of nowhere. I impotently swung my cane in arcs around my body, trying to connect with his head, his arms, anything that might slow him down. There was another painful jab to my arm, and I felt my cane slip from my fingers.

I felt like one of those half-trained boxers that used to go up against Muhammad Ali or Mike Tyson when they were in the twilight of their careers. I was completely outclassed, swinging uselessly while my adversary just stepped in and clobbered me as if I had no defense at all.

There was a painful punch in my midsection, followed by a powerful blow to my right eye, and I found myself against the wall as I fought to stay conscious, the silhouette backing up a step or two to see if he'd finished the job.

There was a sound and a sudden movement, as Jyanette burst through the open door. Her hair was askew, she wasn't wearing shoes, and she was holding — of all things — a chair over her head.

"Leave him alone!" she screamed, bringing the wooden frame heavily down upon my shadowy adversary.

He rolled into a ball as the chair hit him with a resounding 'crack' of wood on bone. She looked surprised, but she now moved into the darkness and became a dim shape herself. Her movements suggested she was trying to lift the chair for another assault.

I tried to convince my arms and legs that this would be a great time to spring into action, but my spring felt unwound.

There was another 'crack' as his hand burst through the chair, knocking the seat out and into the air. He then seemed to compact the piece of furniture like a large accordion, and it fell apart: legs, back, sections of wood.

The two shadows collided, and Jyanette cried out in pain. He pushed her back into the doorway, and she fell to the floor.

That gave me a shot of adrenaline.

I dodged — not an easy trick with my bad leg and no cane — grabbed one of the broken chair legs that had just rattled to the floor, and brought it up with all my remaining strength against the shadowy figure.

I connected wood to bone with a noise that sounded like his skull breaking, or it could have been the wood. He made a grunt of pain, which I found satisfying and energizing.

I stepped forward, trying to swing the furniture leg like a bat, recalling Reuben as he tried to do the same to my head.

As I moved into position, he also moved, bent low, and pulled at my good leg. I lost my balance and fell with such force that I hit my head on the floor. My head reverberated as if an earthquake had struck the entire building. I saw flashes of light and had a fitful grip on reality. I couldn't move. My head hurt as if a weight sat on it, and I couldn't fight the feeling that he had done some serious damage.

I felt my body being dragged like a rag doll into the light of the room. I turned my head enough to see Jyanette as she lay on the floor next to me, her image out of focus as I fought to see straight.

There was another chair in the room with another person in it. I tried to bring that into focus. I fought to see who else was caught in our own private hell.

From where I lay, I saw a pantsuit soaked in blood, and Kate's face. She was lolling forward, and the top and back of her head were nothing but a red tangle.

All of her hair was gone. He had removed the skin from her head.

I shifted, and that's when I saw her long hair lying on the floor with her scalp attached, like a wig of flaming-red hair.

She was unmoving and appeared to be dead.

I fought to stay conscious as the room spun around me, and the even stronger urge to vomit.

"You've been a lot of trouble, boy," the voice said. "You and your friends." The man moved closer into my line of vision.

I'd had a lot of shocks that night, each one more frightening than the last. This one was the worst, and yet cathartic. All the puzzle parts fell into place, and a part of me wanted to burst out laughing.

Jim Stevens stood over me, his dark face shiny with perspiration, but it was his eyes—

They were completely red: blood-red.

"Yes, you've been a lot of trouble," said the deep voice that wasn't his but reverberated through his diaphragm. "But after tonight, you won't be."

My tentative hold on reality unraveled as I tumbled helplessly into unconsciousness.

19. PANDEMONIUM

Being unconscious doesn't mean you are completely oblivious to what goes on around you. I have distinct memories of the operation that the surgeons performed on my leg — three of them, in fact.

I cannot recall anything that happened once they anesthetized me, but for weeks afterward, when I would fall asleep, I could see myself on that table and observe the masked and gowned team as they worked on my leg, the skin open and bone exposed. These dreams would wake me with an adrenaline rush, and it would take hours to drift off again.

I was aware of movement, of being carried, and an accompanying pain in my already sore stomach. I also had a vague memory of an upside-down floor, which made me think I was being transported in a hold known as the 'fireman's carry,' which allowed a rescue worker to carry even a large man using his shoulder instead of a 'dead weight' carry, like one would do with a child.

I still felt that Ashtoreth, wearing the body of Jim Stevens, carried me as easily as a child. I think if he wanted to, he could carry both Jyanette and me, one in each arm.

The entire experience had an odd, dreamlike quality.

When I regained consciousness, the first thing I could hear were Jyanette's sobs. I couldn't see her, but I could hear her convulsive gasps as she fought to control them.

At least she was still alive.

A chill permeated me, and moisture soaked my leg near my shoe. I was lying on my side on a dusty wooden plank floor. Everything came into focus; though there was swelling in my right eye, as from a bee sting, and my vision was limited.

My chest felt tight, as if there was a weight on it. I tried to bring my hands to my face, but heavy cloth restrained them. It was then I realized I was in a straitjacket, a dirty canvas cocoon that was once probably white, but now was a scuffed and dingy gray.

Of course, he loves the dramatic.

I almost expected to see a huge sharpened blade hanging over me, as in Poe's story, *The Pit and the Pendulum*.

But no, there was only a tall conical roof with the slats showing.

We were back in the tower.

One of the large opaque windows was open and rain was coming in. I slid back, shifting like an earthworm to pull my foot out of the rain.

I fought to sit up — a difficult procedure without the use of my hands. I was close enough to the wall to shimmy up it, which put me into a more or less upright position. My head was pounding, and my body was throbbing with pain where he had struck me.

I could clearly see the tower room around me, complete with the candles and the skulls. Jyanette was in the bolted chair, with the leather restraints on her wrists to secure her. There was a strip of black cloth over her eyes.

No sign of Jim or the monster that wore his face.

"Jyanette?" I hissed, trying not to be too loud.

"Len?" she gasped and turned her head to locate the source of my voice. "Oh, God, I thought you were dead! The way he just picked you up and carried you!"

"I'm still alive. Are you all right?"

"I was unconscious for… a while. I don't know what happened then. But he hasn't done any s-surgery," she sniffed, a shudder passing through her as she spoke the last words.

Yet.

I had enough sense not to say it out loud. "How did he get you?"

She exhaled heavily. "It was stupid — I mean, I should've known better. But after he talked to you—"

I continued her story. "He made an excuse and got you away from the party?"

"He said you were on a nearby intercom phone, since I didn't have my cell. It made sense because only you knew I didn't have it. So, I followed him. We walked around the building, where it was dark, and there was this phone hanging off the hook. I picked up the phone and he hit me. I went right down. I woke up in that room, tied up and blindfolded. That's when I heard... her."

"Kate?" I whispered.

"Yes, she talked to me as I became conscious. She told me, 'Ms. Emery, I'm Agent Kate Yearling, I'm going to get you out of here.' S-she told me — told me — that you were right."

"She did?"

"Yes. She said she t-tracked him through the records."

"Records?"

"Yes, employment r-records. She had been tracking a m-man who worked at b-both places." Jyanette wept again.

"Jyanette, darling, stay strong. I know you can."

Although unable to see, Jyanette nodded and swallowed back the tears. "She said she shot him."

"Shot him?" I repeated, amazed that the man who had just bested me and carried me up the ladder might have a gunshot wound.

"She told me it only made him mad."

I tried to think how I could stop a monster that could do what he'd been doing with a bullet in him.

"But it — but it — got w-worse," Jyanette said as her body shook uncontrollably.

"Don't think about it."

"I have to — have to tell you. He c-came back, and apologized to her."

"To Kate?" I queried, not comprehending.

"Yes. He s-said that they would have to d-do his work quickly and quietly."

"What did he mean?"

"He put something in her mouth, a ball-gag. After that, he— he— " An anguished cry came from her lips. "He scalped her. While she sat there, awake and aware."

She wept again, and I could feel tears sting my eyes as well.

"I heard everything. He cut the skin around her head and scalp, and all she could do was make terrible, gurgled screams—"

I saw her wince as the memories flooded her mind.

"Jyanette, stop," I consoled her, as I felt my gorge rise. "Don't do this to yourself."

"Then he pulled it off like a trophy and threw it to the floor, the skin of her head with her hair!" she wailed, all but choking on the words. "She stopped screaming. I think she's d-dead."

I paused for a moment and felt the loss of a woman I admired. "Jyanette, we have to focus on staying alive. Here and now."

She again pushed back the tears and snuffled to stop her flowing nose.

"You hit him with that chair," I said, trying to pull her thoughts away from the grisly scene replaying in her mind.

She nodded sadly. "I worked my way out of the bonds — they were just strips of cloth."

"I'm in a straitjacket."

"I saw you before he put the blindfold on. Your face is all swollen. What are we going to do? I hit him with a pretty solid chair — and his eyes!"

"He… the man… Jim… was the one who told me about Blackshale, and he got me to go to Santos, so you were alone."

"Kate said he worked at the college. What does he have to do with Blackshale?"

"Summer job. He must have been working here when Jeff Hanley passed through—"

"You're saying that the — the demon—"

"It has a name: Ashtoreth."

"It went from Hanley to this guy, but how?"

"I'm not sure, but Jim had to agree to it. The demon can only use you if you agree to be used."

She sat still and sniffled occasionally. I could hear the steady drip of the rain overhead, which was slower now.

Finally, she spoke, "Why would anyone agree to such a thing?"

I shifted, my right arm growing numb from the angle against the wall.

"I don't know, but he tried to influence me in this room a little while ago." I shook my head, even though Jyanette couldn't see me do it. "It felt like it was something I wanted to do. All of us agree to do things we don't believe in. That's how accountants become embezzlers and salesmen become con men. We all fight our own personal demons. In Jim's case, it's a real one. It's—"

I stopped philosophizing and shut my mouth as the trapdoor moved, creaking up on its ancient hinges. I could see a dark hand push it up — a hand covered with a surgical glove. Jim's head and body followed. He wore the stained and faded white lab coat I remembered from my vision.

I noticed a fresh red spot on the white coat near his left hip, just above the waist. I hadn't seen it before in the darkness, but that must have been the spot where Kate shot him. Yet he didn't limp or seem to be slowed down by it at all.

I recalled my anatomy from medical school, and because of the placement of the wound and the stain of blood, I guessed the shot must have missed his vital organs and gone right through him, also missing the important veins and arteries.

Jim turned to look at Jyanette and then me. He wore a ghastly smile, the face of madness. His eyes were still very red, both the cornea and the irises. The only change in color was the pupils, which were large and black, giving them the effect of large cat's eyes.

"Missed me?" he asked and fixated on me. "I know you talked about me while I was gone."

"And Kate Yearling," I snapped.

He laughed. "That stupid cow. You missed a good show, boy."

"I'm also wondering what happened to Jim Stevens. The one married to Ronnie, who raised his kids."

He nodded, the shit-eating grin still there. He walked unhurriedly to the wall and picked up one skull, walked over to me, and held out the dry bone like Hamlet about to give a soliloquy.

"You never met him. His kids moved out long ago, before I reached my stride. But, Ronnie," he purred, and raised the skull to my face for my approval. "She's still nearby."

I looked at the small skull and could imagine the petite face of the woman I'd met the first time I'd seen him a year earlier.

He caressed it with the other hand. "About a year ago, she was getting in the way. Asked too many questions."

He walked back to put the skull in its place of honor. "It's easy to hide things — when you're old, poor, and black." He turned back to me, the grin frozen on his face like the skull he'd just held. "I tell anyone who asks that Ronnie's out of town or visiting her sister or the kids or whatever comes to mind. It don't matter, all the neighbors were used to both of us working all hours of the day and night. Especially the night—"

He spun and opened his arms wide to take in the room. "This is my work, and it is splendid. It took a while to get Jim to go along with it all, but underneath there was a lot of anger."

"Anger?" I asked, as I tried to keep him talking. I figured if he talked, I might slow down the appearance of the scalpels.

"Oh, yes. Everywhere he went, people treated him like the help. All those smart-ass, lily-white college kids, who talked down to the old black janitor." His voice changed for a moment as he assumed a parodied version of Jim's gait. "And that janitor got angry at those college kids. He got real tired of being the 'College Negro.'"

"And you used that anger."

"Used it? I gave him what he truly wanted: power. Power to make people afraid. I gave him the ultimate power over life and death." Reaching into his lab coat, he pulled out a small gray plastic box, like a tiny tool kit. He opened it, and several shiny scalpels of different sizes shimmered in the light. He took one out, held it between his thumb and forefinger, and watched the candlelight reflect on it.

"They're on to you. When they find Stant, they'll find this place."

"And I'm sure you'll tell me that if anything happens to you two, it will be worse for me," he said, as a laugh came from deep within him. "That doesn't matter. I can find another downtrodden soul who will give me what I want. There is no Jim anymore. He's long gone."

He walked up to Jyanette and pulled the blindfold off her eyes with a yank, pulling some of her hair with it. She gasped in pain. Her earlier battle had swollen one of her eyes shut. Her beautiful nose had also swollen, and purple bruises marked the side of her face.

He held her hair with one hand and moved the knife toward her face with the other.

"No, please—" Jyanette squeaked.

"Don't!" I yelled, the throb in my head worse, my gaze transfixed on the shiny implement.

He turned to look back at me, the scalpel inches from her face. He lowered his arm and released her head. I exhaled heavily and saw Jyanette catch her breath.

"Of course, I knew it would soon be time to move on," he bragged, and sashayed around the room, as if he spoke of nothing more than the weather. "That's why I sought you out, boy."

"Sought me out?" I repeated, my mouth dry, as if I'd swallowed salt.

He nodded. "Think about it."

"The map!" I blurted. "You sent the map—"

That elicited a smile. "There was no doubt your friend McGee would put it together. I also knew you would get the vision and see the room. I'm good at sending visions. You've seen some good ones tonight."

This tickled him to no end, and he leaned back as the laughter broke from his gut. "But even with that, you are too slow. I was in that hall so I could tell you about Blackshale. I had to clean that floor for a good two hours before you showed up."

"But why—"

"Time to move on, move out, boy! By the time I killed Ronnie, Jim was gone. I could act like him, but his soul had departed. I need another home." He poked at the wound in his own gut. "That damn FBI agent damaged this one."

He stepped to Jyanette, pulled her hair back again, and put the knife near her face.

"Ah!" she yelped, her one good eye watching the blade.

"Stop!" I shouted. "What do you want?"

He released her head, pushing it forward roughly. "I want you, boy. I want to live with you. In fact, inside you. But you have to agree to it."

The biblical quotes I read on the paper Jeff sent me reeled through my mind. The one that stuck was from the book of Amos: "Can two walk together, except they be agreed?"

"Why me?" I queried, unhappy that I was correct. He had been after me.

"Because, boy, you're the one that released me."

I sat against the wall, confused for a moment. I felt the wood against my head, the stiffness of my neck, the ache that was my eye, and as I looked at the hateful face, a memory appeared in my head, like an epiphany.

20. NON COMPOS MENTIS

I stood in the middle of a living room. I recognized it from the night of the party eight years earlier. It was just as I remembered. The room had lit candles; incense burned fragrantly in the corner. The furniture was cheap, and the sofa was so ugly that only a college kid could own it. There were large bowls of popcorn and potato chips, and a Styrofoam cooler crammed with beer and cheap wine coolers stood in the corner.

Jeff Hanley, holding a beer aloft and a tad wobbly, was at my side. We watched the guests play with the shuttle on the Ouija board.

The thing that struck me was how young we all looked, so unbelievably immature. I turned my head, and there sat Cathy, who looked up at me with a smile that made my heart flutter.

"It doesn't work without your hand on it, Len," she chuckled.

"That's bullshit," Jeff mocked. "Let's do something big."

"Yeah," a boy chimed in.

"Like what?" a girl asked.

"Yeah, Jeff, you've got nothing big," a girl jibed and raised her beer as everyone laughed.

"No, I mean, like… I dunno, conjure a demon!" Jeff offered, and the crowd hooted and laughed.

"How do we do that?" said one girl — a blonde cheerleader type. I recalled from rumors that she was game to do just about anything.

"I dunno." He took a drunken moment to ponder. "We need to form a circle."

With guffaws, prattle, and the movement of beer cans and wine coolers, the group formed a circle, the Ouija board placed in its center.

"Do we chant?" offered a guy. I think his name was Dave.

"Owa-Tagoo-Siam," said another guy, who laughed at his own joke. "Get it! Oh what a goose I am!"

The girl next to him, with far too much eye makeup, playfully slapped him on the head as he giggled again.

I sat down with two good legs next to Cathy, the warmth of her hand in mine.

My God, I'm here. I'm really here. I can smell the beer, the potato chips, and the incense. I can feel Cathy's hand.

"Len, what's wrong?" Cathy wondered, as she pulled my head toward her and spoke quietly, "You look like you lost your best friend."

Not yet.

"I'm okay," I managed. It was my voice, but it sounded as if it came from someone else who was far, far away.

The room already had candles burning, and someone turned off the overhead lights, which gave the room a solemn feel. The change was instantaneous. Everyone quieted down; the jokes and drunken foolery ceased.

I heard Hanley speak next to me. "Everybody joining hands?"

"That's not my hand," one girl protested and smacked the boy next to her.

There were a couple of giggles, but the group seemed more serious now.

"Do you know what the hell you're doing, Hanley?" another guy questioned, but he spoke less jovially than a scant few moments earlier.

"We have to concentrate," Jeff told him. "I want to invite a demon in."

The hair on the back of my neck stood up. He had actually said it. No wonder Ashtoreth moved into his body. Jeff just gave him an invitation. We all held hands, and Jeff swayed drunkenly, a little like the Orthodox men in my father's synagogue, who would daven as they prayed.

There was an energy that I could feel — an evil energy. It descended into the room like a poisonous insect that sought a place to alight.

"I conjure ye anew by the most high names."

I heard a voice chanting. I glanced over at Jeff, but his mouth was closed and he sat in drunken contemplation.

"El Shaddai, Elohim, Elohi, Tzabaoth."

I flashed my eyes through the crowd as I tried to see who spoke in that big, booming voice.

"Asher Eheieh, Yah, Tetragrammaton."

I looked at Cathy, who stared at me, puzzled.

"Come forth, Ashtoreth, show yourself. Fiat, Fiat."

All at once, I knew why she stared at me. I understood Ashtoreth's connection to me.

I was the one speaking.

I wanted to shut my mouth, bite my tongue off if I needed to, but I also knew it was too late. An energy ran through the crowd. The conjuration was complete. I felt something release. There was a flash of blue light, like a giant electric spark. It passed through the room and vanished, and something pushed our hands apart.

Released, Jeff Hanley fell over and passed out. The group giggled; someone turned on the lights, and people relaxed.

"Now that was weird," Dave blurted.

"I really felt something," Miss Too-Much-Eye-Makeup replied.

"I have something for you to feel," Dave retorted.

I wanted to leap up, to tell them we had just released a monster — that we had to do something while all of us were still there.

But at that moment, I also knew that I was merely an observer. Whether I was really there or just reliving a vivid memory, it didn't matter. The events of that night remained fixed and unchangeable: that younger Leonard would soon be crippled and Cathy would soon be dead.

This realization caused the room to shimmer, elongate, and empty. I was back in that dreadful tower, as the creature that was once Jim Stevens gazed into my eyes.

I tried to catch my breath, as if my visit to the past knocked the wind out of me. Tears were in my eyes, and a sound came from my throat. Was I sobbing?

"Good, good. I told you I was exceptional with the visions," the creature explained through Jim's mouth. "Now you remember. You see? We're linked — always have been."

I looked at him, confused, but I knew one thing: he was right.

"But the words — how did I—" was all I could manage.

Ashtoreth found this very amusing and laughed with a deep belly laugh. "You don't get it, do you, boy?" He walked around the room, pointing at the candles and at Jyanette in a way that made her turn from his gaze. "It was your 'gift,' and you didn't even know it. You were psychic and you had read The Key. It was The Key, boy!"

"No," I said, trying to understand. "I got that book at Doctor Kohl's class, years later."

"You got that book when you were a kid at that used bookstore in Morristown. You just needed someone to help you remember the words."

I fought to keep my wits, the lump on my head aching. Suddenly, it was clear in my memory. That store in Morristown called 'The Olde Book Shoppe.' I would save my allowance and buy second-hand books, usually the ones that had anything to do with ghosts or the occult. I found a copy of The *Key of Solomon the King*. I had bought that book and read it again and again. I had actually read that incantation and memorized it years earlier.

He turned to face me. "All I ever needed was to find someone who was willing, then use them. Like I did that chemist, Claude, you fought a few months ago. I had to touch his mind and send visions as a beautiful woman. But you spoke the words because I reminded you of them. I would have moved into you, but you didn't invite me in, boy." He approached me and pulled me upright by my hair.

"Ah!" I gasped and struggled to sit up, as excruciating pain rocketed through my skull.

"But, your buddy, Hanley, he gave me an open invitation. I used his energy to appear on that road to get you on the right path — the path I wanted you on. Boy, you are where you are because I put you there, so that one day, you and I could have this little chat."

He let me go and stepped away. I didn't know which hurt more, my head or the idea that a demon had manipulated my life for the last eight years. The concept that everything I'd done was to benefit this strutting monster made the desire to vomit stronger.

I croaked, "What the hell do you want?"

"Good choice of words, boy," he drawled, and strolled leisurely toward Jyanette. He pulled out his scalpel again. Jyanette's good eye widened in fear. "I'm going to give you a choice. You can freely and openly agree to let me in… or I slice up your pretty lady here, while you watch."

I tried to grasp the concept. "Let you in? You want me as your puppet?"

"It ain't so bad as all that." He smiled. "Jim wasn't sure about me at first. In the beginning, I only came out now and then—"

"Three times a year," I realized, now sure why the murders were so spread out.

"That's right. He wouldn't remember much, except in his dreams. But the seed was there, and Jim began to enjoy it. The feeling of power, the ability to make women beg and cry — that added to it for him."

He walked around and held the scalpel aloft.

"All I want is to keep going, and you would be the perfect host. Get rid of that landlady, and you'll have that big-ass house to yourself. I'm sure we could set up a room like this in that old Victorian."

A picture of one of the upper rooms appeared in my mind. It was a tower room with a slight rounding, similar to this one. I could imagine it set up with the pentagram and candles.

"No," I whispered, the image a little too real. "I won't become your killing machine."

Ashtoreth seemed undaunted by my words. "I've seen civilizations come and go. People have worshiped and reviled me, but I still go on."

"So you can keep feasting on blood and fear?"

"It's what I've done since your ancestors were wearing skins, boy. Deep down, you are all just livestock to me." As he spoke, he walked around Jyanette until he was behind her. He pulled her head back, the blade at her throat.

"No, don't!" I begged, the tears coming unbidden.

"Then agree, boy. You agree to let me in, and I won't kill her."

"How do I know you'll keep your word?" I demanded, as I struggled to find some way out. I thought of the papers in my pocket. They might help, but with me bound like a caterpillar, I couldn't extract them. "How do I know that once you've got me, you won't kill her anyway? Let her go first."

He let go of her head, strode over to me, and swung his open left hand in a resounding slap on my face. My head jolted against the stud behind me.

"I'm not a fool, boy. You can't bargain here."

I brought my head back to face him. "If you don't let her go, I have no reason to believe you'll spare her."

He looked as if he were going to turn away, but he shifted his weight and threw a vicious kick into the small of my back.

"Ah!" I yelled as pain shot down both legs. They twitched and kicked, and I tried to focus through the pain.

"We're playing by my rules, boy. That's the offer. Take it or I slice."

"Wait," a female voice said.

"I don't have time for you, bitch," the demon told her as he looked at me and smiled at my pain.

"I'll agree," Jyanette stated simply.

Ashtoreth turned to face her, and I saw a look of surprise on his now-twisted features.

"You'll agree?" he challenged her as he stepped away from me and toward her.

"I'm willing," she vowed, as the thing inside the tall, black man watched her. "Think of it, a lawyer, an Assistant District Attorney. We could copy a killer's methods, then catch someone and blame them for the murders we do."

The man stood in front of her in deep contemplation. I was still in pain and tried to think of something — anything. I figured Jyanette was buying me some time. Could I roll over and knock him down? Was it possible to slip out of this straitjacket?

My brother, the magician, and I did such tricks when we were teenagers, and I was part of his act. But a straitjacket escape — a real one — takes time and a lot of movement, neither of which I could do and have the element of surprise.

Jyanette spoke, her eyes focused intently on Ashtoreth. "My grandfather was a Nganga, a healer for his tribe and his father before him. I have the blood of generations of healers in my veins."

Ashtoreth considered it carefully and approached her. "It's been a long time since I wore the body of a female. You freely agree?"

"I do. I accept you," Jyanette told him.

Jim drew closer, his eyes focused on her face. I didn't know what he was going to do — slit a wrist or sign something in blood. But as he drew near, I noticed the strap that restrained Jyanette's legs was hanging free, or had she worked it loose when Ashtoreth argued with me?

As Jim drew near, all at once, she lifted her legs in one quick movement and shot out with a vicious kick to his groin. Jim cried out in pain and surprise, bent double in front of her, his impressive strength for a moment abated. Jyanette lifted her legs to his chest, and with surprising force, kicked him with all her might.

Jim fell back, stumbling as he fought to regain his balance. His foot hit the pool of water from the window, and his legs went out from under him. With a cry, his body plummeted past me and out the open window.

I heard his voice fade as he fell to the pavement, a terrible sound as he hit, soft flesh and bone as it struck unyielding cement. I crawled to the window and raised myself enough to peek out. On the ground below lay Jim next to the twisted body of Stant, the dark drizzle falling upon them both.

I turned back to look at Jyanette, gasping air as fast as she could.

"Is he dead?" she demanded through gritted teeth.

"Yes," I breathed, amazed. "How did you—"

"I didn't know if it would work. I was trying to get him close enough. With the open window... I thought I had a chance." She calmed down. "So now what do we do? Sit here until we're found?"

"There's another way," I said, twisting my body. Every movement hurt as I shifted to gain slack. I thought hard to remember how I got out of the jacket the way Thomas showed me — of course, he went on to fame and fortune in Vegas, so he certainly knew.

I could feel the tight jacket loosen, though I felt every sore muscle as I did it. After I struggled for a while, I shifted my shoulder and pulled the long sleeves over my head.

"Magnificent!" Jyanette hooted, impressed by my performance.

"I'm not out yet," I panted. I undid the straps on the sleeves with my teeth, and then reached around and released the back straps, my fingers manipulating them through the heavy canvas. This gave me enough slack to undo the all-important strap between my legs. Another two minutes, and I pulled the jacket up and over my head. I threw it to the ground and used the wall for support to rise unsteadily to my feet. I glanced down at the torn clothing that was once my tuxedo.

"Now, get me out of this!" Jyanette insisted.

I limped to Jyanette and looked at the straps that held her.

"Come on!" she urged. "My arms are killing me!"

"Give me a minute," I cautioned as I looked into her eyes.

Something's wrong…

The buzz stabbed my brain, and a part of me, too tired to continue the fight, wanted to ignore it. I drew closer to Jyanette's face and carefully examined her swollen eye.

"I need to get you to a doctor," I clarified.

"I suppose," she confirmed, then she bent closer and kissed me. Not a quick peck, but a long, hard, and sexy joining of our mouths.

I will always remember that kiss. I had kissed Jyanette many times, and I had experienced her kisses when they were coy and meaningless, and others so arousing it was painful.

But that kiss froze me to the spot, as if ice water had taken the place of my blood. I backed away as terror spread from my lips to the pit of my stomach.

"Sorry," I heard Jyanette say, smiling, "I guess the risk of life and death made me a little excited." She was panting, and I saw her pupils had dilated.

I tried to connect Jyanette to the person who sat in front of me.

"Or else," I stated, as I found my voice, "it's just been a long time since you were a woman."

She smiled innocently. "Len, untie me."

"No, that wouldn't be a good choice. In fact, it might be fatal."

She looked at me seriously for a moment, then smiled. "Len, I just got excited."

"And kissing me is a damn good way to distract me from the fact that you aren't Jyanette Emery."

Her face hardened. "Len, this is stupid. Release me."

"Oh, you look like Jyanette, and you probably have access to everything she knows, so I won't bother with questions. She agreed to take on the demon."

"I was just biding our time. Len, stop this and release me," she argued, getting angry.

I knew my woman, and I'd seen her quarrel with me, discuss with me, and be ready to kick my sorry ass into next week. But this wasn't her. If there were the slightest doubt, it was gone.

This was Ashtoreth.

"For all the talk about using me, that was just another lie. You wanted Jyanette from the beginning. That's why you didn't kill her. In fact, you only hit her because she attacked you with the chair."

"This is insane. No one will believe this."

"I believe it. And it's just you and me right now, Ashtoreth."

"Don't call me that," she spat, becoming agitated. "It's me, Jyanette, the woman you sleep with, that offered you your favorite sexual treat tonight." She took a deep breath and calmed herself. "Now, release me."

"You can't act when you're bound," I recalled what both Jeff and Dennis had told me.

"Len, this is ridiculous. My circulation is being cut off. Release me!"

I reached into my pockets and touched the two parchments. I pulled the one from my right pocket first.

"All right, Jyanette. I'll let you go," I said.

"Thank you," she replied, her demeanor growing calm.

"If you'll look at this." I held up the parchment with the small sigil on it. Within the circle was the figure of a scorpion surrounded by Hebrew letters. It was called the Fifth Pentacle of Mars, and the book claimed it was terrible to demons, and they couldn't resist its presence.

Jyanette saw the paper and cringed. She turned her face away from it.

"Say this," I bellowed. "By this sign, I swear I am not Ashtoreth."

"Len, this is stupid," she fumed, then shifted her head and struggled with her bonds to get away. "You sound like a bad movie."

"I figure no one will find us until morning." I held the parchment close to her. "So, if you want to spend the night tied up, I can go along with that."

Mrs. Higgins' story from the day I had my nightmare came to mind. I had been busy fighting what I thought was a gigantic monster, that suddenly was a lot smaller than I imagined it to be.

I watched her reaction. Ashtoreth was adept at hiding until the right time and also had no problem with lies. But, bound to the chair, and inside the pentagram and the mystical symbol in my hand, he could not deceive. He was now, in essence, a very small dragon.

"You see, I think Jyanette agreed to buy us time, but in that moment, Ashtoreth stepped in, and now she's yours. Jyanette didn't believe in it, but an agreement is an agreement." I grabbed her head and held the sigil in front of her eyes.

"Let me go!" she screamed, and she kicked out at me. I was not in front of her, fortunately, so I didn't go out the window, but her foot clipped my leg, bruising my calf.

"Ashtoreth got what he wanted," I goaded as she struggled against my hand. "A new host, a new life, and the old host neatly eliminated, so that we would say he was insane, a lunatic who believed he was possessed. But you keep going, Ashtoreth. You find new victims, new hunting grounds, and go on for another — what? Decade? Century? Then you'll find another host and another. This ends tonight."

Jyanette set her jaw, her eyes tightly closed.

"So, if I brought you here," I mused aloud, "that gives me the ability to get rid of you, doesn't it?"

Jyanette opened her eyes, but they were darker.

No, they were redder.

The change had no guile. Her face grew angry, her mouth twisted with an evil that had survived since the dawn of time.

"You bastard!" the deep voice bellowed with some of Jyanette's vocal qualities, a higher tone that was lacking when it was Jim. "Release me or die!"

I held out the parchment, and she turned her head to avoid looking at it.

"You're really not the one to make demands. You're bound. Now, get out, or I'll leave you that way."

"You don't have the power to make me go, boy!" she bellowed, her tongue twisted like a snake in her mouth.

I looked at her in the chair, and suddenly I knew the truth. I had the power, just as I had the power years earlier. Folding up the parchment and putting it in my pocket, I retrieved the other one I had drawn — the copy of Ashtoreth's sigil — and showed it to her. I knew what to do. I had memorized the words from the book that very day.

She looked at me with Jyanette's eyes, which were now blood red, aware of my intention. "I can give you anything you want, boy. You want money, I can get it. This woman — any woman — can be yours, to do with as you wish. You'd like that, wouldn't you?"

"I conjure ye, O Creature of Fire," I chanted, as I allowed the words to come.

"No! Come on, you want a threesome, don't you, boy?"

"Be ye accursed, damned, and eternally reproved—"

"You can have women, money, power! Come on, boy."

"By the three principles Alef, Mem, Shin."

"YOU CAN HAVE ANYTHING YOU WANT," Ashtoreth pleaded.

I paused for a moment.

"Give me back my woman."

Her mouth fell open.

I touched the parchment to the flame of the candle. The paper caught fire and burned with the scent of burnt hair.

"Ashtoreth, go ye unto the deepest Abyss!" I intoned.

The monster inside Jyanette pulled at the straps and screamed a hollow roar. I dropped the burning parchment on the floor, and in seconds it melted away. A wind, which felt like a tornado, blew through the room, making the candles flicker and extinguishing two of them.

The roar became a scream of defeat, anger, and malice, and all at once, panes of opaque glass exploded inward, glass shards whipping dangerously through the air. I covered my face as the glass ripped at my hands, the back of my head, and impaled my clothes. I watched Jyanette's body writhe in the chair through a small opening between my fingers.

Jyanette's head fell back as she screamed, but the scream faded into a whine that became more and more her authentic voice, until it faded into a moan. The wind ceased as her voice did, and the glass fell with a harmless tinkle to the floor. Two candles still burned in the sudden silence.

Jyanette fell forward in the chair, spent.

The rain had stopped.

I stood for a moment and weakly drew a breath. I moved to the wall to lean against it for support as I assessed my personal damage. There were several minor cuts and scratches on my hands, red lines of blood oozing between my fingers. I was tired, and every muscle ached, as well as in the many places where Jim had punched and kicked me. I still had the pain in my chest and probably had a broken rib or two.

I looked out of the empty frames which had housed the glass panels, to see the lights of a flashing police car approach. Blue, red, and white lights flickered, but there were no sirens, as they probably didn't want to upset the patients in the wards. It made the quiet even stiller, like a grave.

The car pulled up the drive and stopped about ten feet from the fallen bodies. McGee leapt out and ran to the two figures. He looked up at my silhouette in the window. I hoped he knew it was me. It would really be stupid if I survived, only to be shot by my friend.

"Len?" he called up.

"It's me, Bill," I hollered back, rasping through the rawness in my throat.

"You okay?"

"I think so. We need a couple of ambulances."

Even up several stories, I could see McGee's head nod. "I called for backup as well."

I turned away and hobbled to the secured chair, where Jyanette stirred. Her shoulders shook with wracking sobs.

"Jyanette?" I tried to soothe her.

"Oh God, it was terrible," she wept. "I knew what it said, but I couldn't make it stop."

I took her face in my hands and lifted her chin. I looked in her one good eye with the other swollen shut. "Everything's fine now."

She looked at me, still shaking. "I could hear what it said and watch it, but I couldn't—"

"It's not your fault. You saved us."

"I agreed to it, Len. And a part of me felt so powerful. It wasn't a good feeling, but I knew I had the power to kill." She avoided my eyes. "How can I live with myself—"

I bent forward and put my lips to hers. She pulled back in surprise, then met my lips, as we both savored the feel of human contact, flesh on flesh.

I pulled away, and she looked at me questioningly.

"Just checking," I explained. And I had been. There was no longer the coldness behind that kiss, with a desire filled with darkness. It was a kiss between two humans who loved each other and survived.

She nodded sadly. "Len, I would've killed you—"

"But you didn't. You did it to save both of us. But he wanted you the entire time. That thing manipulated us... but now it's gone." I undid her bonds as I spoke, trying to keep her focused and calm.

As the last restraint came loose, I helped her to her feet, and she pulled in close to hug me. She shivered in my arms, but her hug felt good.

"We've got to go talk to McGee," I said. "And I want to make sure we know what to tell him."

She shook her head. "Get our stories straight, you mean?"

"I don't think you want to tell Agent Petrie or Bill McGee that a demon possessed you, do you?"

"No," she asserted and stood straight. "It's clear that man abducted me—"

"Jim Stevens," I reminded her. "And we tell everything that happened. Without the part about him being a demon or possessed or any of that. We tell them he was insane."

"Got it," Jyanette affirmed with a nod of her head. "Can you handle the ladder?"

"I think so. But I would like the police to help me find my cane."

"We both should go to the hospital."

"Let's get down to the ground first."

She opened the trapdoor. I found a flashlight on the floor and projected it through the opening to the floor beneath. She started carefully down the ladder. I looked at the chair, the still-burning candles, and the grinning skulls that circled the room.

"Beat you, you bastard," I whispered.

21. CHAOS

I spent the next three days in the hospital with my only contacts being Petrie, McGee, Jenny Baines, Mrs. Higgins, and Santos, who usually just brought papers that I absolutely had to sign before the day ended.

I didn't see Jyanette. In fact, they wouldn't even tell me where she was.

It surprised me when McGee told me that when he and his team went through the building, they found Kate Yearling and were shocked to find that she was still alive, though barely. The EMTs removed her first, as she was suffering from tremendous blood loss. How she survived being scalped was beyond my comprehension.

Gabe Petrie questioned me repeatedly, going over my story again and again, and then once more. Then, he changed his questions to trip me up. I think he had a desire to prove that Jim and I worked together, which was how I knew where he took Jyanette.

At first, he spoke about arresting me for our confrontation at the college, but after a talk with McGee, he stopped, and I certainly didn't bring it up. Of course, at some point, I asked him about Kate.

"I called her at about seven-thirty after Stant — or now you tell me it wasn't Stant — called me. I told her that Stant claimed there was a body at Garden State University, and she said something about employment records."

I nodded. "She was checking on employees at Blackshale when I left her."

"That's when our team left Blackshale and went to GSU to dig up Mary's body, which we were told was in a flowerbed near Templeton Library. We now realize that Mister Stevens was probably the one who put her there."

"How did Kate end up at Blackshale?" I asked.

"I've examined her computer, and she left open a window with a list of employees at GSU," Petrie said, a stern look on his face. "Our guess is that she saw Stevens' name on both lists and went to Blackshale to confront him."

"Alone?" I commented.

"She probably thought there were still agents there, but I had pulled the team to help at GSU."

I nodded. "Because you found Mary."

"Right. The one guy we had left at Blackshale says she showed up at the crime scene about nine. Then she said she was going to follow up on a lead, and about nine-twenty our guy got pulled."

"Who pulled him out?"

Petrie looked disgusted. "He said I called him, ordered him to come to GSU."

I shook my head. "Most of the police were called away as well. All tricked by Jim Stevens."

"Yeah." Petrie stared at his hands, unblinking. "So, nine was the last anyone saw of her."

My mouth was in a tight line. "Jyanette was there when he cut her. I'm shocked she survived."

"It's been touch and go. She's been in a coma, there was massive blood loss, and the doctors were afraid of a heart attack or a stroke due to blood clots. But the team here... well, I'll just say it's a miracle. She's still in intensive care, probably will be for a while."

I nodded. "I'm just glad she survived."

The flash of anger on Gabe's face was deep and powerful. "I'd like to kill the bastard again," he rasped, his teeth clenched.

"So would I."

Eventually, a nurse shooed Petrie away.

Bill McGee was easier to deal with and much more accepting of my rendition of events. I never shared with him my possession theory, but as I told him about Jim Stevens' demise, he seemed to know that I needed to keep some things from him.

"And that's the entire story, Len?" he questioned.

"More or less," I replied, not wanting to relive it. McGee had accepted a lot of craziness with his work with me, but I felt that he really didn't need to be burdened with all of it. After all, it wouldn't help his case.

"FBI's been doing real well with the skulls in that tower," he told me. "Been able to track some of them with their dental records."

"And?" I offered.

"Solved several disappearances. And as you told me, Ronnie Stevens. A couple of them we still don't know who they are."

I nodded. "Try going through Blackshale's records and see about missing patients. I think Mister Stevens might have taken a couple of female patients — for practice."

"Good idea," McGee said and made a note in his detective pad. He closed it and then added, "By the way, Jyanette is doing all right."

"Where is she?"

"Down the hall. She's going to be here a few more days — internal injuries from her battle with the perp."

"Can I see her?"

"As a matter of fact, Len, I have a wheelchair just outside the door."

In a matter of two minutes, I was in the chair and McGee wheeled me down the hall, much to the disapproval of my nurse. He pushed me into a private room and backed out gently as he gestured me to go forward.

"Gotta go," McGee nodded. "You two talk."

I wheeled up to the bed. Jyanette lay with an IV in her arm and a tube up her nose. Her one eye remained swollen shut, and deep purple bruises colored several places on her skin.

She turned to me, her good eye unfocused from the drugs they'd pumped her with, but still able to recognize me. I touched her hand, and she returned a feeble grip.

"Hi," I said softly, brushing a stray lock of hair out of her face.

"Hello, Len," she greeted sadly, her voice a strained croak.

"How are you doing?"

"I'm alive… and still me, thanks to you."

"Just a bit beaten up."

She looked away to avoid my gaze. "Len, I've had a chance to think while I've been here."

"Yes, me too. I promise we'll have that talk about the future as soon as we get you out of here."

She moved her mouth, as if to find the words, and went on. "This life — this work of yours—"

"Yes."

"I've thought about it." She gripped my hand tighter. "I mean, I love you—"

"And I love you." I gazed adoringly at her poor, battered face. "That's all that matters."

She turned her good eye to me, as a tear slowly slipped from it. "Yes, it matters. But no — after what happened to me, to us… what I felt in that room. When that thing got inside me—"

I smiled. "You've got to let yourself heal a bit, physically and mentally—"

"Yes, I do, my sweet man. But not with you."

My mouth fell open. "What do you mean?"

"Len, that was darker and more evil than any of the experiences I've had dealing with criminals — the scum of the earth — in my job. It was worse than my abusive ex-husband, and the awful things he put me through..."

I felt the floor drop away as I hung over an endless abyss. "I've always protected you from—"

"You can't, Len. Being close to you, that hypnotherapist used me as a puppet, and now — this monster wanted to take me. It's you, Len. This life you lead, these abilities of yours. It attracts these things."

"I can change," I attempted, feeling lost. "I'll quit McGee. I'll just teach—"

"You can't, my darling man, you can't." She lifted my hand to her lips. "You help people, save lives. But those close to you suffer."

Tears burned my eyes, but I fought for control. "I mean it, I'll quit McGee. I'll just teach," I repeated.

She reached out to touch my head, stroking my hair lovingly as I saw the look in her one good eye.

"Please, don't leave me, Jyanette," I pleaded. "I'll do anything..."

"You've got to heal," she said as tears ran down her face in streams. "And so have I. By myself."

"No, no," I floundered as I shook my head.

She took my face in her hands, forcing my eyes to meet hers. I saw the wreckage of her heart in that look, but I also saw a wall I couldn't climb. "Len, I want a life. I want a family. I want babies and Sunday mornings without shadows."

"I want that too," I whispered, fighting for breath.

"But I could never bring a child into this. My mind tells me it was an illusion—suggestion—but in my dreams, I can still feel that thing's thoughts inside my head. I can't live like that. I won't."

"Jyanette, I'll do anything—," I begged.

She stared at me in abject wretchedness. "Every few weeks, you show up broken, half-dead, or haunted. How do I raise a child with a man who might not come home at all? Or worse, a man who brings the monsters home with him? It would break me, Len. It's already breaking me."

I went silent. The grief was a physical weight, crushing the air from my lungs. A cold, distant part of my mind whispered the truth I'd been outrunning: I had lost the chance at a "normal" life the night Cathy died. I was marked.

"I'll just teach…" I muttered, all but inaudible.

She opened her arms, and I collapsed against her on the hospital bed. We held each other and wept—not for the pain, but for the beautiful, impossible life that was dying between us.

Eventually, the sedatives pulled her under. Her grip loosened, her breathing leveled out, and she slipped away into a sleep I couldn't share. I pulled myself back, away from her warmth, and began the long, silent journey to my room.

Alone.

More alone than ever.

EPILOGUE

A week later, I was drowning the ghosts in a dive bar on Bloomdale Avenue. A half-full snifter of brandy sat before me, the amber liquid shimmering under the neon hum of the overheads.

"How ya doing, buddy?"

I looked groggily at the bartender, but his mouth hadn't moved. I turned my head, squinting as all six-foot-five of Bill McGee materialized beside me.

"Hey, McGee." I offered a loose, lopsided grin. "Have a drink!"

"This is what you do your first day out of the hospital, Len?" McGee asked, his voice heavy with disappointment. "Hitting the bars?"

"Yup." I tried for jaunty, but it came out as a slur. "Single guy, hitting the town." I downed the brandy in one fiery, throat-scorching gulp and signaled the barkeep. "Another, my good man!"

McGee didn't say a word. He just flashed his shield, a brief glint of silver that sent the bartender retreating to the other end of the bar.

"Party pooper," I muttered.

"Come on, Len. You've had enough."

"Am I con-con... conscious?" I tripped over the syllables, my tongue feeling like a lead weight.

"Yes."

I shook my head, nearly toppling off the stool. "Then I haven't had enough."

"I'm taking you home. You have a staff meeting at the university tomorrow."

"Don't care. I quit," I whined, the words coming out with the petulance of a tired child.

"You don't mean that."

"Yes, I do. I'm quitting everything. I quit you, too."

McGee's expression softened into something agonizingly pitying. "I heard about Jyanette, Len."

The name hit me like a physical blow. I stared into the empty snifter, the silence of the bar suddenly deafening. Then, the dam broke. I collapsed into racking, ugly sobs that tore through my chest.

McGee's massive hand settled on my shoulder, a steady anchor. "It's okay, buddy."

"No! It's not!" I howled.

The few regulars at the end of the bar glared our way. McGee gave them a calm, warning look before leaning in close.

"Don't make me take you in for disturbing the peace, Len."

"You can't. I quit," I mumbled into my sleeve.

"Let's go."

"No. Not until you let me buy you a drink. For Christ's sake, Bill, you're a cop. Don't you need a drink when your guts are lying on the floor? When they've been pulled out through your heart?" I sobbed again, pressing a shredded bar napkin to my face.

"Yeah," he said quietly. "I do."

"Then have a freakin' drink!" I blustered, trying to find my anger again.

"I can't."

I forced myself upright, gripping the edge of the bar to look him square in the eye. "Why the hell not?" I spat.

"Because I'm an alcoholic."

Drunk as I was, my "gift" was gone; I couldn't read a single thought in his head. But the raw, hollow truth in his voice cut through the fog and took the fight right out of me. I slumped back onto the stool, the room blurring behind a fresh haze of tears.

"So am I," I whispered.

"Then it's time to go home," McGee said. He hauled me to my feet, tucked my cane under his arm, and with my weight draped over his broad shoulders, he guided my limp, broken frame out into the night.

AUTHOR'S NOTE

Hello again, peruser of the odd.

Asylum In the Mind is a dark book, and it comes from all the dark places in my head. Since I also write horror, it seemed a good fit, but even for me, this has a lot of unpleasant elements.

This book was actually the second book I wrote for the good doctor, and this final version fits in well in its place in the series, and brings the demonic story arc to its conclusion. It also bespeaks of just how difficult Len's life can be and how dangerous it is to anyone who gets close to him.

I originally created Kate Yearling for this book, and despite her terrible fate, don't count her out. She's a tough lady, and we haven't seen the last of her.

For a mental image of this book, I visited the grounds of the old Greystone Psychiatric Hospital here in New Jersey. This was back in the 1990s, when the main building and the old wards still stood, dilapidated and unused. Every time I visited the site, it was raining.

I cannot read the epilogue of this book without bursting into tears. Even though Len emerges victorious and defeats the demon, the events leave him a mere shell of a man.

Len needs to recover and renew his sense of purpose. He will seek that in the next book, *Specter In The Mind.*

—Arjay Lewis

FREE PREVIEW

SPECTER IN THE MIND

DOCTOR WISE BOOK 7

ARJAY LEWIS

MIND
BENDER
PRESS

SPECTER IN THE MIND

The sun was a dying ember, bleeding its last light across the San Francisco Bay, when Joseph Thompson turned his back on the view.

He didn't care for the fiery horizon; he was looking at the monster behind him. The mansion sat atop the hill like a gargoyle of stone and soot-stained brick. Its twin turrets reached into the darkening sky, silhouetted like the horns of a buried titan.

Encircling the property, a wrought-iron fence stood like a line of spears. Jagged and threatening points marked the eight-foot metal posts, which rust had pitted. If not meant to keep people out, the fence kept something very specific trapped within.

Parked at the curb was a windowless white van, in stark contrast to the overgrown driveway. From its rear doors, thick black cables spilled out, snaking across the dead grass to the house.

Joseph reached into the back of the van and gripped the pull-cord of the gasoline generator. With a violent yank, the machine coughed, sputtered, and then roared into a rhythmic, grinding life.

Up the hill, the house reacted. In the hollow sockets of the windows, yellow light flickered on — wan and sickly. The glow didn't make the place more inviting; it only highlighted the neglected abode.

Joseph ignored the sudden prick of dread at the base of his neck. He marched up the carved stone steps, stepping over the thick power cables to walk through the front door, propping it open like an unblinking eye.

He told himself it didn't matter. There was nothing left to steal. The house had been a hollow shell for years, its true treasures — the artifacts and the "echoes" — stripped away two years ago.

By him. Leonard Wise.

Joseph's jaw tightened. Even here, in the silence, Leonard's shadow felt heavy. He could still hear Doctor Kohl's voice, thick with academic worship, droning on about his "most brilliant protégé."

He remembered the way Anna Chou's almond-shaped eyes would soften, lit from within by a flame Joseph could never kindle, whenever anyone mentioned Wise's name.

To Anna, he was just "Joey." A diminutive. A child's name. It sat in his gut like lead, especially knowing that even her roommate, Zabella, seemed to command more of her attention than he ever could.

Joseph had the gift — the tests proved he had psychic potential — but it was a flickering candle compared to Leonard's bonfire.

Tonight, Joseph thought, his fingers twitching, the candle becomes a sun.

As he stepped into the foyer, the cool air hit him. It was August in California, a sweltering evening, yet the interior of the mansion was tomb-cold. The scent of stale dust and damp masonry filled his nose, thick enough to taste. He pulled his jacket tight, his boots echoing hollowly on the scarred wood paneling of the great hall.

In the center of the room stood the Accelerator. It was a jury-rigged nightmare of wire coils and copper plates bolted to a cheap folding table. It looked small, almost pathetic, beneath the towering fireplace.

Joseph caught his reflection in the massive mirror above the mantel. The silvering was peeling away, making his face look fractured and ghostly. On the top of the mirror, in red spray paint, the words GET OUT stood. A gift from a squatter who hadn't lasted forty-eight hours in the house before fleeing into the night, screaming about "the sounds."

Joseph's thin lips twisted into a jagged smile as he looked at the machine. Leonard hadn't built this. He had. Taking Kohl's cryptic notes and the University of Maine's raw specs, he breathed life into them. He hadn't just replicated the machine; he'd optimized it. He'd rewritten the software to do what the others were too afraid to try.

The plan was a team effort. Safeguards. Peer reviews. Boring, cautious science. But Joseph knew the machine could be more than a sensor. It was an amplifier. If he ran it alone, the feedback loop would funnel directly into the only psychic receptor in the room: his own brain. This was his chance to one-up Leonard

Wise in a single night. The Accelerator would allow him to see things Leonard couldn't imagine.

He would earn that adoring look from Anna.

His fingers danced over the laptop keys. The activation sequence hummed, a low-frequency vibration that he felt in his teeth. It would take ten seconds for the machine to warm up.

"Ten minutes," he whispered to the empty, freezing room as he set the sequence timer.

Even if the "bad things" the rumors whispered about were real, ten minutes wasn't enough time for a haunting to take root. It was a calculated risk.

He hit 'Enter.'

The countdown began: 10... 09...

Joseph stepped back, his heart hammering against his ribs like a trapped bird. Outside, the last sliver of the red sun dipped below the Pacific, plunging the world into a bruised purple twilight.

He closed his eyes, surrendering to the growling, electric roar of the Accelerator as it surged to full power. The air ionized, and the scent of ozone struck his nose. He felt a sudden, sharp pressure behind his eyes — a door unhinging in the back of his mind.

It was the last thing Joseph Thompson ever did in his right mind.

TO BE CONTINUED IN

SPECTER IN THE MIND

DOCTOR WISE BOOK 7

ALSO BY ARJAY LEWIS

Doctor Wise Series
Fire In The Mind
Seduction In The Mind
Reunion In The Mind
Haunted In The Mind
Devotion In The Mind
Asylum In The Mind
Specter In The Mind
Vengeance In The Mind
Echoes In The Mind
Infection In The Mind
Justice In The Mind
Ritual In The Mind
Vanished In The Mind

Horror
The Muse
Kept In The Dark
The Vanishing
Digger
Ghost Writer

Romantic Suspense
(with Debra Snow)
A Study In Murder

NYPD Wizard Detective
The Wizards Of Central Park West
The Vampires Of Greenwich Village
The Werewolves Of Washington Square